MIGHT MAKES RIGHT

MIGHT MAKES RIGHT

THE KURTHERIAN GAMBIT™ BOOK 18

MICHAEL ANDERLE

DISRUPTIVE IMAGINATION®

DON'T MISS OUR NEW RELEASES

Join the LMBPN email list to be notified of new releases and special promotions (which happen often) by following this link:

http://lmbpn.com/email/

Copyright © 2017 Michael T. Anderle
Cover by Gene Mollica and Sasha Almazan
https://www.gsstockphoto.com/
Cover copyright © LMBPN Publishing

LMBPN Publishing
PMB 196, 2540 South Maryland Pkwy
Las Vegas, NV 89109

Version 2.02, March 2023
eBook ISBN: 978-1-64971-585-2
Print ISBN: 978-1-64202-035-9

THE MIGHT MAKES RIGHT TEAM

Beta Editor / Readers

Bree Buras (Aussie Awesomeness)
Timothy Cox (The Myth)
Tom Dickerson (The man)
S Forbes (oh yeah!)
Dorene Johnson (US Navy (Ret) & DD)
Dorothy Lloyd (Teach you to ask...Teacher!)
Diane Velasquez (Chinchilla lady & DD)

JIT Beta Readers

Erika Daly
Paul Westman
John Findlay
James Caplan
Kimberly Boyer
Keith Verret
Peter Manis
Kelly ODonnell

John Raisor
Alex Wilson
Sherry Foster
Melissa OHanlon
Mike Pendergrass
Thomas Ogden
Micky Cocker
Joshua Ahles

Thanks to our JIT Readers for this Version
Rachel Beckford
Dave Hicks
Deb Mader
Diane L. Smith
Veronica Stephan-Miller
Peter Manis
Kerry Mortimer
Timothy Cox (the myth)
Dorothy Lloyd

If I missed anyone, please let me know!

Original Editors
Stephen Russell
Lynne Stiegler

This version edited by
Lynne Stiegler

**Thank you to the following Special Consultants
for MIGHT MAKES RIGHT**

**Jeff Morris - US Army - Asst Professor Cyber-Warfare,
Nuclear Munitions (Active)**

To Family, Friends and
Those Who Love
To Read.
May We All Enjoy Grace
To Live The Life We Are
Called.

CHAPTER ONE

The two women set up near their favorite tree. It had grown in the years since they had first used it as a backdrop for their reports, but it was still recognizable.

The woman in front of the camera ran a hand through her hair as the other winked at her from behind her HUD Reporting setup.

Not that Giannini could see Sia's wink.

There were a total of five drone cameras around Sia, the one high overhead setting the shot. Giannini was always amazed at Sia's ability to control so much.

"Hello," Giannini began. "My name is Giannini Oviedo, and I'm coming to you from Mark Billingsley Park located inside the QBBS _Meredith Reynolds,_ currently on station within the Etheric Empire. This is our last report before additional Etheric Empire ships depart to support the Karillians in their fight with the Leath. You will remember that the Etheric Empire supported the Karillians' efforts to stay free from the Kurtherian-backed Leath."

Outside the range of the cameras, two men glided through the trees, their eyes searching everywhere for anyone or anything that might suggest the two women were in danger.

YAREE

ART BY ERIC QUIGLEY

Giannini continued speaking, her voice dubbed over video footage of a battle. "We will be conducting an interview with the Empress later today, but for now, we were able to confirm that the videos which have circulated of her on the Yaree or, more properly, the *Karillian* home world, are unaltered. Empress Bethany Anne, Stephen, Gabrielle, John Grimes, Eric Escobar, Darryl Jackson and Scott English are seen in these videos fighting the Leath from an odd pyramid structure in a jungle."

Sia cut back to Giannini only. "The following scenes were provided by Cheryl Lynn and were taken from the HUDs of those fighting." Giannini looked straight into the camera.

"If you are bothered by graphic scenes of violence and death, please turn to a different channel right now."

. . .

QBBS _Meredith Reynolds,_ Main Military Meeting Room

"We are," Admiral Thomas stated in answer to Bethany Anne's question, "outmatched in numbers. Best estimate is they have us by fifty percent in new production and eighty percent on existing tonnage."

The Admiral listened to an update from his earpiece, thought about his response, and added, "The Leath ships are, class by class, close but not equivalent to our capabilities. However, with their numbers and a bit of luck, they could take us in a major action so long as it is not here in our system. We are dropping puck defense satellites as quickly as we can right now."

"How many attacks," Bethany Anne asked, "have we sustained on Karillia in the last four months?"

"Three," he answered. While both of them knew these numbers, the operations people in the large meeting room needed to be reminded of them again. They should have all this information as well, since the updates for each attack by the Leath into Karillian space were shared with all relevant personnel, but question sessions like these reminded everyone about the issues at hand.

LEATH MILITARY

THE KURTHERIAN GAMBIT

Bethany Anne raised an eyebrow. "Timing?"

"Exactly twenty-two-point-four days apart."

"Another one coming in?" she asked.

"Three days, four hours, twelve minutes."

Bethany Anne paused for a moment.

TOM, why are they so predictable?

The Phraim-'Eh clan are very regimented in their belief system. However, that major clan is broken down into five smaller clans. One of them, the K'gurth, is regimented to a fault.

That is a Kurtherian assessment?

No. That is a Kurtherian-with-years-and-years-of-working-with-humans assessment. Most Kurtherians would only see the symmetry of the math and revel in it. We would, perhaps, love the math and believe that it is sacrosanct, deciding that to mess with it would disparage its meaning.

So they won't change?

We don't know that it is the K'gurth clan. It might be one of the other four. Even so, it depends on how much the Leath themselves believe in the rightness of the plan before they contemplate changing it.

Well, it's annoying that they could change it at any time.

Very.

She spoke to the group. "TOM says that the clan of Kurtherians that is most likely behind the Leath revel in the symmetry of their math. However, we can't absolutely depend on them remaining so regimented since the Leath themselves have some leeway with what they choose to do."

"Well, that's annoying," General Lance Reynolds grumped.

"Very," Admiral Thomas agreed to the general chuckles of the group. A dependable opponent was a godsend. A dependable opponent who could change when you most needed them to stay dependable was an invitation to have your ass handed to you at the worst possible moment.

Hey. That's what we said!

Like father, like daughter, she replied.

QBBS *Meredith Reynolds*, Guardians' Workout Area

Ashur dodged to his left, jaws clamping on the wolf's hind leg. The two of them arrested their momentum as Ashur kept his jaws locked, and it felt like his teeth were about to be ripped out of his jaws.

The two canine bodies slammed to the floor. Over at the side, Peter winced at the sound.

"That had to hurt," Todd commented, followed by Peter's nod of agreement.

"*Hold!*" Peter called. "Change, Tim," he ordered the wolf. A moment later, a very large man replaced the wolf on the ground. The white German Shepherd barked.

Tim turned towards Ashur. "No," he told him. "I'm fine, but that was a hell of a grab." He flexed his rapidly healing leg, stretching it out and back a couple of times. "See? Good as new, buddy!"

Peter tossed a pair of sweatpants to Tim, who slid them on after he stood up. "For a dog, you're wicked fast."

Tim raised an eyebrow as Ashur barked to him, "Yeah? No fucking wonder. Glad it's your ass that has to work out with the Empress, not mine!"

Ashur's chuff caused all of them to laugh in sympathy with the canine. With everyone having the latest updates and upgrades in their implants, they could understand both the parents and the pups easily, plus any other alien languages the Etheric Empire ran into.

"Okay, Ashur." Peter smiled evilly, looking at the German Shepherd.

Ashur cocked his head sideways. *OH, DAMN!* he thought, *that expression means trouble for me.*

Tim looked at Peter as he yelled, "Jian!"

Over on the far side of the workout gym, a Chinese man turned to look in their direction. "Cat time!" Peter called, and Jian nodded, starting to jog over to their position.

Ashur whined as Peter and Tim chuckled.

Someone please get me the body armor! Ashur chuffed.

Peter smiled as he headed toward the wall. Bethany Anne had told him Ashur was trying to get away with working out without his armor, but he needed to learn that while it was constricting, it was necessary. It had taken Ashur exactly one match with Jian to learn he didn't enjoy healing from cat claws ripping through his side.

QBBS *Meredith Reynolds*, Mark Billingsley Park

Samuel walked over to the three adults standing by the tree. Richard turned to him, "Anything?"

"Like there would be anything going on in the middle of the *Meredith Reynolds*!" Sia told the two of them.

The brief flash of pain across Richard's face caused Sia to remember. To Richard, Mark's death hadn't been that long ago. The vampires remembered, and they still felt the pain.

Especially Richard. Why, Sia had yet to understand. She had tried to talk with him about it, but he had been reticent. She then cornered Samuel instead, and he admitted that Richard had seen a piece of himself in Mark and had liked him much more than any other normal human in a century or more.

Plus, at his core, Richard was a romantic, and he had wanted to see the two of them hook up. Or Mark and Giannini; Richard wasn't particular.

"So," she had asked Samuel, "he's like a blood-drinking Cupid?"

Samuel's eyes had lit up at that, and Sia put her hands on his chest. "Don't you *dare* tell Richard I said that!" She'd eyed his mischievous grin. "I swear I'll think of something to cause you …" Here, Sia had to stop talking a moment and think the threat through. Samuel had been trading practical jokes with people for centuries.

What the hell could you do to embarrass someone who wouldn't care if he walked naked through a book-reading event held by a bunch of nuns?

She'd narrowed her eyes. "I'll tell Gabrielle a complete lie that will cause her to come looking for you."

That had caused Samuel's smile to disappear. "Sia," he sniffed, looking down at the young woman, "I applaud your Machiavellian ways. You have graduated to sophomore status."

At that he had turned and walked away, and Sia had realized she was proud of herself. That feeling lasted for about a second, until she realized he had never promised her he wouldn't say anything to Richard.

Dammit!

Sia came back to the present and offered a smile to the two men. "We appreciate you signing up to help us with this project."

"You aren't just reporting here, are you?" Richard looked between the women.

Giannini answered, "No, I think this is going to open everything up for the Etheric Empire. For the last few years, everything has been about internal issues, specifically the Yollin assholes or the other governments which have attacked us. This time *we* are sending ships to another planet."

Samuel shrugged. "We've sent out our ships before," he told her. "What's different this time?"

"Pirates," Sia answered as she turned and started packing away the drones. "All those other times pirates caused the Empire's military to leave our little area. Now those who feared we would start expanding are going to flail their arms."

Sia paused, then clarified, "Or tentacles or claws or whatever sort of appendages they have."

Richard pursed his lips. "You two have experience with this?" He flicked his eyes to Samuel, who nodded.

"Humanity has," Giannini told them. "Sia and I have spent a good while on Yoll and Straiphus tracking down stories, and we have come to realize that the universal glue that holds us together isn't genetics." She noticed the look that said, "Go on already" from her two friends. "It's self-interest."

"Which," Sia picked up her drone case and stood, "if it is a hive-mind-type alien, just means the self-interest is on a larger scale."

Samuel took a second to sweep his eyes through his sector. "Hope we don't see any large creatures with a hive-mind attitude."

The two ladies stared at him. "You know," Sia told him, "I had forgotten how you could take a somewhat normal thought and make it far worse."

Samuel shrugged. "When you live hundreds of years, you experience a lot of bad things."

"Only to have life demonstrate it really was fucking with you," Richard finished. "Which is why we continue to watch for threats, even on the *Meredith Reynolds*."

Sia and Giannini stepped toward the men, who were surprised when the girls gave them each a hug. "I wouldn't feel any safer with John Grimes around, Richard," Sia told him, her words muffled by his jacket.

She could feel his body relax, and then his arm pulled her tight as he hugged her back.

QBBS *Meredith Reynolds*, Main Military Meeting Room

Bethany Anne nodded to her advisors and stood. She turned to the audience, which was made up of second- and third-line management and operations personnel. "You have tasks, challenges, and opportunities ahead. We came out here to find and stop the Kurtherians, if possible." She stepped away from her chair and walked toward the front of the long table, looking up at the rows of faces gazing back at her.

"Unfortunately, the Leath are stronger than us, and frankly are on a better war footing. Right now, them being anal-retentive about timing is giving us a chance to restrict the fight to the Karillian system. The Karillians are pulling their people home, those they can take away from trade. That means we have the monumental task of training a race that needs to grow a little backbone. We *are* that backbone for the moment."

Bethany Anne looked around. "It's time to kick our efforts into overdrive, people. I encourage all of you to go back to your jobs, kick ass, and work with your staffs. We need you to come up with new ideas and new solutions. Find ways we can close the distance between our expected delivery times, and yesterday. Am I *understood?*"

"YES, MA'AM!" the crowd yelled back.

She smiled at them. "*Dismissed!*"

She stood at the front and spoke to the few who came up to talk to her. She listened to a few ideas and smiled, sending them to the appropriate person in the organization who would be addressing that problem.

Lance walked up to her. "Bethany Anne?"

She turned to him. "Yes, Dad?"

A couple of the people around her nodded and stepped back. They could tell when it was official business because the General would refer to her by her title, and she would reply in kind. They walked away with smiles on their face; just the little moment of the Empress calling the General her dad made her more human.

Less of a figurehead.

"Patricia was wondering if you would have time to stop by

this week, maybe touch base on some of her thoughts about the war packages?"

"Of course," she told him. "Do we have the archives set up to print the books and comics?" She thought for a moment. "And the cards for the games?"

"Yes, yes, and yes," he told her. "Plus, we have limited the print run with scarcity in mind so that they will have something to gamble with."

"Can you go right now?" she asked him.

He checked the time. "I've got a conversation with Kevin about the new mobile Reynolds he's building in ten minutes."

Bethany Anne checked her schedule.

ADAM, move my meeting with Jean until tonight before dinner. Tell her I'm tagging along with my dad to see about the new Reynolds.

>>Done. She says that works out better for her anyway.<<

There was a pause...

>>Sorry, I wasn't supposed to admit that last part.<<

Humans have been copping out on stuff for more than a thousand years. We are all busy.

"Why don't we swing by, see if Patricia is around, then I'll go with you to see Kevin?" she asked him.

He nodded. "Works for me."

"Hey!" The two turned to see Admiral Thomas walking toward them. "Give an old man a lift?"

Bethany Anne reached out to them both as he neared them. "You don't look a day past thirty, Bartholomew." She smiled when just the tiniest part of his lip curled in annoyance.

Hey, it wasn't her fault his parents named him something he didn't care for. She wasn't about to call him Bart, for fuck's sake.

Why not just call him "B" like he had requested for all his life, and was one of the points in TQB's favor when they made the initial call to contact him about the job?

ADAM, where is Patricia?

>> **Shopping, fourth floor, men's section.**<<

Seconds later, the three of them popped out into the large shopping area, seventh floor, in front of a shop.

They all heard the indrawn breath.

"Empress?" a woman's voice inquired softly.

CHAPTER TWO

QBBS *Meredith Reynolds*, Prime Guardian's Office

Peter looked at his two subordinates, and then at Todd and *his* two. "Guys, we need more recruits. We can't just shanghai people willy-nilly into the Guardians."

He leaned back. "It's time we started accepting others if we are going to implement our own version of Death Dealers to another planet."

The sucked-in breaths from around the table amused Peter as they realized who he was talking about. "She isn't *that* strange, Tommy," Peter told him.

"Sir," he nodded, "all due respect, she is fucking frightening."

"Well then," Todd told them, "I guess it's a good thing she's on our side, isn't it?"

The four men and two women nodded their agreement.

"Okay," Peter asked the group, "who's *volunteering* to ask Gyada if she is ready to take point again?"

"I think that kind of risk belongs at the top." Todd smirked, looking at Peter. "Besides, you heal quicker."

He eyed his friend. "Yeah, I figured as much. Just seeing if I had any abnormally courageous individuals here."

"Sir, she isn't going to hurt you, right?" Tina, his second, asked.

Peter shook his head, "No, she's actually very pleasant. She's incredibly old. Her time trapped in those caves in Russia, stuck in a Were form thinking about her children hurt her. It's taken a lot of time for her heart to heal since Boris and his team saved her, and I'm sure it hasn't fully healed yet. However, I can tell you she is walking death and I'm the one who is going to potentially be sending her down a road that is going to cause her pain. And frankly?" He looked at them all, "I hate to ask a friend to do that."

"But needs must when the devil is driving," Todd quoted.

QBBS *Meredith Reynolds*, Open Court, Level Seven

Sarah recognized the three who appeared in front of her office and a whisper escaped her lips. "Empress?"

She was surprised when the Empress turned towards her. "Sarah!" She wore a smile.

Sarah's internal voice was screaming, *Oh shit, oh shit, oh shit! She's coming in here!*

Sarah stood up from her desk and stepped out from behind it, calling to her son over her shoulder. "Johnny?"

Bethany Anne winked at Sarah as the little boy came out of the back of her office. He was playing with two model spaceships, using his hands to fly them around. "*Pew*! Take that, you Skaine slavers!" He twisted the first ship in his hand, then flew it into the wall and bounced it off, dropping it with a shouted, "*KABLOOIE!*"

He bent down to pick up the ship and stepped forward as he looked up. His mouth opened, and he couldn't speak.

He stared at the Empress, who was smiling down at him with a glint of humor in her eyes. "Hello, Johnny."

Beside her, Sarah surreptitiously wiped her eye. This woman was everything she could ever wish for in a monarch, and then some.

About three months before, she and Johnny had been guests on a tour of the *ArchAngel II*, the preeminent ship in the Etheric Empire's fleet, conducted by the head of the Empress' Rangers, Barnabas himself.

Sarah was a single mom, and she hadn't told Johnny much about the military side of the Etheric Empire. The fact that Johnny's dad had been killed in an operation back in human space was all she could share before her heart folded in on itself. She didn't hate the military; it was just too hard for her to talk about it.

Even to her son. Someday, she had promised herself, she would tell the young man all about his father—just not that moment. The someday moment had yet to occur.

Until Barnabas had stopped in front of her little business and rented a chair from her son.

The visit to the mighty *ArchAngel II* had captured Johnny's attention, and she could see Earl's, her husband's, blood flow through her son's veins as he soaked it all up. God, she felt like she had let Earl down.

But it was so damned *hard*.

Sarah had thought the tour would be a fast thirty minutes, but Barnabas seemed to know exactly what Johnny wanted to see, and he found the right people each time to explain things to the young boy. Her heart broke as she realized Barnabas was providing the kind of detailed explanation Earl would have given their son had he been alive.

He had always been the teacher, no matter the subject.

About an hour into the tour, Barnabas had turned to her and pursed his lips. "Sarah," he had asked, "may I show Johnny a video we have on the corporal?"

Sarah's mouth had hung open for a few seconds. "You have footage?" she had finally asked. She had quickly nodded her agreement before Johnny figured out whatever Barnabas had decided to surprise him with.

She noticed when Barnabas reached up to his collar and spoke softly. A full hour later the three of them entered a small theater with a table at the bottom. They took seats in the bottom row as a voice greeted them.

"This is *ArchAngel*. I have a video of your father, which ADAM compiled at the direction of the Empress for you to see, young Master Brunner."

Johnny turned to his mom, his eyes glistening. "Dad?" he whispered, and she nodded.

"Would you like to see it now, or would you like to wait until you are older? The Empress says it is your choice," the AI asked him.

"Please?" he asked. "Please, *ArchAngel*, Empress?"

It wasn't a short video. It ran for over twenty minutes, showing Earl first as a young man going to college to be a teacher before he received that fateful phone call.

One that informed him his friend Samantha had been killed in a terrorist attack in France. He had told Samantha's mother that he understood and appreciated her call.

He slowly hung up the phone and grabbed his keys. He didn't have class for another four hours, but his classes had become irrelevant to him now anyway.

He never went back to that college. Rather, he left his apartment and went to the Navy/Marines recruiting station. Standing in front of the two doors, Navy to the left, Marines to the right, he looked at their posters. Pressing his lips together, he realized he wanted…no, he *needed* to be on the sharp end of the stick.

He had turned right into the Marines' office and never looked back.

Two years later, in a nowhere little dirt town protecting a group of civilians who probably didn't appreciate his support, Earl's vehicle ran over an IED, and in the blast that tore up their vehicle, he lost a leg. When he woke up on a stretcher, he could see his sergeant's face and knew something was wrong.

"All I want to know," he ground out through the pain that the meds were nowhere near taking care of, "is can I go back?" A moment later, he pressed his eyelids together as the sergeant shook his head.

A knock on his apartment door a year later changed his life. It was an invitation to visit TQB's medical ship, which was based in France at that time. He hadn't been sure it wasn't a joke, but thank God he had taken them up on the offer.

When they told him he could get back into the game against the foes of Earth, he couldn't agree fast enough.

Sarah had been his physical therapist and had gone with him to France. When he had healed, he asked if she would marry him.

She had questioned him before answering, and he had admitted that he wouldn't have asked her when he wasn't a whole man. She had told him he was beyond stupid for thinking something like that would matter, then given him an emphatic *yes*.

His story, including the tale of his lost leg, unfolded on the screen to their son's rapt attention.

An eternity and a few seconds later, the film ended, and the lights brightened. During the film, Johnny had slid out of his seat and sat on his mom's lap as she wiped tears away, reliving the love she still felt for Earl.

Johnny had given her hugs during the video to comfort her, and she had returned them.

In the aftermath of the footage, the two of them were blankly watching the white screen. The next second, they both were shocked when the Empress and John Grimes appeared in front of them.

Johnny couldn't figure out which of the two he had wanted to look at first as John walked towards him, "You can handle this, Johnny. Your dad's story is incredible. You were damned lucky to have had him, both of you." He nodded to Sarah, then stepped out of the room to take up his position outside.

That left only the Empress, who had once again smiled at him.

Just like she was smiling at him right now as he clutched the two forgotten spaceships in his hands.

"Are you playing Rangers?" Bethany Anne asked him.

Johnny nodded.

"Well, Barnabas is going to be happy to hear that," she told him, then winked. "But I've brought two other people who want to make sure they get a word with you before you make any choices for your future, young man." She stepped aside and waved to the two men behind her. "Let me introduce you to General Lance Reynolds, Military Commander of the Etheric Empire, and Admiral Thomas, Space Navy Commander of the Etheric Empire."

Both men smiled, and they playfully jostled each other to be the first to shake his hand.

Johnny stepped forward, moved the ship to his left hand, and reached up. "I'm honored to meet you both, sirs. My name is Johnny."

Sarah had groped to try and find some tissues as she watched. When someone handed her a handkerchief, she used it to wipe her tears. Realizing it was soft, she saw that it was made of silk. She turned to see a young-looking woman in a purple dress, wisdom in her eyes, smiling at her. "Keep it. I bought it for Lance, but I think maybe it would be an excellent marketing tool to offset Barnabas' influence."

And she was right.

Leath System, Sanctified Ground, City of Truth

Torik, the Third of the Seven, looked over to the Supreme Fourth, Head of the Military Maliki, and asked him. "Our efforts to drive them from the testing's system is going how?

"Stalemate, Your Holiness," Maliki answered.

Torik nodded. It was the same answer he had received three

times before. Now, with their most recent effort a week in the past, it was just another example of a waste of their resources.

His role was to handle resource management for the efforts to elevate—and incidentally modify—this race. The actual killing of participants in the Testing was designed to facilitate the Prime's effort to genetically enhance the Leath as a people. That the Leath believed Torik's clan were gods was to be expected.

Because they effectively were. Power and ability to change whole races and worlds did put them into the godhood bracket. Clan K'gurth, and specifically their branch, were the future of Clan Phraim-'Eh. Now they would explain to those who had cast them out why they reveled in the purity of chaos.

The math that finds ways to predict the unpredictable chaos of life providing insight, power, and wisdom.

"I will take the information you provide and consult with the Seven. We will have instructions before the next Testing for you to implement, Supreme Fourth."

The Leath military head bowed and left the holy location. He always felt exalted when he spoke to any of the Holinesses. But why would he expect any less when speaking with gods?

QBBS *Meredith Reynolds,* Military Bases Development Offices

Kevin was working at a large table, space displayed by a holographic projector above. Stephanie, beside him, was arguing with him as Bethany Anne, Lance, and Admiral Thomas entered the Base Development offices.

Neither of them turned as the three started talking softly between themselves.

"Do they realize we are here?" Bethany Anne asked her father.

"Doubt it," Lance answered. "Occasionally Kevin would get into arguments back in Colorado having to do with the base, and he could become laser-focused on the situation. Especially," he nodded at Stephanie, "if it was a spirited debate about engineering versus proper base arrangement."

The trio listened as the two deliberated the merits of the latest project they had been assigned.

"*That*," Kevin pointed to a rather large asteroid and highlighting the huge chunk of rock, "is *not* going to work well for defense purposes. There are too many odd angles, and it would take a goddamned lifetime to install enough protective emplacements to cover all of the—"

Stephanie, the bi-racial engineer Bethany Anne and her father had hired years ago, wasn't budging an inch. "We can cut the peaks *down!*"

Bethany Anne thought she noticed Stephanie's hand twitch as if she were considering emphasizing the statement with a slap to the back of Kevin's head.

"Why would we want to spend the time cutting this shit down," he shot right back, "if we have three other selections, each of which is better?"

"I swear, if I have to force-feed you the mineralogy reports for options 21, 88, and 221B, I will do it, page by page."

Kevin looked at her, "I've read them. What I don't understand is why the percentages matter since the numbers don't seem to be that far apart."

Stephanie stopped a moment, mouth open. Closing her mouth, her eyes narrowed. "You read them?"

"Hell, yes, I read them. I've learned to make sure I am prepared. Are you?"

Stephanie ran her tongue around her lips a moment. "May I?" She nodded to the display and Kevin waved a hand, offering her the opportunity to take over. She stepped up and touched the four rocks hovering above the table in the display, then spoke. "Reynolds, please get rid of everything but these selections and then provide me the top five types of rock which make them up by percentage, listing below each."

MICHAEL ANDERLE

The three watched, entranced, as the two continued their discussion.

"Left is my selection labeled one, the other three are options. Now, the difference," she swiped a couple of controls, causing small space ship animations to start attacking all four rocks, "is what can create an unstable dissonance in the core of each asteroid. You will notice that Asteroid 21 has a dissonance frequency similar to Asteroid 88." She pushed up the controls as Kevin watched, mesmerized.

"Granted, this isn't the most likely event, but should someone attack 221B using two asteroids at points," she lifted a hand to indicate, "A here, and B over there, the asteroid will crack. There is a small problem with it." She pulled her hand back and crossed her arms over her chest. "We could engineer a method of reducing the risk."

"But why take the chance?" Kevin finished. He was chewing on the inside of his lip, deep in thought. "Okay, you are saying it's a small chance, and I agree. But," he nodded to the asteroid she had listed as her first choice, "how are we going to get that hunk of rock prepared in a timeline that works worth a damn?"

"En route," Stephanie told him.

"En route?" Bethany Anne asked, startling the two in front of her.

"Damn," Kevin put a hand over his heart, "don't scare a man like that, Bethany Anne. He's likely to have a heart attack and need mouth-to— Ooof." Kevin finished, Stephanie having punched him in the ribs.

"If you don't focus, I'll give you mouth-to-mouth."

"That was my intent," he interrupted.

"You didn't let me finish!" Stephanie eyed him.

"That's right," Kevin agreed, "and that is because whatever you have to say will be infinitely less enjoyable than my version."

Bethany Anne wondered how, after all these years, these two maintained both a working and a personal relationship.

Stephanie preferred to keep the two separate, and Kevin preferred to annoy her.

Bethany Anne would have thought the ex-Army man would have been all prim and proper, but not so much.

"En route." Stephanie ignored her husband. "My thought is we figure out the best solution for the external design for the mobile ESD and then emplace a field like we have here on the *Meredith Reynolds* to push attackers into a defined funnel, moving them away from locations we are concerned about."

"To some killing fields." Kevin nodded. "How long would that take?"

"Depends on how many and where," Stephanie temporized. "If we can agree where the ESD beam will be set up, then we can—"

"Have we heard enough?" Lance asked the others. "I know these two can continue like this for a while."

"I'm good," Admiral Thomas admitted. "I think they will have a satisfactory solution…sometime."

Kevin put up a hand to pause Stephanie and turned to the three. "Give us three days."

"Two," Stephanie added after him. "He's padding our effort here. We will have the core worked out by tonight."

"The morning," Kevin corrected. "She won't be sure about her answers until she has slept and confirmed she agrees in the morning."

Stephanie paused a moment before nodding. "Yeah, he's right. Assuming I'm good in the morning, we'll do the calculations and have our temporary solution to you before noon."

Bethany Anne nodded. "How long until we are functional?"

Kevin and Stephanie looked at each other. "Twenty-four months?" he asked, and she nodded her agreement.

"Good." Bethany Anne smiled. "You have eighteen." Reaching out, she grabbed the two men, and they disappeared.

A moment later, Stephanie broke the silence. "We didn't need twenty-four months." She eyed her husband. "Why did you tell her that?"

"Because," Kevin replied, "I know Bethany Anne. We really need what, about twenty months?"

She nodded.

"If we had told her twenty, she would've given us fifteen," he finished.

CHAPTER THREE

Planet Yoll, Second Outer Orbit, New Yollin Navy Spaceyard G'enysis

Admiral Thomas nodded to the Yollin mate who opened the door for him. The Admiral and his Guardian detachment exited the shuttle, stepping into the receiving bay for the new navy spaceyard.

Waiting for him was Minister of Defense E'kolorn, with his guards as well.

Admiral Thomas walked over and took E'kolorn's outstretched hand. "Good to see you again, E'kolorn."

"Likewise, Thomas," he answered. The two turned from the large shuttle bay towards the exit and headed to the operations deck of the massive complex. Since the Straiphus Rebellion, Bethany Anne had placed a premium on building a new shipyard for the Etheric Empire. First task was to repair ships damaged in the conflict, then start construction on the latest designs.

"G'enysis tells me," E'kolorn continued the conversation once they had stepped out of the shuttle bay, "that we have new ship designs in the works that will allow me to share capabilities with the ones you have out here?"

"Sort of," Thomas admitted. "Perhaps the better way to say it is, we need to come to an agreement on how we should share the budget." The two of them, guards walking in front and behind, turned a corner. They left a four-person-wide hallway to enter one that was only wide enough for two.

"The new Defender series of destroyers is going to be capable of either fighting inside the atmosphere or taking the battle to space."

E'kolorn caught on and completed the thought. "Or be in space and take the fight into the atmosphere."

"Yes," Thomas admitted.

"Similar to the *ArchAngel I* and the G'laxix Sphaea-class ships."

"Right," Thomas agreed, "except we are going to have bigger weapons on these ships, and they are each going to carry up to one hundred Marines."

The two men walked another hundred paces while E'kolorn thought about the ramifications of having this type of resource in his arsenal. The group slowed and came to a stop when they had to pass through security before entering the operations area.

Another two hundred steps beyond security, they were stopped again before being allowed into the operations room, where they left all but one of their guards outside.

As the three stepped through the doors, the remaining guard stepped to the side and took a position against the walls.

Thomas addressed the EI running the station. "G'enysis."

In the middle of the large circular room was a table. The room itself had seven circular rows of workstations with desks and screens inlaid into the surfaces for the staff. The center table had a holographic representation of the huge shipyard and tiny little dots scooting around.

E'kolorn stepped to the circular table, noting that he could see Yollins in space suits scampering around a superdreadnought that had to have been brought over from the original shipyard, considering how complete it was.

"Nice detail," E'kolorn murmured as he watched the display.

"Thank you," G'enysis replied. "I like to keep it up-to-date as the ships are completed for the crew working in here."

Thomas looked at the eighteen docks that seemed to have activity. "Are we on track for all of them at the moment, G'enysis?"

"Yes, sir, we are. Should production proceed as planned, we will probably be deploying most of the ships two percent earlier than currently scheduled."

"How does that timeframe compare to what the Empress wishes?" E'kolorn asked. He heard the Admiral snort beside him.

"We will be five percent late compared to the Empress' wishes," the EI answered.

"What is causing us to miss the Empress' dates?" E'kolorn looked at the screens embedded in the table and started flipping through them to view the tasks which seemed to have the most flags.

"Mining and materials," Thomas answered at the same time as G'enysis. "We are working with that group ourselves, but until we figure out the best way to bring the materials from the outer asteroids here at the right time," Thomas shrugged, "I'm not sure what we can do about it."

E'kolorn looked back at the enormous hologram. "G'enysis, would you please show me the system?"

The shipyards shrunk as the Yollin planet, the orbiting space stations, and the *Meredith Reynolds* all came into view as the EI started showing the path to the asteroids. "The problem we have had," E'kolorn pointed to the small dot representing the mining facilities, "is that we already mined the areas close to us a generation or two back."

"That is why you use the Eubos system." Thomas pursed his lips. "You find the Gate system easier?"

"Well," E'kolorn tapped his mandibles together in thought, "it was until we required this much material at one time. Now we are searching for the right method to procure materials on schedule."

"Time to get the two bricks out, as Dan would say." Thomas ran a hand through his hair. "But I'm afraid we are going to be receiving a lot of pain and still not figuring out anything."

"Sirs," G'enysis interrupted, "if we could use the time in transit for production, we could meet the Empress' optimistic request."

"Optimistic is a euphemism for?" Thomas asked, not considering he was speaking to the EI.

"Impossible," E'kolorn inserted.

"Challenging," G'enysis answered. "I have been in contact with Jeovanni Deteusche in Mining, and he is working on the problem.

"Jeo?" Thomas narrowed his eyes. "Why the hell didn't I think to ask him?"

"Shall I call him?"

"Yes, please, G'enysis," Thomas confirmed.

It took a moment before Jeo popped into view in the hologram. He started looking around, and the human and the Yollin realized he was figuring out where he was.

"Sorry," he mumbled and seemed to take a step back, his head shifting to the edge of the hologram. Then he turned so that he was looking at the hologram himself.

E'kolorn considered it eerie to have a human's head with its little neck just floating in the air.

Aliens, he thought.

"I see. This is our project management problem, right, G'enysis?" Jeo asked.

"It is, Mining and Materials Senior Engineer," the EI answered, conferencing everyone into the conversation between the two of them.

Jeo's head turned toward the Admiral and the Defense Minister and winked. "So, our Empress is up to her standard operating procedure of figuring out how long something should take and then taking away your slack?"

The two nodded their heads. "Yes."

"Okay." He blew out a long breath. "We fixed this before by manufacturing some of the materials on Earth instead of in space."

E'kolorn spoke up. "We have already tasked all the manufacturing resources we can down on the planet. I don't believe we can build any of the bigger pieces there. It would take too much time to pull them up through the gravity well, with too much risk of twisting them, or worse, of the whole ship being destroyed."

Thomas started nodding. "Are you thinking of the effort required to lift the three ocean liners?"

"Something like that, sir," Jeo admitted. "But I'm also thinking about the space stations."

This time E'kolorn started nodding and Admiral Thomas looked confused.

"You are thinking about building additional manufacturing facilities near the space stations and then hiring the workers already on board?"

"Yes," Jeo admitted. "Do you think the people on the stations might go for that?"

"If they don't, or we need more, we can move them down to the planet." E'kolorn's voice seemed to get hard. "I'm not going to allow someone who won't work where we need them to dictate to us where they live."

E'kolorn looked at Thomas. "Would the Empress have a problem with that?"

Thomas snorted. "If anyone on the space stations gives her any lip, she will open the hatch to space, point outside, and tell them to walk back to the planet or choose the ship that is leaving." He smiled. "Those would be their only two options."

E'kolorn nodded sharply. "Good."

Thomas kept a straight face when he heard E'kolorn mumble

under his breath, "That is the kind of leadership I was *born* to support."

QBBS *Meredith Reynolds,* Jean Dukes R&D Lab

The large black German Shepherd walked around the R&D lab, easily threading through the crowd to find his way to Jean's office.

Jean?

Jean looked up to see Matrix standing there. "What's up?"

I'd like to understand why TOM is saying that the specifications for my latest armor are not adequate to allow me to wear it.

Jean looked down at the results of the latest implosion device, which used the smallest version of a black hole they could temporarily create. So far the math worked, but the reality was far from the math.

She sighed. It wasn't going to be built any time soon, and she needed a break anyway. "Walk with me."

Matrix followed Jean out of the lab and ignored the two Guards who immediately attached themselves as Jean headed towards the nearest park.

"The problems with the armor," Jean started explaining to the inquisitive dog, "are the potential issues of vacuum and space. Like if you get ejected during an attack on a ship you are on. The links that enable the armor to move with your body stretch and flex."

Jean started making motions with her arms. "The speed and direction your legs move will create a friction problem at that point, and they will hypothetically stick." The four of them walked into the park. A few of the people pointed towards Matrix, who ignored the attention.

He really didn't like the popularity he inspired. If he could just sit in an office and review new information, he might be a truly happy dog. However, nanocytes or no nanocytes, he did need to exercise.

"This is as much for me as it is for you," Jean admitted as she pulled out a small yellow ball. "I need the exercise as well."

I didn't think you read minds, he asked her.

"I don't, but you have bent my ear enough for me to know playing any version of fetch isn't your idea of a great time."

True, but I get it. Fire away, he told her, then ran as she threw the first pitch. Her method was to throw it high into the air, allowing Matrix a moment to try and figure out the apogee and guess where the ball would land. Matrix scored himself.

Nineteen out of twenty.

He figured the light source messed up his calculations. While he could have intuited where the ball would go, that wasn't what he wanted to accomplish. He tried instead to calculate the ball's angle and velocity as it left Jean's hand and determine the height and distance it would travel. Then he would convert the distance into running strides and project from where he was. He allowed himself to be off by one stride to either side of his calculation.

It wasn't perfection, but perhaps he would get closer if they went through another twenty tosses.

An hour later, Jean had to beg off since her arm was starting to hurt.

Leath, the Gods' Chambers

Torik was deep in thought as he wandered into the general meeting rooms for the Seven. His ruminations were interrupted when a female of his clan greeted him. He looked up to see her working at their central table.

"Torik, what has you so deep in concentration?"

He nodded a greeting. In centuries past they had dropped their Kurtherian names to allow those they manipulated to more properly address them. "Var'ence." He joined her at the table, slipping into the chair next to her and turning his body in her direction.

"I am having trouble calculating the correct options related to the new challenges the Leath are encountering with the Karillians. Their efforts to overtake the planet have been rebuffed multiple times."

Var'ence pondered. "I imagine it is due to a problem in the calculations." She put up a hand, "Not with your calculations, but some lack of information. What don't we know about these new aliens?"

He temporized. "I've used all variables for aliens inside and outside the range of what we have encountered before." With a thought he sent his efforts to Var'ence, whose eyes opened when she realized the scope of the effort Torik had undertaken so far.

The two sat quietly for a moment and digested the data before Var'ence offered, "Why don't we get more information, so the calculations can be completed?" She looked at him. "Presuming that there is something missing?"

It took a moment for the beauty of the probabilities to spread through Torik's mind. The colors created as the new options interlaced brought a smile to his face. "Yes, let us do that."

CHAPTER FOUR

QBBS _Meredith Reynolds,_ Prime Guardian's Office

Peter closed down the screens on his tablet. "Meredith?" he asked as he locked his desk. He made the effort to physically lock his desk simply so Meredith would know that he didn't want anyone going through it.

That way if someone did, she would notify him immediately.

"Yes, Peter?"

"Can you tell me where Gyada is at the moment?" he requested as he stood and reached for the ceiling, stretching his back. He could feel his spine crack in a couple of places. Perhaps that last fall he had taken during his workout with Tim had required a bit of a cool-down and recovery, which he hadn't done.

Teach him _to walk away as if being slammed to the floor from six feet in the air was something to shrug off._

"She is presently walking toward a bar she enjoys."

"All Guns Blazing?" Peter asked, trying to remember if he had seen her in that place.

"No, she is heading towards NS Squared."

Peter thought about that for a moment. He knew he had been there but was trying to remember with...*ah!*

"Pearl's place? The one Tabitha likes to go to?"

"The same," Meredith answered.

Peter closed his office door for privacy and walked over to his locker. Dropping his military fatigues, he pulled out a set of civilian clothes—some jeans and a large cotton shirt with gray, green and black lines running through it. His black belt and some black leather shoes completed the outfit.

Taking a quick glance in the mirror, he winked at himself before placing his military clothing into the locker and closing it and heading out of the Guardians' operations wing.

If he was heading for Never Submit-Never Surrender, he wanted to fit in. He knew Gyada wouldn't be there in anything but blue-collar clothes.

It was a bar many of the Guards and Guardians visited from time to time. You didn't need to have your uniform on for the people there to know you were *family*.

The family of *doers*, not talkers.

Whether it was cops, firemen, engineers, military, or just those who had put in the time and honored the ones who had made it possible, NS Squared was the place you went when you needed a beer.

And a chance to talk to Pearl.

Gyada strode along the hallway, keeping to herself. She had signed onto the *Meredith Reynolds* as a way to distance herself from her children—those who had been killed so long ago by that madman in Russia and the others she had taken on her team.

Bethany Anne had received her gratefully and treated her like an aunt. Older and wiser in some ways, but mostly Bethany Anne had been worried about Gyada's fragile emotional state.

Queen at the time, Bethany Anne had simply looked into Gyada's eyes and told her, "All things will heal in time. You will know when you are ready. Until then, teach, train, and keep yourself in shape. Because," the Queen's eyes went from soft to hard, "if I have to, I'll take those who are broken-in-heart and require their service. So you will need to be ready if it happens."

At this moment, Gyada wondered for what had to be the hundredth time if the threat in the Queen's voice had been real.

Would Bethany Anne make her fight? She had heard about the Leath, and she was familiar with the battles.

But she had not been asked to join.

Even now, months later, she knew about the Guardians and their efforts to ramp up enrollment and bring more teams on board.

And still she had not been asked.

Was she too damaged to belong to a family again? Did Bethany Anne mean for her to volunteer?

Would she volunteer, or did she just want to continue this lonely existence and maybe learn another trade—one that didn't require her to kill.

Pearl nodded at her when she saw who had come into the bar. The place was smaller, with a long row of seats on the left. The backs of the seats "could cover John Grimes' head," Tabitha had told her one time.

Gyada smiled at the memory. The feisty Ranger had been introduced to her at a meeting with Bethany Anne over a year ago. It had taken Tabitha about three sentences to place who Gyada was and what she was suffering from, and then the two of them left by a side door.

"Won't the Empress be upset?" Gyada had asked.

"She's cool with it," Tabitha answered as the two passed the Guards in the back hallway.

"How would you know?" Gyada had looked behind them, trying to remember if she had noticed the two of them talking.

"Mental communication," Tabitha admitted, tapping her head. "I asked her if I could take you to Pearl's, and she told me Pearl's was more important than the meeting."

"What is Pearl's?"

"It's a bar," Tabitha answered. The two of them took a right down another hall, heading towards the tram. "We need to go inward about a kilometer and up three levels."

Gyada murmured, "That's not close."

Tabitha turned to look at her. "Did you think it would be?"

Gyada stepped onto the tram with Tabitha. Wearing her official Ranger outfit, which was, Gyada thought, whatever made her happy, Tabitha cut a dashing figure. "I thought it would be back on the outer docks."

"Oh, no." Tabitha shook her head, "This place is strictly for Inner Etheric citizens. Basically, you have to be able to get inside the *Meredith Reynolds* to get there."

Memories aside, Pearl was waiting for an order as Gyada slid into her customary table at the back. "One on tap," she told Pearl. "Who's on the grill?"

"Sean," Pearl answered, reaching under the bar. "I got an order in from Yelena's brewery. You want pale or dark?"

Gyada eyed Pearl, who chuckled and put the pale ale back. Coming around the bar, she placed a cold glass and the bottled dark beer on the table. Gyada appreciated that the bottles were recyclable. No extra trash up in space.

"Why does Yelena sell to you if her guy owns All Guns Blazing?" Gyada wondered.

Pearl waved a hand. "Distribution and production are higher than even Bobcat's group can handle. Plus," Pearl smiled, "Bobcat is always out to make a buck. I understand from Yelena that the two of them are betting William and Marcus that they can sell more beer than the other two for a year."

"Couldn't you cheat?" Gyada asked, pouring a bit of the beer into the cold glass. Most dark beer drinkers would give Gyada grief for drinking it cold. "Thanks for allowing my beer weirdness into NS."

Pearl shrugged, "If you want to drink a beer extra-cold, that is your prerogative. You don't have to abide by the rules of a planet so far away I can't even put enough zeros at the end of a number to represent the distance."

"Still." Gyada relaxed. Being around Pearl was, she imagined, the closest she would get to having a friend who accepted her for who she was. Celebrating the good things and helping her through the bad.

Gyada heard the door chime a moment before Pearl's eyes flicked up to see who was coming in. The look on Pearl's face let Gyada know that she wasn't expecting whoever it was. Whether it was due to not knowing the person…

Gyada had to slide out of her seat and turn to look. The suspense was killing her.

"Peter?" Gyada's question was left in the air as Peter turned towards her voice to see his quarry's face peeking around the corner of the booth's partition.

"Ah." He smiled, walking towards her.

"My, oh my." Pearl whistled under her breath. "Mr. Hot Stuff is looking for you."

Gyada whipped her face back to Pearl. "I'm old enough to be his umpteenth grandmother!"

Pearl winked at her. "And your point?" she asked as she slid out of the booth.

"What are you having, son?" Gyada heard her ask Peter.

"Not sure I'm staying. I need to speak with Gyada," he answered. Gyada watched as Peter came into view and was surprised.

He was in casual clothes.

"I'd say fancy meeting you here," Peter smiled at Gyada, "but since I had Meredith track you down, it would be kinda pointless." He pursed his lips. "And inaccurate."

Gyada ignored Pearl's motion from behind the bar as she focused on the Empress' top Guardian, the captain.

She kept her mouth shut.

"Okay," Peter announced as he laid both hands on the table, "I will make this quick and to the point." He looked her in the eye.

"Gyada, I need you."

There was a snort from the bar, and Gyada almost turned to give Pearl an evil glare.

Instead, she picked up her glass, and before taking a sip, asked, "Would you care to clarify that?"

Peter's eyes narrowed before they rolled as he realized how she might have taken the comment. "If I was going to come on to you, be very assured I would offer a certain amount of wining and dining." He looked at her drink. "Or perhaps a little beer and fear." He shrugged, "You can never tell the needs of a lady."

Gyada almost snorted the drink out of her nose, and she started coughing as she choked a bit. Too bad she'd taken that sip. Peter chuckled but handed her the rag Pearl had tossed him. Gyada wheezed a few more times into the towel.

"Wow," she rasped, "you know how to really choke a woman up."

"It's a gift." He shrugged, his mischievous eyes sparkling. "Or a curse."

Gyada set the towel down on the bench next to her. "Okay, since we aren't talking wine and dine or beer and fear in the service of Venus…" When she looked up, she could tell she had lost Peter with her comment about Venus.

"Give someone a green gown?" she asked. Peter shook his head. "Horizontal refreshment?"

Peter smiled broadly and pointed at her. "Horizontal mambo, got it!" His smile disappeared as he asked, "Service of Venus?"

"Back in the thirteen hundreds people talked about Venus as the Goddess of Love."

"And green gown?" he asked. "I could have figured out Venus, given enough time. However, I got nothing for green gown."

Gyada nodded her understanding. "That is one activity that can't be accomplished in outer space. When you laid with a woman on a green patch of ground—grass or clover or something— you got green stains on her clothing."

"Which were dresses back then, got it." He nodded. "And I apologize. I wasn't proposing a romp with Willy the One-eyed Wonder Worm."

Gyada snickered.

Peter smirked. "It really is a gift."

Pearl set a beer on the table, "Bullshit. I've seen the company you keep. Hell, I remember a challenge about all the ways you could say sex without using fuck. You were in the top three spots."

Gyada looked at Pearl. "Who won?"

"Well, about that," Peter answered, "it was Bethany Anne."

"The *Empress?*" she asked, looking at the two of them.

"Oh, yeah." Pearl nodded. She turned to Peter, "Move over, Scrumptious, and give a very slightly older lady some room to park it."

"Don't let her tease you!" a male voice called from one of the front booths.

Pearl leaned into the aisle to yell back. "J.D., if you don't keep your yap shut, I won't be cooking for you when we get home."

There was a squeak beside Pearl, then Peter asked, "That was your husband?"

Pearl looked at Peter. "Yes, of course. We *are* married. Don't you fret, I'm harmless."

There was more cackling and hands-slapping-on-wood noises coming from the front of the bar.

Pearl leaned back into the aisle. "Keep it up and I'll put cilantro in the food." She waited for a second to confirm the lack of commotion from up front.

Pearl turned back to Gyada and Peter, then inclined toward them over the table and eyed them both as she whispered, "Can't get cilantro any more, but he doesn't know that."

"Uh," Peter told her, "if you really, really need it, I can get you a pinch."

"Oh?" She leaned back and looked Peter up and down. "How?"

"I have...sources," Peter admitted. "It's a special project, but if you wanted a very small amount, just enough to spice something," Peter nodded up the aisle, "I'm pretty sure I could make it happen."

"Hmmm. I can't stand the stuff either, but it always works to keep J.D. quiet. I think you might be a good contact." She tilted her head toward the beer he was drinking. "Consider that a freebie."

"Well," Peter shrugged and took a sip, "if you insist. My teacher always said to be polite to ladies."

"Who was that, your mom or your dad?" Pearl asked.

Peter put the bottle on the table. "Neither," he told her. "My teacher was John Grimes."

Pearl gave him a pat on the arm. "My sympathies. That had to hurt."

"All the damn time," Peter admitted. "And that was before I started mouthing off. Then life became miserable."

"How often did you get in trouble?" Gyada asked.

Peter looked at her. "Pretty much constantly. I was a spoiled rich kid with no sense and very little idea just how close to death I was."

"Death?" she pressed him.

"Yeah," Peter's eyes unfocused as he remembered. "I had done some stupid things back on Earth. Had some regular girls take pictures. It was a massive breach of the rules, and Bethany Anne stepped in when the Alpha of the Weres in the US was about to kill me for stupidity beyond the pale." Peter stopped a moment, thinking. "Or something like that. Anyway, I was really stupid."

"John put a stop to it?"

Peter reached up to touch his mouth, then moved his jaw left and right. "You might say he knocked the smartass right outta me. Along with a tooth or two. My own father told me to get my shit together or they could and would be willing to kill me. I kept my mouth shut that trip on the airplane, but from time to time stuff slipped out and John was there. One time we were in the garage of this house they had renovated to have weights and a place to spar. I said something stupid, and John tossed the barbell he was using for curls to Eric."

Peter told Gyada. "It took Eric two hands to catch it at that time."

Leaning back and grabbing the bottle, he continued, "Anyway, he tossed the barbell and weights, backhanded me, and caught the barbell Eric tossed back to him. I ended up with my feet above me against the far wall, wondering what fucking day it was." He took a swallow of his beer.

He smiled, thinking back to the memories. "God, those guys would work out to AC/DC all of the time. Their favorite song was *Big Balls*, but they changed a line to 'Bethany Anne's got the biggest balls of them all.'"

"You accepted this treatment?" Gyada asked.

Peter looked at her, eyes serious. "If John hadn't cleaned me up, I wouldn't be the man you see here. I owe him more than I can ever repay."

"No, that wasn't a judgment, Peter," she told him. "Rather, I come from...let's say a long time ago, when rough and ready treatment taught little warriors to grow up fast."

"Oh?" Pearl turned to Gyada. "You've never told me how old you really are."

"Well," Gyada smiled, "perhaps age is the last wall to fall between friends?"

"Well, for women," Peter agreed. "Not such a big deal for men."

"Don't you know everything *about* women is *for* women?" Pearl asked him.

"That isn't true," Gyada protested.

Pearl turned to Gyada. "Of course it isn't true, sweetie," she answered. "but Big-and-Strong-and-Not-Necessarily-Bright-about-Dating-Women here doesn't need to know that right now."

"Who says I'm not bright when it comes to dating women?" Peter protested.

Pearl just shook her head. "Boy, I've seen how you dress."

"Hey!" He pulled the shirt up a little. "Flannel is comfortable."

"And ugly." Pearl patted him on the shoulder and slid out of the seat to allow Peter more room. "There is no woman in history who has ever looked at a man in flannel and said, 'I want a hunk of that flannel-wearing man-candy.' In fact," she pointed at Peter, "I'm going to make him show up wearing flannel only."

Pearl turned and stepped across the small aisle to lift the board and slide behind the bar. "Nothing but flannel, head to toe. Just to test the theory."

Peter looked at Gyada, who was just as flummoxed as Peter. "In a very, very odd way, I think she is right," she admitted. "But wow, very odd."

Peter shrugged his shoulders, "After being around Gabrielle and Bethany Anne, Pearl is tame."

Both of them heard Pearl snort. "Tame?" she called. "I will have to up my game."

Gyada watched Peter stare at Pearl. He commented in a whisper, "Wow, Bethany Anne exerts a hell of an influence."

"Why do you say that?" Gyada asked, pulling his attention back to her.

"It's just…" He shrugged. "It seems I don't understand women well enough to know the answer. But it doesn't matter if she is kicking ass or making up smartass comments, Bethany Anne causes others to want to stretch themselves. Well," he smiled, "learning how to fight better so you can stop the ass-kicking I understand. The whole one..." Peter stopped for a moment, looking up and thinking. "Never mind, it's just people."

Gyada nodded, "That is how it has been through the ages."

"Really?" Peter asked, "How many?"

Gyada shook her head, "I'm sorry, youngling, you don't have enough game to get that answer out of me."

CHAPTER FIVE

Cheryl Lynn was sitting on one of the couches in Bethany Anne's suite, waiting for the Empress to arrive.

Bethany Anne eyed the PR lady as if she were a bug as she walked past her.

"You forgot," Cheryl Lynn observed, her head tracking Bethany Anne as she left the meeting room and went into her bedroom.

"Did not!" Bethany Anne responded a moment later. "I remember I'm meeting with Giannini just fine."

Cheryl Lynn raised an eyebrow as she heard her changing clothes. "Uh-huh, and by remember, you mean someone told you?"

"That would be me," ADAM's voice announced over the loud-speakers.

"You rat fink!" Bethany Anne groused from inside her bedroom. "I was about to tell you to keep that to yourself."

"But you didn't"

"But I was!"

"I can't read your mind, Bethany Anne," ADAM continued

over the loudspeaker. As far as Cheryl Lynn knew, they could keep up another conversation in her mind at the same time. However, Bethany Anne was normally considerate enough to include others.

Well, when it was convenient for her. Cheryl Lynn didn't want to give her friend too much credit.

Bethany Anne walked out of her suite wearing a dark red pantsuit with a formfitting, black, long-sleeve shirt under the jacket and a gold chain around her neck. "Well, that *is* probably to my benefit," she admitted. "Wouldn't want you to know all the good things I think about."

Cheryl Lynn noticed ADAM was quiet, leaving the last word to the Empress.

Bethany Anne thought for a moment, then scrunched up her face. "Where are we meeting them?"

"If your head wasn't screwed onto your shoulders—" Cheryl Lynn started to say as Bethany Anne's arm jetted out and grabbed her shoulder. The two of them disappeared.

QBBS *Meredith Reynolds*, Mark Billingsley Park

"When do you think they are going to be here?" Giannini asked Sia.

"Soon," a male voice answered, and the two women turned to see Scott nodding to Samuel and Richard, who were walking around the park to keep an eye out for trouble.

Scott turned to speak to them as he walked closer. "She doesn't want to sweep in here with an entourage, so we are trying to keep it low-key."

"Low-key?" Sia asked. Scott noticed she was already looking at her HUD, and the drones had started flying. She had three of them about fifteen feet from Giannini, and two circling at about forty feet to provide images from above.

"Sure. It can become a bit of a circus anytime she goes somewhere," Scott admitted. "Plus, this is supposed to be a rather quick interview, right?" He looked at Giannini, who nodded. He continued, "She figured she could pop in here, answer your questions, and then pop out. The guys will watch for any issues outside. I'll take care of anyone coming too close."

Scott looked around as he spoke to Giannini. "You don't get scared easily, right?"

"I've been baptized in fire twice," she answered. "Three times, if you include the riot on Yoll a few years back."

"Yeah, that was nasty," Scott admitted. "Sorry it took so long to pull you, Sia, Samuel, and Richard out of J'loong."

"Well," Giannini looked down a moment, "it's not like we had asked permission or for protection. We went there on our own and got stuck in the middle."

"Good footage, though," Sia commented. "Any reason we can't use it, Scott?"

Scott could hear ADAM answer in his implant. >> **Nothing was said that would be a problem.**<<

"Sure, go ahead," he replied. "It's not like you don't already have permission from Bethany Anne to run around and interview everyone."

This time it was a female who interrupted the conversation. "Did someone call my name?" Bethany Anne asked.

Inside her HUD, Sia already started editing the footage from when Bethany Anne appeared with Cheryl Lynn next to her. She caught Scott's reaction to her appearance and compared it with Giannini's. She kept the surprise off her face and made sure to follow the Empress with Drone Two, keeping Drone One on Giannini and Drone Three on Scott.

Drones Four and Five she set to fly in pre-programmed patterns. They would give her plenty of setting shots to intersperse. She hoped some people would show up so she could get crowd reactions.

She was going to need to request another two drones. That

meant a resource request up the chain—which ultimately went to Bethany Anne.

Normally that would cause Sia to be concerned about catching the Empress' good side so that the video would help her argue for more resources. With Bethany Anne, there wasn't a bad side.

Bethany Anne greeted Giannini and it was go-time.

"This is Giannini Oviedo, reporter and researcher, and I've been granted a few minutes with Empress Bethany Anne to give a little background to the latest concerns of those inside and outside the Etheric Empire." Giannini turned from her camera, the pink one, and focused on Bethany Anne. "Thank you so much for finding the time."

"You're certainly welcome," Bethany Anne replied.

"First, can we get an update about the Yaree, or Karillian, disagreement?"

Bethany Anne raised an eyebrow. "Well, first let's clarify the terms, shall we?"

Giannini nodded.

"The disagreement, if you will, is a war of opposing belief systems. The Leath are led by a group they call gods. We call them Kurtherians, and they want to exterminate the Karillians who are living on their homeworld. Approximately six months ago, a Karillian contingent headed by Delegate Tomthum requested an audience. During this conversation, they provided the background on six previous attempts by the Leath to subjugate the Karillian world and eradicate any sentient species."

"For what reason?" Giannini interrupted.

"We only have educated guesses at this time, I hope you understand?" Bethany Anne asked, and waited for Giannini's nod of agreement. "We surmise that the Kurtherians want to elevate the Leath to a state where they can overwhelm other species. Basically, advancement by warfare."

"If the Leath are dangerous, why haven't we heard from other groups about them?"

"We don't know that others have not been approached, unfortunately," Bethany Anne answered. "It could be that the Leath have implemented alliances with other races. Or, another reason might be that the Karillians are the nexus of two separate spheres of influence. The Karillians have been very insular in their own relationships, and only explained the situation once they felt we could help them."

"When was that?" Giannini interrupted. "Or rather, what allowed them to believe we could help them?"

Bethany Anne paused a moment to consider her answer. She finally responded, "It was a multitude of things. However, the main ones were the unexpected display of our abilities with the Ixtali Delegation, who happened to be attending the Etheric Empire court during the same time, and the fact that we had information on them already."

"Many are asking what the Karillians provide the Etheric Empire—"

Bethany Anne's eyes flashed red as she put up a hand. "They needed our help against the Kurtherians," she told Giannini. "That was sufficient for me." Bethany Anne put her hand to her mouth and tapped her lips. "Let me be clear. No matter what country our people came from back on our home planet or what type of government they may have previously lived under, the Etheric Empire is not a monarchy with a House of Commons, nor is it a republic or a representative form of government."

Bethany Anne's voice went soft, but with steel resonating in every word. "My charge is to keep our home planet safe from any group who would wish to go there and take control. For those who have joined us and forgotten this point, that was your reminder. For those who were born since we came to Yollin space or have grown into an awareness of things outside yourself, you might need to get a refresher on our history. Ask Meredith to get that for you."

Giannini nodded. She had received the message loud and clear. The problem was that her reporter mouth wouldn't shut the hell up. Before she could slap a hand over the traitorous mouth, she blurted another question. "If we aren't a monarchy with a House of Commons or a republic, what type of government are we?"

Bethany Anne smiled, her eyes flaring red. "We are a benevolent dictatorship. Those who don't like it will be shown the door."

Bethany Anne nodded to Giannini and then to Sia. As she turned to walk away with Cheryl Lynn, Giannini asked no one in particular, "The *Meredith Reynolds* doesn't have a door, so where would they go?"

Bethany Anne turned to answer over her shoulder, a smirk on her face. "Beats the fuck out of me, but I'd suggest they make sure they have plenty of air. This Empire won't bend a knee to anyone. Not as long as I'm the Empress."

Bethany Anne winked at the reporter, then touched Cheryl Lynn's arm, and the two of them disappeared.

Giannini finished her closeout and waited for Sia to signal all the drones to return with their cameras off. "She really doesn't give a shit about the growing concerns of some of those here about another war, does she?"

"Is it a lack of concern?" Sia inquired as she gently socketed her five drones into the small suitcase she used to store them. She had filled five spots with drones, but the suitcase could hold ten. Making sure Giannini wasn't watching, she reached in and petted two of the drones. "My sweet little video birds, Momma loves you." She closed and locked the case.

Picking up her case, she finished her thought. "So, is it a lack of concern, or is it a healthy step the fuck up? You got on this horse, so to speak, so stop bitching and cinch your belt, and let's move on."

Giannini shrugged. "I don't know, but the trip to meet with some of the other races ought to be fun."

"Did we get invited?" Sia asked. The two of them started down one of the paths toward Exit Four of the park.

"Yes," Giannini answered. "She told me in here," she tapped her head, "just as she disappeared."

"Well, I guess that last question didn't bother her, then."

"Thank God!" Giannini answered. "That damned question slipped out. I'm lucky Bethany Anne doesn't get pissed over those types of questions."

Sia reached out, grabbed Giannini around the shoulders, and pulled the woman close. "I think she likes that you are willing to ask those questions, not run from them."

"I think you're right," Giannini answered. "What do you think I should pack to meet with the Noel-ni assemblage?"

Sia was quiet a moment. "We are going to meet the Noel-ni?"

"Yes."

"Is it too late," Sia asked as the two of them were about to leave the park, "to ask for my vacation time?"

"No," Giannini answered. "But then I'll have to take another video producer with me."

There was a long pause as the two ladies entered the hall. Seconds later, Samuel and Richard swung in behind them. Sia's voice echoed from just a bit ahead.

"Sometimes, G, you can be *such* a bitch."

Leath Dreadnoughts *D'leet* and *Touk*

There were seventeen Leath ships in the queue, waiting to Gate to the Karillian system. The master Gate ship was in position, waiting for the final command.

The military advisors had worked very hard to bring a new tactic to the translocation defense. So far, each time their forces had left the Leath system, they had almost immediately been attacked by uncountable little metal disks. They drained the power of the shields, allowing the real weapons of the Etheric ships waiting on the other side to attack.

The results had been devastating.

Now, their latest ships with their latest technology were arranging themselves to transit. However, the new ships had ten older vessels in front of them.

Those ten ships were barely manned. The job of the ten in front was to run interference. The ships were massive energy sinks, running powerful shields to absorb any attack and push back, creating a large donut of protection with the center open for ships to enter behind them.

Once the ten ships created a beachhead, they would seek to break free of the Gate and in the confusion, the rest of the group would transit the Gate and break through the defenders. Then, after raining fire down onto the planet, their plan was to use additional ships to land the army and capture key ground areas.

Provided the navy could keep the protection overhead, those on the ground would take over the final centers of governmental power, and the Leath would claim the world as their own.

The signal went out and the ten shield ships started pushing forward, the first disappearing through the Gate.

Ten shield ships, four battleships, and the two massive dreadnoughts slipped through the Gate, all guns powered.

Karillian System

Admiral Thomas sat in the belly of the superdreadnought. "Reynolds, where are we going?" he asked the EI of the ship in a calm voice, grabbing his cup of coffee.

The Admiral hadn't even finished his question when a hologram of the system was displayed above his operations table. The Karillian planet was to the left—behind them for all practical purposes—and there was a small red spot halfway through the system. "Well, damn." The Admiral exhaled, looking at the new Gate.

The little spy EI they kept in the Leath system had let them know how many ships they would be facing, but the Leath had been too damned smart. They had changed their entry area, so his group would have to fight all of them.

Right now he was in *Reynolds*, of a design similar to *ArchAngel II*'s but with fewer people aboard. Reynolds had not worked with humans in his efforts before and therefore preferred to have bots on his ship. The only reason Admiral Thomas was on *Reynolds* along with his staff was because they had left *ArchAngel II* back in the Yollin system to transport Bethany Anne on her goodwill tour.

Internally it was known as the "We aren't out to eat your babies tour." It seemed a few of the newsies were starting to paint Bethany Anne as a horrible monster.

Nothing like kicking serious ass to make some groups scared of you.

Plus, what was attractive to humans had scared the hell out of a couple of the alien groups and caused a couple of others to send marriage contracts. Cheryl Lynn didn't even bother with asking Bethany Anne if she wanted to answer the requests.

Cheryl Lynn figured it would be less inflammatory that way.

"What the hell?" Admiral Thomas exclaimed as he looked at the best information they had at the time. It wasn't real-time, but their closest sensors were only a light minute away.

Captain Natalia Jakowski stood up from the captain's chair and wandered over to the Admiral's area. As of this moment, she had confirmed all of Reynolds' questions related to permissions for the ship's movement, and it would be a little while until their group reached the Leath.

"Natalia," Admiral Thomas pointed to the ships that had come through the Gate, and how they were building a large sphere, the later ships sliding into the protection provided by the first ships, "thoughts?"

"Seems like what you would typically do, protect the..." She paused a moment, leaning forward. "Are those their two big ships sliding in late?"

Reynolds answered through the speakers. "Yes, those are their two largest ships. This is in direct contrast to the last operation where they brought the big ships in first."

"And had their asses handed to them," Natalia added. She reached forward and zoomed in on the ships as close as she could. "Those ships in front look...wrong."

Admiral Thomas put his mug of coffee to the side and rested his elbows on his chair arms. Leaning forward, he twisted the hologram so he was looking from the back. "They have set up a defensive position with those ten ships. I imagine they are a bitch to bust through to get to the inner core, which is another set of ships that won't be easy to crack."

He leaned back in his chair. "Sonofabitch, they are upgrading their tactics." Thomas looked to his left and flipped a tablet screen to review other sensors. "We don't seem to have any other ships coming in sneaky."

"Well, none that we've found." Natalia walked back to the captain's chair. "If they are sneaking *properly*, we won't."

"Too damned true by half," Admiral Thomas admitted. "I hate this defensive bullshit, but we can't attack their system any more than they can attack ours." He looked at the screen where Lance Reynolds' face stared at him. "Dammit, Reynolds. Can't you give me another avatar to look at?"

"Why?" the EI replied. "Does the General's face bother you, sir?"

"It's like having BA looking over my shoulder," he told the EI. "Lance is good, but I don't need to see him all the time."

The visage on the screen changed, and Admiral Thomas

looked at it for at least fifteen seconds. "You know what, Reynolds, forget my complaint." He could hear Natalia trying to cover her snickering. "I'd rather look at a general of the Army than a brewmeister. Take Bobcat's face and flush it. I'll look at Lance."

"As you wish, Admiral," Lance's face replied.

Thomas looked at the map. "Reynolds, provide me with the locations of our asteroids with offensive capabilities on the hologram."

The map started exploding with different colored areas all over space.

"Good." Thomas nodded as he cracked his knuckles. "Let's get to work."

Ixtali System, Ixtali Nation's Floating Court, Two Months Later

Ixtali Court Member Addix stood in front of the giant two-story clear membrane in the dark. The room, easily big enough to hold a hundred who were mixing and mingling and up to a hundred and fifty if they got close, was empty but for her and one other who had just entered.

Addix continued looking out into space at the massive ship of the human Empress and the ship's escorts.

"It is impressive." Court Member Jondence spoke quietly, maintaining the reverent feel of the moment as he stepped up beside Addix.

"The ship?" Addix asked, turning to Jondence.

He nodded.

"Jondence, that ship doesn't compare to the Empress. I know you and the others think she played with my head, my emotions. Just do me a favor, if any of you intend to be inflammatory, give me enough warning that I can get out of the way."

Jondence's hissing laughter soon had Addix laughing as well. "We laugh, but I'm serious."

He put up a hand. "I'm well aware you are serious, Addix. If you weren't, I wouldn't have backed you for so many years. Of all of us, you had the clear eyes we needed to meet with the Etheric Empire in the first place. It would be devastatingly stupid to choose you for the negotiations and then ignore your recommendations."

"Even when the recommendations are ripping apart the fabric of our society?" she questioned, a hint of doubt in her voice.

Jondence's four mandibles made the sign of confidence. "You have now survived two attacks on your life to bring us this information. Those who would use our own technology against us have proven your argument, probably better than you might ever have done. This," he pointed to the Etheric Empire superdreadnought, "is but the proper time to announce what we have already approved in the court. The die of the future has already been cast. Now we wait for time to show us what the future holds in its hands."

The two of them took another long look at the superdreadnought. While they were watching, a battleship slid down the flank, dwarfed by the motionless ship.

"Is that a Skaine battleship?" Jondence asked.

"Yes," Addix answered. "It seems one of their police groups—Rangers, they call them—captured a Skaine battleship."

"Remarkable," Jondence muttered, his mandibles chittering in surprise. "Simply remarkable."

CHAPTER SIX

QBBS _Meredith Reynolds_

Yelena pursed her lips. She could see Bobcat sitting at their kitchen table, his shoulders hunched. She could tell he was sipping a beer and thinking.

He wasn't happy.

She folded the towel in her hands and inhaled deeply before letting the breath out, and with it, the hope that he was happy with what he and his two best friends had accomplished over the years. She had not only listened to the stories Bobcat had told her but had also sought out a few of Bobcat's friends in the past couple of months.

He was slipping into a sort of funk. Not a depression really, she reassured herself. He was here for her. She had his heart, but she needed to trust that by supporting him, she let him fly and be who he was born to be.

Kicking ass and taking names in a way only he and those two brainiac kids could. In the last few years, she had been happier than she deemed would have been possible for a woman who had previously thought going to work in an expensive suit would provide her bliss.

Now she was happy with Bobcat, the dogs, and beer. Oh, they had close friends, but for a while, it had mostly been her, Bellatrix, and Bobcat.

A siren call had him as well, and Yelena had felt the jealousy and fought it. Both the jealousy and the siren call. Just because she understood it didn't mean she didn't have selfish reasons for it to go the hell away.

She opened the closet door and placed the towel inside. Closing the door, she settled her shoulders and started toward the man she loved.

Sometimes there was pain in doing the right thing.

QBBS _Meredith Reynolds_, All Guns Blazing, Viewing Deck

"So," Tina, Cheryl Lynn's oldest, glanced at the scientist, a smile on her face as the two of them looked at stars they couldn't have seen worth a damn from Earth, "do you remember the first time we went out in a Pod?"

Marcus pulled back from looking through the ancient telescope the two of them had set up in the glass-walled room of All Guns Blazing.

He looked at the young woman and smiled. "That was a while back!" Marcus chuckled. "What I specifically remember is your mom chewing my ass out for not asking her permission."

His eyes glazed over for a moment, but Tina caught it. Since the fateful time Marcus had interceded on her behalf, and because of her time in the Etheric Academy, she had grown into a perceptive woman who cared about what this man did with his life.

And what he didn't.

"How come you haven't gone sightseeing or done other things?" she asked him.

Marcus frowned. "I've done other things!" He pointed down

the stairs to her left. "I'll have you know I'm part-owner of the most famous bar in multiple systems."

"Uh-huh," Tina tapped the telescope, "but was that your goal in life?"

Marcus chuckled. "Well, to be honest, I just wanted to prove the existence of aliens."

Tina slowly looked around the large room with its two-story-tall glass window that provided a view of space and the planet Yoll in the far distance. In this room she could count three different alien species. "I count three right here, and I bet if I went downstairs, there would be another four."

"Five," Marcus corrected.

Tina turned to him. "Five?"

He nodded. "Yeah, I have everyone let me know when we get a new alien species in the bar. Two months ago, we had a multi-alien group show up, and we had twenty-two different species at the same time." His eyes glinted in humor. "Bobcat thought I was going to shit a..." He stopped, eyes wide, and looked at Tina in alarm. "Oh, shit, woman present! I'm so sorry, Tina." He fumbled a moment. "I've been around Bobcat and William too long to place a filter on my mouth."

"Well." She patted his hand. Marcus looked young until you noticed his eyes. Right now, they were looking way older than she had seen them in a long time. "I appreciate your concern, but given that Scott is my dad, my uncles are John, Darryl, Eric and Peter, and my aunts are Gabrielle and the Empress, and that doesn't even include..." Tina scrunched her eyes. "Well, shit. Just about everyone who cares about them cares about me. I tend to be around some harsh and brash language."

Marcus nodded in agreement. "I bet you are, at that. But in my time, there were a few things we didn't casually talk about to a younger woman, and I'll ask you not to have me change too much."

Tina moved her hand to pat the older scientist on his arm.

"That is why so many women don't understand the amazing person you are, Teacher my Teacher."

Marcus smiled and placed a hand on hers. "You know that there is never going to be a good enough guy for you, right?"

Tina snorted. "Do you know how hard it is to get a date? Hell, my dad is a Queen's Bitch, and my uncle is famous, or infamous anyway, in how many systems for the death and destruction he can cause?"

Marcus turned to look out the window. "Do you regret it?" He waved toward space. "There is a whole galaxy out there you could lose yourself in, Tina."

She took her hand away. "You think? Do you really believe that my mom and dad wouldn't know exactly where I was?" She tapped the side of her head. "I know these wonder gadgets inside my skull can be used to track me as well as let me translate and all the other badass stuff they do."

"So," Marcus asked, still looking at the stars for a moment before turning back toward her. "Do you want it removed?"

"Haaayllll no, as Uncle Darryl would say." Tina laughed. "I have ADAM and everybody, including you, on instant connect. Plus, you allow me to wake you up whenever I want." She shrugged as she looked at the stars. "I'm special."

Marcus chuckled. "Tina, you will *always* be special, and not just because you're my favorite student."

"I'm your only student."

"Not true!" Marcus grinned. "I have a lot of students."

"No, you have a lot of people you help in the Etheric Academy from time to time. Those are 'here today, gone in six weeks.'"

Marcus shrugged.

"I'm the only one you seek out to show the latest cool stuff that's going on," Tina proclaimed

"Maybe."

"Maybe, my ass," Tina responded.

Marcus looked at her, shocked.

"What? Marcus, I'm pretty old now. You think maybe I can cuss a bit if I want to?"

"You still look like a young woman."

"I look no younger than you do."

He stared at her.

"Okay, maybe five years younger," she amended. "However," she tapped the side of her head in a different location, "I'm smart, and you know it."

Marcus smiled. "Why do you think I keep pestering you?"

Tina turned to the bar table next to them and picked up her glass. This time she had gotten one of the guys in the back to try brewing Dr. Pepper. She mumbled an answer under her breath to Marcus before she took a sip, wrinkling her nose.

"What did you say?" he asked. Still facing away from him, she rolled her eyes.

I said, she thought to herself, *well, you don't pester me because I'm beautiful.* Aloud, she told him, "This Dr. Pepper might be an acquired taste."

He raised his eyebrows, so she grabbed her drink and passed it to him. Surprised, he accepted the drink and took a small sip, then another one. "Hmm." He looked down into the glass. "Actually, from what I remember they got it right." He took another sip. "This came from Texas originally." He looked down the stairs. "Who did you bribe to make it?"

"Like I would rat someone out!" Tina told him. "I have my sources."

"Probably Chester," Marcus continued, ignoring Tina's remark. "He's the best down there, and he's already married."

"What does being married have to do with anything?" she asked.

Marcus turned to her and raised the glass and one eyebrow in question. She shook her head so he shrugged, then upended the glass and finished the drink. "God," he reached around her to put the glass on the table, "that was good."

"Elementary, my dear Tina," he told her. She didn't get worked up about his comment since she had read all the original Sherlock Holmes books. "It's in our glass, so it's one of our people. Besides Chester, we have only two others who are good enough with brewing this stuff that you would even bother asking. Barry is young and still deathly afraid of Scott, and the other is so scared of Bethany Anne; she probably wouldn't even touch the ingredients."

"She wasn't even willing to look at a printout of the recipe," Tina answered, thinking back to her conversation with Jackie before she looked at Marcus, smiling. Then she played back the conversation and realized she had given up the truth. *"Gott Verdammt!"*

Marcus chuckled some more. "Okay, my little Padawan, why are we up here?" He pointed to the telescope. "We aren't really looking, so what did you want to talk about?"

ADAM? Tina reached through her connection, the technology placed in her skull behind her ear.

>>**Yes, Tina?**<<

Would you please ask Meredith to give Marcus and me some space?

Moments later, Tina noticed the small conversations start to diminish. Fortunately, a couple of years back, Bethany Anne had had the same technology installed up here on the viewing deck that she used in the throne room.

Startled, Marcus looked around before returning his gaze to Tina. "Seriously? It's so important you want audio privacy?"

"Yes." She looked straight at him. "I need to tell you something, and I want your full attention. That is why we aren't in the lab."

Marcus nodded. "Good choice."

"Tell me about it," she agreed. "If we were, I wouldn't remember what the hell I wanted to talk about because we would be concocting something."

Marcus looked at her a moment before barking a laugh, his

smile wide and his eyes crinkling in delight. He pointed at her. "That's *right!*" He smiled some more, the most fully animated he had been so far with her, and it caused her to stare back at him.

"What?" she asked.

"I wouldn't be the problem child in the lab, *you* would!" He stepped around the woman and pulled out a bar stool for her to sit on at their table before he pulled out one for himself. When she was seated, he continued, "I think you might be worse in the lab than I am."

"No," she shook her head, "I'm just a little younger and more excitable in the lab."

"Yeah, there is that," he mused. "Okay, Padawan, you have my full attention and your own."

Tina took a deep breath, running through the speech she had been working on all week. She folded her hands and placed them on the table.

Here goes nothing, she thought to herself.

QBBS *Meredith Reynolds,* William's Manufacturing Cavern

William slid the bolt into the last hole and grabbed a nut. Reaching around to the other side, he found the threaded end and quickly spun the nut onto it. The large cavern was peaceful. He had ten large copper brewing kettles and their associated piping in various stages of completion around him.

While the Yollins and others appreciated manufactured products for brewing, there was something about owning a handmade William's Kettle (TM) product. He charged fifteen times more for a handmade product than a manufactured one.

Hell, he even had a black-market product he shipped through other sources that promised "You can't tell the difference between ours and a William's Kettle, or your money back." He sold that one for half the cost of a William's Kettle.

He had become stupidly wealthy just by using his hands and for the joy of making stuff that it wasn't funny.

There was a soft meow. William frowned and bent to his left, looking down the aisle toward the sound. He waited a moment before leaning back.

Meow.

He jumped into the aisle this time, his eyes glancing into the shadows. He looked at the lights above the doorway into his little sanctum.

One of the twelve was red.

"Okay, who's here?" he called. "I'll give you one second before Meredith initiates a security alarm."

William leaned back toward the large kettle he was working on and grabbed a foot-long wrench.

"It's me, old friend," a voice stated calmly.

William recognized the voice. "Goddammit, Stephen," he tossed the wrench back on the bench, "stop scaring a man like that. I'd likely be upset if I brained the fuck out of you." He reached up and scratched his chin. "Then Bethany Anne would be annoyed until I explained the situation."

Stephen chuckled. "I'll be more careful next time," he answered as he came around the corner of one of William's tall shelving units.

He was carrying an all-black cat.

"Huh." William reached out to take the cat from Stephen. "I was wondering where your furry black ass went." He scratched the cat behind its ears and then turned, the cat fairly leaping out of his arms to land on the ground and run after God-only-knew-what.

Stephen put his arms behind his back and looked at William's projects. "I've come to tell you that it's time to close up the shop."

William narrowed his eyes, turning his head a bit. "Whatcha talkin' 'bout, Willis?"

Stephen pursed his lips. "William, first of all, be thankful I understand the reference. *But*, this isn't an episode of *Diff'rent Strokes*! Bethany Anne says to get your lazy ass up and shake out the fucking cobwebs."

"She said those exact words?" There was a huskiness to William's voice, a yearning Stephen recognized.

Stephen pulled his arms around to his front and crossed them. "You want her exact words?"

William nodded.

"Tell my lazy-ass tinkerer that it's time he stopped pretending he's happy building a manufacturing company and get back on the fucking horse, for fuck's sake. If he doesn't understand that, tell him I need a *Gott Verdammt* genius with ships, antigrav, and stuff that fucks up annoying motherfuckers. So, Winnie-the-fucking-Pooh-bear needs to get on Tigger's back and get back to work. We got shit to do, people to protect, and others to fuck up."

William eyed Stephen for thirty seconds, the vampire waiting for his response. Stephen wasn't surprised as he watched the tension drain from William's shoulders. Some needed to see the light, some needed to be told it was okay, and some needed a foot up their ass.

William turned, pulled the rag he had been using out of the kettle, and tossed it on the bench. "Meredith?"

"Yes, William?" she replied.

"Please sell my remaining inventory and let anyone interested in William's Kettle products know the old man has taken a sabbatical. Then when I leave, please shut down this area, pumping the air out and mothballing it."

He turned and started toward the door that led out of the workshop. "Team BMW has shit to accomplish."

"I thought you guys *had* been doing stuff?" Stephen queried as the two walked out through the double doors. William stopped to punch in some security code or another before waving Stephen to walk ahead of him.

"We've been living life and doing a job," William answered, "but our Empress just kicked me in the ass."

"And how does that make you feel?" Stephen asked.

"Pretty fucking good, old man." William chuckled. "Pretty fucking good."

Team BMW Offices, Two Hours Later

Bobcat, Yelena, and Bellatrix were the last three to enter through the security doors. Bobcat was surprised to see that Cheryl Lynn, Tina, and Stephen were there with William and Marcus. "Uh-oh," he nodded to his friends, "I'm not the only one who got 'the talk,' am I?"

William and Marcus both smiled and shook their heads.

"Since I've got permission—" Bobcat started before Yelena cut him off.

"You don't need permission, but you have my blessing," she told him. "You need to be who you are for Bethany Anne and your friends. I'm not going anywhere, Bobcat, so stop fretting about me!"

Bobcat reached out and wrapped an arm around Yelena. Then, surprising her, he quickly pulled her up, grabbed her legs, and started carrying her.

"Let me down, you goof!" She beat at his chest. "I'll kick your ass!"

"A good reason not to let you down, I'd say," Bobcat told her.

She stopped beating him and reached up to grab him around his neck. Using it for leverage, she pulled herself up and whispered in his ear.

He damned near dropped her.

"*Hey!*" she shrieked, her legs dropping to the ground.

He helped her stand up. "Sorry." He smiled. "Your offer surprised me."

"Too much candy?" Tina asked, smiling wickedly.

Yelena smiled. "I promised to try out a new recipe at home."

"Uh-huh." William grinned. "You don't have to share what kind of recipe it was."

She eyed him. "Beer!" she retorted. "We have a book of positions we are still working through for the other kind of recipes."

William reached over and snagged his tablet. "Kamasutra?"

"No," Bobcat answered as Yelena looked at Cheryl Lynn with a "what?" facial expression.

"Human or alien recipes?" Marcus asked.

"Alien," Bobcat answered.

William chuckled. "Lucky bastard."

There was a sharp *whack* as Yelena finally caught up to the conversation.

"Hey!" She pointed a finger at him. "That number seven hundred and forty-five was something I've been waiting to try for sixty-four positions, so don't piss me off!"

Bobcat grabbed a bar stool from under the table everyone was sitting at and pulled it out for Yelena. "Why do you think I thought it was safe to answer the way I did?"

She snorted. "Because you are Bobcat, and thank you for the chair."

Bobcat sat down next to her and glanced around the table. "Okay, Yelena helped me figure out why I have been acting like a mopey dog for the last three months."

"Because you're Bobcat?" Marcus asked.

"Because your last four barrels of beer have sucked tiger titties?" William responded.

Bobcat looked at Marcus and answered him first. "No." He turned to William. "Seriously? My last brew kicked your ass so bad we had to carry you out on a stretcher."

"Pshaw!" William waved a hand. "I was just trying to make you feel better."

"Dude," Bobcat looked at his friend and pointed down the

table, "you asked Tina here if she was going to have babies like Gabrielle."

William turned to Tina, a blush starting to form. "Tell me I didn't!"

"Okay," Tina shrugged, "you didn't."

"Oh, thank God." William was slowly turning toward Bobcat when she shook her head and spoke again.

"But that wouldn't be the truth."

Everyone winced when William's head hit the table. A moment later, a slow moan came from him. "Ooooowwwwwww," he groaned. "That fucking hurrrrrrrrrt."

They waited a moment for him to lift his head up. When he didn't, Cheryl Lynn reached over and patted him on the back. "It's okay. At least you didn't ask her to marry you."

William's head turned enough that one eye could peek out, straining to look sideways at the woman. "Tell me the truth. My head is already on the table."

She winked at him. "You didn't, but it is true that the beer took you out."

William slowly lifted his head back up from the table. "I wondered how I got back home."

"Would you like to see the video?" Bobcat asked. William just gave him the fisheye, so Bobcat shrugged. "Just asking." He took a deep breath and looked at everyone there.

"Okay," he nodded to Stephen, "I understand you probably went to William to have a talk, right?" Stephen nodded. "Coming from Bethany Anne?" Stephen nodded again. He turned to Tina. "You and your Mom for Marcus?"

Cheryl Lynn turned to her daughter. "Uh, not me."

Tina smiled. "It was me." She paused a moment. "Well, except Bethany Anne stopped me last week and asked…"

There was an intake of breath beside Bobcat. He turned to see a look of surprise on Yelena's face. "Oh. My. God!"

Bobcat slowly nodded. "She got to you too, didn't she?"

Yelena just nodded.

He turned to everyone there. "She is getting us off our asses again. We've been calling it in for too long."

"So," William asked as he looked at his two friends. "Who do we trust with All Guns Blazing?"

CHAPTER SEVEN

Stephen, William, Marcus, Cheryl Lynn, Tina, and Yelena all turned to stare at Bobcat. His eyes went unfocused for a moment, then he looked at everyone who was staring at him.

"What?" he asked. "I figure we ask Yelena, Cheryl Lynn, Stephen, and Tina to run it," he answered, a small smile on his face. "After all," he jerked a thumb in Yelena's direction, "she can brew as well—"

"Better," Yelena cut in.

Bobcat ignored her, but his smile gave away that he had heard her. "As I can, or will with a little practice." He couldn't ignore the elbow to his ribs. His voice squeaked just a bit. "Apparently that opinion isn't universal," he concluded, to general chuckles around the table.

"Why am I included in this?" Cheryl Lynn asked.

"Marketing," Yelena replied.

Cheryl Lynn turned to Tina. "Was that why you asked me to come?"

Tina shook her head. "Actually, no, but I'll get to that in a moment because I think it would be awesome if you got involved in All Guns Blazing, Mom."

Cheryl Lynn's eyes narrowed. "Why?"

"It fits with your present job responsibilities very well," Tina pointed out. "You are supposed to keep your finger on the pulse of what's heard and felt about the Etheric Empire, and how better to accomplish that than talking with patrons at a popular bar?"

"Like a bartender?" Cheryl Lynn's eyes opened wide.

"Sure," Tina continued. "Short skirt, pantyhose…"

"I'LL DO NO SUCH THING!" Cheryl Lynn turned on her daughter, then noticed the barely-restrained smile. "Oh!" She pointed a finger at Tina. "I'll get you for that. You can be wait-staff and wear tiny tight tops!"

Bobcat and William looked at each other, both trying to push back a little way from the table.

"Sorry, I can't do that," Tina answered, putting her hands on the table, "but I have another suggestion."

Yelena looked at Stephen, who winked at her but kept a blank face.

"And what's that?" Cheryl Lynn asked. "Bouncer?"

"No." Tina took a deep breath. "Guys," she looked from Bobcat to William and lastly at Marcus, "I'd like to formally ask to be a part of Team BMW."

The room got deathly quiet for a moment as the three guys in question searched each other's eyes for answers.

Bobcat pursed his lips. "So," he turned to Yelena, "will you take over All Guns Blazing as primary manager and brewmeister?"

"Only if you let me grow it," Yelena answered. "I don't want to have only the one bar."

"Sonofabitch," William breathed. "Those are some…" Yelena looked at the big man, "ovaries," he finally got out.

"I'm in, if I get a cut." Cheryl Lynn told them. "I like a challenge."

"What," Stephen asked from her right, "trying to corral Bethany Anne's antics isn't enough?"

"Hell," Cheryl Lynn replied. "I have all my core responses to anything Bethany Anne does as templates. I just pull out the appropriate template, fill in the details, and have ADAM shoot it to the news agencies and my contacts around the systems. We occasionally add some video if we have it, or if we need to give our news a better shot at being seen." She shrugged. "Frankly, Bethany Anne doesn't surprise me anymore."

"Those sound like famous last words," Yelena whispered. Bobcat nodded just a little in agreement, she saw from the corner of her eye, and she noted the twinkle in Stephen's eye and his lip upturned just a bit in amusement on her other side.

Marcus was amused. He hadn't expected Tina to ask to be a part of the team, but frankly they needed a new catalyst in the group. The three of them had been together too long, and could read each other's minds. They would be better for some new blood, and if anything, he wanted one more voice on the side of reason.

Bobcat smiled and directed his attention across the table. "Stephen?" Bobcat was surprised when he answered something besides, "Not interested."

"I think I'll take the occasional bouncer job, among other things," he agreed, then smiled. "For a cut."

Bobcat looked at William, who shrugged. "A smaller percentage of something we don't have is a bigger amount than a third of nothing."

Bobcat turned to Marcus. "Do the honors?"

Marcus smiled. "Of course." He turned to his right. "Tina, would you like to join Team BMW in the science area?"

Her whoop of delight had everyone clapping and laughing as she leaned over to give Marcus a hug, then got up to squeeze Bobcat and William.

Stephen looked around the group and wondered, *Just how* did *Bethany Anne make this stuff happen?*

And… *Hell, did I just agree to be a co-owner in a company again?*

He nodded. Bethany Anne needed Team BMW to make stuff happen. The guys needed to know All Guns Blazing and Yelena were going to be okay.

Stephen sighed. *Needs must when Bethany Anne was the driver.* Later that evening, when everyone agreed to get back together the next day to hammer out details, he realized he felt ten years younger.

It didn't hurt that Jennifer wanted to be involved as well.

When she didn't have to ship out with the Guardians, she figured she could bounce with the best of them.

QBBS *Meredith Reynolds*, Guardians' Workout Area

Peter walked into the workout area and turned to his right. A few of the teams in the huge area nodded to him before they went back to their activities.

Peter's hackles went up, and he smiled as he stripped off his normal clothes and put on the workout suit. It was made of a resilient material that stretched if he changed forms.

He was careful to not look toward the front door when Gyada came around the corner, but he was straining with his other senses to hear the change in the heartbeats, to smell the chemicals emitted by the other teams, and to generally see if he could sense a difference.

Not surprisingly, there was one.

Further, Peter could hear the almost-silent whispers as many in the teams stopped what they were doing to see what was happening, and tried to determine who was causing the interruptions and curiosity. When those who made killing their business sensed a threat, it was their nature to scrutinize the newcomer.

What they saw confused them. She wasn't that tall, and she

seemed out of sorts within the large group of people. A little uncomfortable, in fact.

But that didn't hide her easy grace or the eyes flicking from group to group, registering their existence and moving to the next. Peter could sense when her attention turned to him, and he pivoted to face her and nodded.

"Shun?" Peter called. The Chinese team lead was about thirty yards away, working with Zhu and Jian. He waved them over. While Jian would easily have heard his request, Shun and Zhu were upgraded humans, not Weres. They were Jian's backup when the Were changed to his cat.

The three men bowed to their testing team and started jogging in his direction as Gyada approached.

"Gyada," Peter nodded to her, "I sincerely appreciate—"

She cut him off with a small upraised hand. "The Empress has spoken, and her Shield Maiden will answer."

Peter looked at her. "Have you worked out with Bethany Anne much?"

The guys arrived and waited as Peter and Gyada finished their conversation.

"Yes. When I first arrived from Earth, she tested me to see how my control of the beast worked. Then she had me change and tested me as a creature as well."

"And by tested, you mean…" Peter asked.

"She kicked my ass up and down the floor mats," Gyada acknowledged. "She wanted to make sure I had control before she put me through reconditioning in the Pod-doc with TOM and ADAM."

"Okay, just seeing if she worked any differently with you than me," he told her before he turned toward the guys. "All right, you three are going to work with Gyada and form a team with some new recruits we are looking to bring on board. Make sure we think of everything we can, especially how to strengthen the Guards with minimal Weres." Peter jerked a thumb behind him. "Kiel will meet you four in the smaller training area in 04-2."

Peter looked at Gyada. "It's time to remember your berserker training. We might need it."

Gyada pursed her lips. It had been centuries, but sometimes it felt like last week. She nodded her understanding, and the four of them started heading toward the exit.

Planet Yoll, R'Chkoklet

Drk-vaen pulled open his clothes drawer and picked out two shirts and a hat. He wasn't sure what he should take, but he didn't want to be out of fashion if he could help it.

He closed the drawer and turned toward the door as he heard footsteps coming down the hallway.

Then, a knock.

"Son?" the deep voice of his father called.

Drk-vaen walked toward the door and pulled it open. "Hello, Father."

His father greeted him, and Drk-vaen stepped back to allow him to enter the suite. The older male looked around and grunted to himself before turning to his son. "You have decided to join the Empire?"

There was a silence. "I owe it to him," he finally replied. "He didn't save me so I could sit on this planet doing nothing."

Drk-Zehn tapped his mandibles in agreement. "You have come a long way since the human John Grimes spared your life. Taking the family's power armor was foolish. The fact that he could understand told me all I needed to know about the Empress and the aliens who took over." This time Drk-Zehn paused before asking, "Are you doing it for yourself, or because you feel you shamed us?"

Drk-vaen shook his head. "I accepted the shame, and I walked my two years in it. If anyone doubts my honesty, they can come tell me personally. I am more than old enough to answer for myself." He tossed his two shirts on the bed next to the other items he planned to take with him. "When the news told us the humans had accepted a new race into the Empire, I was intrigued. When they went to battle for them, I was impressed."

Drk-vaen looked out his window, across the city to what planet or star system his father couldn't tell. "But when they called for those who would fight for others?" Drk-vaen turned to look his dad in the eyes. "My heart burst. I cannot fail to take up the call. I will help. My shame is behind me, and helping others is my future, beyond what I have done so far."

"Then you should know," his father began, reaching into a pouch he had clasped around his waist, "that your mother and I are very proud of you. We would have you represent our family." His father pulled his hand out and opened it, showing Drk-vaen the small gold family sigil that could either be worn on a sash or a shirt and told every Yollin that Drk-vaen's clan supported him and claimed him no matter what he did.

Basically it was the clan's crest of trust. With it, Drk-vaen could commit the most despicable crimes and the clan would never turn their back on him. It was rarely shared, and as a young Yollin, Drk-vaen had made up stories for himself where he was given the family sigil in a grand ceremony where all would celebrate his awesomeness.

He had long since given up those childish dreams for the reality of his stupidity years before. That his parents hadn't thrown him out on his ass was something he had finally come to understand as a blessing he hadn't deserved.

However, he could tell how much he had hurt his father by taking the family's armor and using it to try to fight the Empress' edicts. Apparently, his father had blamed himself for Drk-vaen's rash actions.

And yet, Drk-vaen had never felt unloved or unwanted.

Drk-vaen reached out to touch the sigil in his father's hand, a tear forming in his eye. "I am not worthy of this, Father." He looked up to see him smiling, a look of pride in his eyes.

"Drk-vaen," he nodded at the sigil, "no family member who has *ever* received the sigil has felt they were worthy. If you thought you were, it would be a sign that the person offering needed to pull it back for their own honor."

"So, your father?" he asked, a question in his eyes.

"Told me the same thing before I myself left." He nodded at the sigil. "In fact, just before giving me this very sigil."

Drk-vaen looked down to see his father hold it out to him. Drk-vaen slowly took the sigil and pulled it closer to see the small cut in the bottom corner that hadn't been visible when his father held it. Drk-vaen closed his hand before he took two steps and threw himself into his father's embrace.

His father's voice reverberated in his mind. "You will do us proud, Drk-vaen. Just know that we are already prouder of you than perhaps you ever knew."

"I will never," Drk-vaen released his father and stepped back, "fail the family."

Drk-Zehn touched his son's chest. "Never fail the Empress, and you will never fail the family." His father clicked his mandibles together. "Now, come down and eat. The whole family has a surprise for you."

Drk-vaen grabbed his clothes, tossed them into his bag and slung it over his shoulder, and followed his father out of his room. Together they went down the stairs, and Drk-vaen could hear chattering as he followed his father around the final few steps and looked up to see who was there to send him off.

His father was right. Every family member was present, with one *additional* guest.

The Guardians' captain and Empress' Bitch was waiting in his family's home, smiling at him.

"I got a call from John Grimes, who is with the Empress," the human told Drk-vaen in Yollin. "He asked if I would do him the favor of picking up a special package on Yoll. Said he's been watching you since you guys met the first time."

Drk-vaen's mandibles froze. He looked at his mother, who nodded ever so slightly to him and then at his father, who popped him on the back and smiled. "We have a video from John Grimes himself explaining he would be protecting the Empress and asking if it would be okay if his protégé paid it forward."

"Protégé?" Drk-vaen finally sputtered.

Peter took a step forward. "Let's just say you aren't the first stupid teenager John has saved despite themselves. When we finish here, I'll treat you to a drink at All Guns Blazing and tell you about an idiot by the name of Pete who almost got himself killed. John Grimes saved him from death by youthful stupidity with a wicked punch to the jaw."

Drk-vaen thought the going-away party was the best experience ever. Then, when the two of them left his father's house, the experience was made better when he came out of the house to find a massive ship sporting the Empress' skull and fangs logo floating in the air.

Everyone now knew that Drk-vaen had joined the Empress' Guards and John Grimes' protégé Peter, the captain of Empress' Guardians, had picked him up.

The ship had been stationed over the house for an hour. There were news people taking video as the two came out of the clan's gates.

That evening after the news reported Drk-vaen had joined the military, thousands of Yollins tried to shove their way into the recruiting stations to follow the young male's lead.

A new generation of Yollins was going to war, following an alien Empress into the deep, frozen darkness of space to do the right thing for a species they had never met.

CHAPTER EIGHT

<u>**Ixtali, High Council Meeting Room**</u>

IXTALI POLITICIAN

THE KURTHERIAN GAMBIT

Bethany Anne arrived in the large auditorium and looked around. There had to be twenty thousand seats rising from a circular table in the middle. The chairs at the table faced each other, but there were monitors above that displayed those sitting or standing at the council table to those in the audience.

Bethany Anne had known the council had a public venue, but it was a bit larger than she had expected.

>> **We have located four persons with energy weapons and six with obvious edged metal weapons.**<<

John's voice came over the channel. "Ignore the edged stuff for now. Show energy weapons on HUD."

Three of the locations looked like they were plants, and another was way up in the balcony so that was most probably a personal protection weapon that had been allowed in somehow. That person was highlighted for the Ixtali guards.

"Okay, guys, we are going to take out the other three—"

Bethany Anne interrupted. "You guys get close, I'll fry them."

"We kinda need them alive if possible, boss," John replied as he sent Eric and Scott toward the two ADAM had tagged with his nanospies. Each looked like he was going to take up a spot where the floor stopped and the wall and the seats started going up.

John headed left.

Darryl stayed with Bethany Anne, who had slowed her descent of the stairs as the guys moved ahead. The auditorium's buzz had increased in volume when Bethany Anne appeared and started coming down the VIP stairs to the floor to meet with the council.

"Ready," Eric commed.

"Ready," came Scott's reply, quickly followed by John's.

"Here goes nothing," Bethany Anne exclaimed, lifting her hand as she continued walking.

Patch me into the auditorium's speakers, ADAM.

>>**Done.**<<

"Ixtali people." Bethany Anne's voice, speaking Ixtali, surrounded everyone in the area.

Down below, one of the councilors leaned over and asked Addix, "Did you give her access?"

Addix just shook her head as her mandibles clicked in a "What do you want me to do?" pattern. Addix sat back to watch the show. She had seen the Guards in their formfitting armor suddenly start coming down the steps and surround the table. One of them had stayed with the Empress.

Addix knew the one named John Grimes was behind her, and even though she trusted them all, his presence was causing an itch in the middle of her back.

Bethany Anne's hand went up, and a blue energy glow appeared. The crowd started quieting down at her display.

It got larger and larger until it was at least as large as her own head, and then it broke apart into three smaller globes that started orbiting her hand.

A second later, they shot off to hit three people in the audience. Addix turned, hearing the commotion behind her, in time to see John Grimes run up the stairs to an Ixtali who was writhing on the chairs, unable to fall to the ground between them. She watched, fascinated when John's left hand touched the male and the blue arcs of electricity that had been causing the Ixtali to spasm went up his arm and disappeared.

Then the Empress' Guard reached into the coat of the attacked Ixtali and pulled out a laser pistol.

Those who were around him pulled back, fearing they would be associated with the threat to the Empress.

Addix turned to look at the other two Guards who were lifting their marks, retrieving their pistols, and bringing the comatose Ixtalis down to the council's area.

Addix was surprised when Bethany Anne's voice came through the speakers and she heard her just feet away as well.

"I have to apologize," Bethany Anne continued, "for taking out the trash, but I refuse to allow the ignorant, the stupid, and the selfish to possibly hurt those here who wish for a stronger future."

Bethany Anne smiled at the audience. "Now that we know who our enemies are, let us work on creating a stronger, more protected future for the Ixtali nation as the Etheric Empire hears the official request of the Ixtali council and accepts your application for membership."

Three Days Later

Bethany Anne stepped from her shuttle, John and Scott beside her with their battle helmets under their arms. She waved to everyone as the three of them walked through the huge landing bay. As soon as she was out of the bay and they had turned a corner, Bethany Anne reached out, and the three of them disappeared.

Reappearing a moment later in her outer suite, she pointed to the main door. "You guys go get into something comfortable. I need to change out of this stuff."

John mumbled something and Scott went out. A couple minutes later he came back and relieved John, who left to go change.

As John came back into the suite, Bethany Anne came out of her rooms, her hair damp from a shower, wearing a black tracksuit.

John raised an eyebrow as he looked at her, a frown on his face.

Bethany Anne looked down at herself. "What is it?" she asked, looking back up at him in confusion. "No shoes? I do that all the time."

"No." He took a seat on one of the leather chairs. Scott had parked himself on the loveseat, leaving the couch for Bethany Anne. "I'm just wondering why you haven't figured something out..." he waved his fingers near his head, "to dry your hair."

Bethany Anne rolled her eyes and dropped onto the couch. "I did."

There was a pause as the two guys looked at each other before turning back to Bethany Anne. "And?" Scott asked.

"You know how my hair does that floaty thing when I pull Etheric energy?"

"Yeah." Scott nodded. "I figured it might dry your hair."

Bethany Anne grabbed a pillow and stuck it in her lap. "It does. But imagine my hair, freshly dried, frizzy, and sticking out like I'd stuck my finger in a light socket."

John snickered. "I'd pay good money."

"No." Bethany Anne forowned.

"Please?" Scott added. "I mean, c'mon. We," he pointed to John and himself, "promise to take a bullet for you, and you won't even share a little frizz between friends?"

Bethany Anne looked between the two of them. "Seriously? You guys want to see El Frizzo?"

"Well," John's face flushed a bit, and he scratched his chin, "uh, yeah, actually. I think it would be funny as hell."

"Well, don't market the shit out of your request or anything," she grumped.

"That's Cheryl Lynn's job," Scott replied. "And if I brought back a story of you being human for once instead of perfect, it would help her immensely."

Bethany Anne's eyes narrowed. "Is she still having issues after all these years?"

Scott shrugged. "Not like you think, no. But there *is* a little bit of 'she's so damned perfect' bugging her still." He flipped his hands above his knees. "What do you want me to do? She's a woman!"

Bethany Anne eyed him.

"You're an anomaly, boss. Just live with it."

Bethany Anne shook her head, looking from one to the other and rolling her eyes. "Oh, for God's sake, call in the other two."

"Whoop!" Scott jumped off the couch and jogged to the door, leaving it open to run over to the guys' suite and call them in.

Bethany Anne looked at John. "How long did you guys work on your argument?"

"For what?"

She narrowed her eyes again. "To get me to share this." She put her elbow on the pillow, cupped her hand, and placed her chin on it. "It seemed like such a good setup."

"Oh," John made a throwing-away gesture, "we have half a dozen good arguments cooked up. I can't believe Scott used that one just so we could see this hair thing, but he's right in a way."

"Close the door!" Bethany Anne called. Darryl stopped, his teeth flashing in a huge smile as he closed the door behind him. Moments later, Eric was next to Scott on the loveseat, and Darryl was standing behind them with his arms crossed and a twinkle in his eye.

Bethany Anne pointed at each of them. "You guys will go to your grave very quickly if this gets out beyond you and your spouses, got that?"

All four men nodded solemnly.

"Archangel, make sure there is no video of this event."

"Yes, Empress," the ship's AI responded.

"Fine." She shook her head twice, running her hands through her hair. "I feel like a little girl with all the guys trying to sneak a peek."

"C'mon, this is cool shit," Scott told her. "Hell, if I could, I'd dry off using the Etheric."

Eric turned to look at him. "You'd try it?"

"Maybe," Scott admitted. "And if I did, and it singed some curlies that smelled horrible, I'd never admit to it, so don't ask."

The guys turned to Bethany Anne when they felt her pull the energy in. Her eyes flashed red, and the lines on her face became pronounced as her hair started to float. They all leaned forward as the larger strands dried, the hair levitating. After about ten seconds, Bethany Anne put her hand out and created a scintillating white ball, draining herself of the energy in her body. She turned and flicked her hand, the white ball zooming to the corner of the room as a floating light.

When she turned back to the guys, she saw all four of them staring at her, their mouths open in shock.

"That—" Scott started to say, but just stopped. Bethany Anne raised an eyebrow, but he shook his head.

She turned to John. "You?"

"I got nothing, boss," he replied.

She turned to Darryl. "You?"

He shrugged. "There would be some women of my persuasion who would be jealous as hell. But on you? Yeah, that doesn't work."

She turned to Eric and raised her eyebrows in a question.

"I never thought," he murmured, "I'd ever see a living example of someone sticking their fingers in a light socket."

"That's the best you have?" she asked all of them as she pointed to her hair, which was now frizzy and pointing straight out from her head. "I look like a Barbie doll on Halloween night."

"Oh, good one," Scott agreed. "That's how I'll tell it to Cheryl Lynn."

"Words only, Shakespeare," she told him. "If I ever find a picture of this bird's nest," she pointed to her hair, "I'll concoct seriously painful repercussions for my personal embarrassment."

"How long have you known this," John pointed to her hair, "would happen?"

"Hell, I tried it back on Earth a couple times."

John stood up and walked over to her. She eyed him dubiously as he put a hand out to touch the ends of her hair.

"MOTHERFUCKINGSONOFABITCH!" he yelled, yanking his hand back after a sharp *crack* of electricity jumped from her hair to zap him.

"Oh yeah," she nodded, "and it still has a charge."

"It's like Cousin Itt is sitting on top of your head." John leaned forward with his hand out again. This time it didn't shock him. "That's pretty stiff."

"It takes really hot water to get it to relax again," she admitted.

"Huh." John pressed the hair down, but it wanted to stick back out. "I wonder what Marcus would think about this?"

Bethany Anne's eyes locked on John's as he kept playing with her hair. "I will kick your gonads up into your throat if he so much as whispers he wants me to become a science experiment."

"Don't worry, boss, I won't say anything," he agreed, "but you have to admit it's kinda funny. However," he turned and took a couple of steps before dropping back into his chair, "what if he could figure out how you could dry your hair without the negative side effects?"

Bethany Anne's eyes narrowed as her mind raced in different directions.

"John Grimes," she told him. "You can be *such* a bastard sometimes."

John's smile took over his face. "You're going to ask him, aren't you!"

"*No,*" she told him. John's smile became a frown.

"Why not?" he demanded.

"Because I'm going to figure it out with ADAM and TOM," she replied.

He cocked his head. "You think they'll have better ideas?"

She shrugged. "Oh, I've no idea," she admitted. "I just know that fewer stories will get around if only they work on it with me."

"So," she finished, looking around the group, "if I ever hear of anyone talking about this mess?" She pointed to her hair. "There will be hell to pay, gentleman!"

Karillian System, Shield Vessel *Tormucht*

"Sir!" Under-Captain Threan braced as the third set of asteroids slammed into their shields. "We can't hold under this onslaught!"

"Those despicable humans are throwing rocks at us." The captain of the Shield Vessel *Tormucht* gritted his teeth. "ROCKS!" he spat. He turned to the under-captain. "Give the signal that all unnecessary crew are to eject and aim for the ships behind us. Hopefully one of our other ships will grab them."

Two seconds later, their shield collapsed, and the Shield Vessel *Tormucht* cracked when a multi-kiloton asteroid penetrated their shields and hit the ship just forward of center. The explosion of detritus and bodies was viewable for a moment before the concussion reverberated to the enhanced energy core, and the ship grew white, expanding into a ball of energy and taking all crew with it.

Leath Dreadnought *Touk*

The calm voice of the Strategy Oracle spoke through the speakers to those on the bridge. "Eighth shield ship down. We are fifty percent to target."

Captain Therov of the *Touk* nodded his head and turned to his communications specialist. "Get me the *D'leet*."

Moments later, an image of the captain of the *D'leet* popped up on his secondary screen and spoke without a preamble. "We ready to call it?"

"Yes," Therov growled. "Those humans have been sneaky again. We have tested our strategy, and I am showing at best a twelve percent chance of success."

"I doubt it is that high," the other captain answered. His bridge lights dimmed a moment before coming back on. He looked around. "I don't think we have seen all of their tricks in this system."

"You may be right," Therov agreed. "I'm with you on this. The gods commanded us to test our theory, and we have found guidance and knowledge."

"Okay," he turned his head and nodded to someone off-screen, "give the fallback codes. No, to the third location. Yes, send the command."

Twelve hours later, the Leath ships left the Karillian system.

Admiral Thomas reviewed the damages to the two respective navies. The Leath lost eight of their protective shield ships and one frigate, and three destroyers were damaged.

On their side, they had lost a close-in combat vessel and would have probably six ships that needed repairs. One would certainly have to go back to the shipyard.

However, none of that worried the Admiral.

What did concern him was that the Leath had officially stopped following their own doctrine. That meant bigger problems trying to fight them in the future.

When would the Leath show up next time?

CHAPTER NINE

<u>Leath System, Sanctified Ground, City of Truth</u>

Torik, Third of the Seven, pulled his robes around him as he sat at the table, shrouding his whole face and body. A black mesh veil covered his face, which allowed him to see and speak while concealing his identity.

That was how the Kurtherians kept the Leath from wondering about their looks changing. When they needed another body, they took one from those in the service of the Seven.

He looked at the operative and nodded. "Prime Intelligence One, we appreciate your attendance."

Prime Intelligence One bowed before the god. "My Lord," he straightened, "I am at your service."

"Tell me, what do you hear about our adversaries?" Torik asked.

One was an intelligent Leath; he didn't believe the Seven were gods. That they asked this question was a stain on their omnipotence. However, the Seven *did* seem to have abilities so far above those of his race that he understood why some would think them gods.

"We know they are new to this area of space. They took over the Yollin people by besting their king in battle."

"One on one?" Torik asked, familiar with the king of that system.

"Yes, your Lordship," One answered. "I understand it was declared official. Once the king was replaced, the leadership of the Etheric Empire started removing the existing caste system from the people. This caused a lot of rancor with the upper classes. Due to the unrest, they had to focus on making sure their new Empire did not disintegrate from the inside." He paused a moment before adding, "That took them some years."

Torik waited. When One did not continue, he asked, "Why are they on our target planet?"

"I cannot express complete knowledge of this, my Lord," One admitted.

"What is your plan for locating the necessary information?" Torik asked. "How are we, the Seven, going to help the next group of beings if we fail to teach the Leath the necessary strategies to implement in our absence?"

"My Lord?" One blinked a moment. "You will be leaving?"

"Of course," Torik answered. He lifted his hand to capture One's attention, then insinuated his mind into the spymaster's, pressing to capture his full attention. *Your questions on our godhood have been noted. You will believe we are the gods that we are. You need to realize that you Leath lack effective strategies and tactics. If we were to simply provide you the answers, you could not spread your wings and grow.*

A little while later, the door to the meeting room clicked closed as the spymaster left. Seconds later, the door behind Torik opened and the Sixth of the Seven, Var'ence, stepped in closing the door behind her. She too was fully dressed in her official robes.

"Did it go well?" She asked.

"Yes and no," he admitted. "He will search for more intelligence on our adversaries, but I had to go into his mind to adjust his beliefs. He felt that us not knowing the answers was an indication we were not gods."

"A logical assertion," she pulled out a chair and sat down.

"Yes," Torik agreed. "Sometimes striving to uplift these peoples is so trying." He looked at Var'ence. "Did you know that our adversaries have killed one of our people?"

"*Our* clan?" she asked, leaning toward him.

"No, Clan M'nassa. The Yollin king."

"That pompous ass?" Var'ence leaned back in her chair. "He was always so sure of his own superiority."

"Yes, but that doesn't mean a normal alien should have been able to kill him in one-on-one combat, regardless of his arrogance."

For a moment both stayed quiet, then Var'ence asked, "You said combat?"

"Yes," he nodded toward the door the spymaster had just left through, "that is what I'm told."

Another moment of silence.

"M'nassa aren't known for playing fair, so whoever beat him was either very good or very sneaky."

"I would imagine both," Torik mused.

Noel-ni Mother Planet Dorasei

D'leck looked around for her daughter. As a Yollin on a Noel-ni planet, she and her daughter were barely second-class citizens.

NOEL-NI

THE KURTHERIAN GAMBIT

Noel-ni protected their own. They allowed others to enter their space to be seen as good galactic citizens, but in truth, they were a very insular society.

Staying in their space meant you followed their rules, whether you liked them or not. D'leck had followed her husband W'ell to this side of space to get away from the changes that had happened in Yollin space ten years ago.

Her husband had feared the aliens.

She and her daughter had been trying to scrape by when W'ell allowed his own belief in Yollin self-importance to have free rein and had struck a Noel-ni. D'leck had heard about his deportation from a friend of hers at the apartments.

That was three days after his failure to come home.

She wished she felt regret, but truly their marriage had ended years ago. W'ell had figured wrongly when choosing the planet for their migration. If anything, the level of insularity the Noel-ni felt was strongest on this world, where other aliens made up more of society due to political importance.

D'leck and her daughter Sis'tael barely noticed W'ell's

absence. For D'leck it was a little harder, but there was certainly less stress.

With his departure, she had only two of them to worry about. As far as D'leck could tell, W'ell would never be seen again.

There were many worlds the Noel-ni could deport those who broke their laws to. W'ell had struck the child of a mid-grade bureaucrat, who had exerted enough pull to put him on a ship headed for their prison planet. He would not be a prisoner on arrival, but the jobs for an alien there were either going to kill W'ell or cause him to become something he had never been in his whole adult Yollin life to this point.

Humble.

At this moment, she was searching for her daughter in the crowds lining the streets. D'leck wasn't sure what was happening here, but for the Noel-ni to be out like this, it had to be something that tweaked their curiosity, or it was a major event in their history.

D'leck could barely keep up with the annual events; she didn't track the holidays based across years.

She considered standing up on her back two legs to see across the tops of the Noel-ni, but if she were to accidentally hurt someone, it would go very badly for her and even worse for Sis'tael. They might allow her daughter to be deported with her, but if they couldn't find her in time, D'leck would be exiled, and her daughter would be here on her own.

Not the best situation for a Yollin teenager.

Sis'tael couldn't see over the heads in front of her. She was careful every time she stepped since her heavy feet would certainly hurt others, and she didn't want that to occur.

What she *did* want was to see the alien Empress whom her

father had said ran them off their planet. While she had listened to her father when she was younger, her eyes had been opened over the years to his belief in his own superiority.

Frankly, her father was a jerk, and while she hadn't wished him to go to a prison planet, she wasn't missing him too much at the moment.

He had truly received punishment for his actions. Sis'tael had heard her mother and father argue many times over the years. Her mother had warned him, badgered him, pleaded with him, and finally told him to do what he needed to.

Two months later, he was on a ship heading to the prison planet for striking a bureaucrat's child. It wasn't a fair punishment, but what could he expect? Noel-ni could be very touchy, and if there was an infraction, it didn't go well for the alien who committed it.

Ever.

Jhrex, the son of a prominent businessman, looked at his friend and winked, a grin on his face. The Yollin in front of him was taking up too much space with her long body, and it was annoying him. His friend looked at him quizzically. Jhrex looked down and opened his hand enough that his friend saw the pin.

It was long enough that it would cause quite a bit of pain, and probably much distress. Jhrex heard the sirens *whoop* at that moment, and a sneaky smirk graced his face.

When his friend saw the look on Jhrex's face, he started moving slowly away. He wasn't sure exactly what Jhrex was going to do, but that look on his face was usually the first indication something was going to go dramatically wrong.

For both Jhrex and whoever was near him.

John and Darryl walked on the road in front of the low vehicle Bethany Anne was riding in while she sat and smiled at the crowds. Eric and Scott walked behind her. The guys had played a round of poker, and the last two to fold had won the front position.

No one expected anything to go wrong, but this was Bethany Anne's first trip to this planet, and it had been a bit of a circus so far. It seemed the Noel-ni had a strong militaristic core to their society. They had seen the videos of Bethany Anne fighting on Karillia and wanted to see what she looked like without the video touch-ups.

John could hear the whispers as Bethany Anne came into view. Most were surprised to see she looked just like the videos, no special effects required to make her prettier.

Unless the Etheric Empire had technology that made someone look good to regular eyes?

John smiled at that. Here they were in yet another solar system so far removed from Earth he couldn't figure out the distance, and Bethany Anne's beauty was a point of consternation with the females. He didn't think the males noticed as much.

"It's all real, folks," John muttered between his teeth as he looked around. More than a few people pointed to the Bitches. The four of them were in their armor, and John was singled out about half as often as Bethany Anne.

"Seems you have a fan club there, buddy," Darryl remarked over the private channel. "I've got three on the right who seem to be taking multiple pictures of you. In fact—" Darryl dropped off the net for a moment.

John glanced around to see who he was talking about before quickly resuming his focus on his area. Darryl finally came back on the channel. "Okay, I've got some drones checking them out."

"Problem?" Scott asked from behind them.

"Just being prepared," Darryl answered. "We probably have some Intel weenies taking close-up shots of our armor."

"Fucking good luck with figuring this armor out," Scott replied. "I've stared at it for hours and still can't figure out how the hell the interlocks work."

"That's because you suck at geometry," Eric told him, keeping an eye on the three in the crowd as the car moved past them.

"New group on my side," John interrupted. "Seems like we have new activity on extra-high bands to try and... Oh shit, they dropped their electronic devices, and someone is squalling like it hurt."

"Bet it was BA," Darryl commented. "Wow, I now count four groups that seem to be focused on themselves and their feet. Probably everyone dropped their devices like hot potatoes."

"Nope," Scott answered. "I got one guy causing a ruckus. From what I can tell, looks like he had it locked to his arm for ease of use."

"Sucks to be him," John was listening on his private channel with Bethany Anne. "Yup, it was the boss. She did some hocus-pocus to their equipment. Okay, new trouble, guys, front and center."

John and Darryl saw the commotion about fifty yards in front of them as six bodies fell into the street. It took them a second to see that a fairly young four-legged Yollin was in the middle of the mess.

The bodies all seemed to be making a hash of themselves, probably hurting each other in the effort to get back up.

The group of Noel-ni jumped up quicker than the young Yollin could get back on her four legs, and they turned on her, kicking her for an unknown reason.

"Guys!" John called, but he was overridden on the command channel.

"I've got this," Bethany Anne stated. The four Bitches started running then when their Empress appeared ten feet above the fighting, and the fireworks started in earnest.

Sis'tael felt a harsh pain in her hindquarter. Her body reacted by surging forward, trying to get away from whatever was stinging her.

The only problem was, there was nowhere to go except over those in front of her. She and a handful of Noel-ni surged into the street. She rolled to the side to make sure she didn't land directly on an older mother Noel-ni.

Panicking, Sis'tael turned to look into the crowd to see if there was any reason for the pain.

Two of the Noel-ni started cursing her, and she realized she was in serious trouble.

The two yelling at her started kicking her, their feet slamming against her hard exoskeleton. She tried to curl on her side to protect herself from the kicks of the larger Noel-ni, but another person's foot slammed into her head from the back and she screamed in pain.

D'leck's head twisted to her left when she heard a scream of pain. It was Sis'tael. D'leck's mandibles clacked in fear when she couldn't see what was going on, and the crowd between her and the noise was impossible to get through.

She turned to see if there was any other way to get around the crowd without running them over—which she was probably capable of doing. If she could get Sis'tael out of this situation, there was a chance they could stay together. However, if D'leck ran over the Noel-ni in front of her, she was surely going to be seeing her stupid-ass husband soon.

Another cry caught D'leck's attention and she set her mandibles together. She was about to start through the crowd when a *crack* sounded, and just thirty paces away, floating above and looking down on the crowd, was the alien Empress.

It was the alien who had taken over her home planet.

The alien pointed down from where she was floating and looked at the crowd, who was pulling back.

The alien's glowing red eyes found D'leck, and she pointed to her.

Sis'tael felt the third kick hit the arms she was using to protect her head. She cried out a second time as a deafening *crack* above her hurt her hearing.

The crowd surged back, and Sis'tael wasn't being kicked anymore.

"John," a voice called above her.

Sis'tael moved an arm and looked up, right into the flaming red eyes of the new Yollin Empress.

"Oh, bistok shit," Sis'tael whispered, trying not to move. "Mom is going to kill me."

The Empress pointed at Sis'tael. "Carry her. She was being kicked."

Sis'tael turned to see another of the aliens, this one in dark red armor and a helmet, looking at her.

Sis'tael swallowed. She had watched enough videos to know this was the alien her father had said did the killing for the false Yollin leader.

She went limp as he knelt next to her.

"I..." Sis'tael started as he gently moved his arms underneath her. "Can...do this..." She looked around when he picked her up easily and kept her legs tight against her body.

Jhrex laughed his ass off as he watched the group in front of him collapse into the street. He started egging on the fallen Noel-ni as they regained their feet. "Kick the alien!" Others took up the chant, and the violence started.

He noticed their kicks hurt her, but not too badly due to the Yollin's hard skin. He was about to yell again when a large *crack* sounded and not ten paces away, floating in the air above the Yollin, was the alien Empress.

Her eyes were glowing red, and her hair was floating loose around her head.

Seconds later, Jhrex started when he felt a hand grab his arm. "C'mon!" his friend hissed, but suddenly his friend's face showed fear, and Jhrex turned to follow his friend's focus back to the alien Empress. His heart sank.

The Empress was aiming a finger at him, and it glowed blue.

Bethany Anne was multitasking as fast as she could think. She confirmed John had the young Yollin protected, then she searched out the Yollin cry of worry she had heard.

The girl's mom was easy to find.

She pointed toward the mother, and the crowd parted where she was pointing.

Score one for having a bunch of videos about your badassery. "Come here!" she commanded the female Yollin.

>>To your right, we believe we have found out why the Yollin teen surged ahead.<<

What happened? she asked TOM and ADAM.

I read her thoughts, TOM answered. **She felt a large sting and her body reacted, then the natural tendency of Noel-ni to hate aliens took over and someone, most likely the one ADAM is pointing out, instigated the attack from the sidelines.**

Bethany Anne lifted her arm, her fingertip glowing blue as the crowd moved away. She spoke in the native tongue. "Come here!"

The Noel-ni had turned to flee, but Bethany Anne released the electrical charge and the one she was pointing at collapsed, spasming on the ground.

>>**INCOMING!**<< ADAM yelled a warning on all channels.

Police Protector Tellek was hot, tired, and annoyed.

He didn't pull many of these official gigs, but when he did, he made sure to inform his upper command how much he despised them.

This time it didn't matter how much of a pain in the ass he was; since practically the whole damn force had been called to duty to help protect the foreign dignitary. He wasn't exactly sure which one this was since they had two coming this month, and frankly, with this being his fifth shift in two days, he could care less.

When he heard the squawk on the radio that said there was a disturbance behind his position, he started jogging in that direction. The least he could do was show up. He imagined others would do the hard part.

Which meant they got the paperwork, as well.

He was a block away when the alien just appeared above a group of his people and another alien.

One of her guards picked up the alien and started to carry her away. Tellek's lips pressed together when the alien, still floating in the air, lifted her hand, which started glowing blue.

Tellek reached over his shoulder, grabbed the radar-guided explosive missile, and pulled it around.

"HALT!" he screamed. Whatever this alien was doing, it was something that looked like it would hurt his people.

She released the blue ball into the crowd, and the screaming started.

Tellek put the weapon to his shoulder, locked onto the alien, and hit the firing switch.

CHAPTER TEN

Minor Planet Howz, City of Chaht, Bar

"I'm sorry, but you want what, exactly?" Nathan asked the odd-looking alien across the table.

He and R'yhek were sitting in a dark, dingy bar where Nathan would have been concerned about taking off his boots. He was sure some insect would crawl onto his feet and infect him with God-knew-what.

While the darkness of the place didn't hamper his eyesight, it might have bothered R'yhek if the Pod-doc hadn't upgraded his low-light vision abilities to the best a Yollin could expect.

The alien, one Nathan would describe as a cross between an emaciated robot and a thrift store, leaned toward him. "I want you," he struck the table with one finger, his one good eye glowing brightly in the gloom, "to provide me with a contract that grants me all your Straiphus output for the collin plants."

R'yhek jumped into the conversation, "You want roots?" Nathan looked at his companion and smirked. The large Yollin continued, "You are trying to shake us down in this dingy place for some damned plants?"

Nathan turned to the Yollin. "You owe me. You lost the bet."

Beethlock eyed the two in front of him. "I am not sure," his sibilant tones seemed annoyed, "you understand the gravity of your position."

Nathan turned back to the black-market businessman. "Oh, I'm pretty sure I know." He leaned back in his chair. "You tried to go to Straiphus and get your own supply of the collin plant, but you can't."

"It doesn't grow anywhere else like it does on Straiphus. Too expensive to cultivate," R'yhek interjected.

"Then," Nathan continued, "when regular business channels didn't work, you tried to strong-arm a few people on the planet. Unfortunately," Nathan's eyes flashed yellow, "you never asked the criminal underground for permission, and they ran your ass out and killed some of your people as a warning."

R'yhek shook his head. "Truly shouldn't piss off the local criminals."

"Finally, you reached out to us to set up a meeting, not realizing that same criminal organization might have let us know that someone was trying to strong-arm our farmers." This time, Nathan tapped the table with his finger.

"Why would they tell *you*?" Beethlock asked, narrowing his good eye.

"Call it professional courtesy," Nathan answered. "These negotiations are over. No one threatens us."

Beethlock's chuckle irritated Nathan. "I think not."

"Yeah?" Nathan looked around the place. He could count about fifteen beings he didn't know. "You and what army?"

"I'm glad you asked," Beethlock told him. Nathan flinched as a high-pitched whistle emanated from the alien in front of him.

Four of those in the bar seemed to go from drunk to sober in seconds, and another eight entered the establishment from outside.

"This army," Beethlock answered.

"Not bad," R'yhek admitted. "Didn't see the outside options coming in."

"Last chance, Beethlock." Nathan's eyes glowed yellow.

"For what?" Beethlock asked, ignoring the warning.

"To accept that you don't fuck over Bad Company, as opposed to learning it the hard way," Nathan answered, but he wasn't really listening to Beethlock anyway. He was confirming everyone's location.

Nathan tapped R'yhek's foot with his boot.

"Time's up, asshole," Nathan told Beethlock.

R'yhek turned in his chair and dove to his left.

"Arrgh, bistok shit!" R'yhek spat when he realized he was now halfway sticking to the gunk all over the floor.

Nathan roared, his body transforming as he grabbed the table in front of him. The nails of his clawed hands raked huge gouges in its top as he shoved it violently forward, crunching Beethlock against the wall. He then twisted to his left and tossed the table toward the larger group of Beethlock's minions who had come in.

After the table had soared over his head, R'yhek jumped up from the floor and laughed. "Is that all you got, Beethlock?" he yelled as he saw Shi-tan's green arm grab one of those who had been in the bar and throw him several feet. "We got an army in green!"

R'yhek heard some noise behind him and turned to see Nathan in Pricolici form ripping off Beethlock's metal arm. "Oh, never mind. Looks like you're busy with death-by-pissed-off-Pricolici." He turned back around when he heard a woman yelling.

"Uncle R'yhek!" Christina shouted as she jumped on the bar and ran down its length, sidestepping all the glasses and plates in an amazing feat of dexterity until one of the people at the bar realized she was working for the other team.

The alien shoved the bar stool out of his way and turned to catch the speeding human, red in his eyes.

"Oh, for…" R'yhek almost closed his eyes, but Christina was on the alien, her clawed hands slicing from his head, behind his neck, under his arm, and down his torso as she twisted around him like he was a pole. Then she jumped back onto the bar as the alien was left screaming, blood cascading down his flesh, eyes blinded.

The girl was giggling.

R'yhek opened his arms as she jumped fifteen feet across two tables and landed on him. She used him like a pole as well, but thankfully, no claws. Then she was next to him. "Dad called it!" she told him and looked behind her. "Oh, sucks to be him."

Nathan appeared next to them, his huge hand on his daughter's shoulder. For this battle, she had chosen to be the size of a full-grown woman, but he easily pushed her behind R'yhek. She smiled into the monster's eyes. "Mom's over there behind Shi-tan!"

The Pricolici turned and scanned the rest of the bar.

It was chaos.

The large group that had entered was mostly down already in various states of damage, thanks to Shi-tan. To his left, Bastek, the female cat-alien, had bounced her charged baton off two heads, and two aliens who had brandished weapons had been shot.

The barkeeper had his hands up, eyes taking in the scene around him in fear.

"*Whoomp!*" Shi-tan yelled as he jumped up in the air and replicated the human wrestling move he had been studying, turning sideways in the air and slamming his elbow into one of the aliens who had been struggling to get back up.

Christina flinched when she heard either bones or exoskeleton crack.

Nathan stayed in his monster form and walked over to the

barkeeper, who needed to look higher and higher as he approached. The monster reached into a large bag dangling from his hip and pulled out Beethlock's head.

He was still alive.

Nathan stared at the head in his hands, "Youuuu willll payyyy forr thiisss messs. Givvve theee barrrkkkppppeeerrrr yourrr crrredit nummber!"

Nathan turned the head toward the barkeeper, whose eyes flicked between the monster and the literal head of the criminal group in this city.

"Why?" the head asked.

Nathan slammed Beethlock's head into the bar, which caused the electronics in the eye to fritz, before holding it in front of the barkeeper again.

"Two Two Frile Frile Con-temm," the head spouted.

Five minutes later, Bastek had provided medical assistance to as many of those in need as she could before the six members of Bad Company left the bar. Nathan had shoved Beethlock's head back into the bag and Shi-tan was carrying the pieces of Beethlock's body, chuckling the whole time about the can of whup-ass they had just opened.

"The spies show nothing between us and the ship," Ecaterina told her husband, "so why don't you change back?" She put a hand on his arm.

A moment later, Nathan was back with them.

"Beethlock," Nathan growled as he walked down the sidewalk, a few aliens giving his group uneasy glances, "you don't come into our backyard and fuck with us. My people will kick your ass and then they will tell the big bosses."

Christina had moved up next to her dad, and she opened the bag and peeked in. She smiled at the robotic head looking up at her, "Which also happens to be us, bistok-shit-for-brains," she told it before she closed the bag again.

Bastek walked next to Shi-tan, who looked down at her. "Yes?"

She looked more closely at his arm, "I'm going to need to give you a couple of stitches, or you should spend a bit of time in the Pod-doc."

Shi-tan twisted his arm to see the cut she was talking about. "How did I get this?"

"Probably that wrestling move," Ecaterina called back. "The guy you hit on the ground had some metal on him."

"Huh." He nodded. "Was probably that." He put his arm back down and looked at Bastek. "I'll take the stitches. The Pod-doc takes away my scars."

"You want them?" she asked before rolling her eyes at the smiling Shrillexian. "Of course you do. Marks of honor and all of that."

"Of course." He shrugged as they all paused a moment to let some mechanical traffic cross in front of them. After crossing the street, Shi-tan kept nodding at those they passed, who stared at the robotic body parts he was carrying. His smiles caused them to avert their eyes and hurry off to whatever it was they had been intending to do.

He laughed when one young alien turned and ran into a wall, bouncing off it and grabbing its forehead in pain.

Bastek slapped his shoulder. "Don't be mean!"

"I'm not mean!" Shi-tan shot back. "Mother Ecaterina up there told me I needed to work on not looking so angry all the time, so I'm practicing my smile."

"Your smile," Ecaterina called, "is a faceful of sharp teeth!" She dodged a small stump jutting from the concrete. "Try being nice without looking like you intend to eat someone."

They walked another five steps before she added, "And I'm not 'Mother'!"

The five of them chuckled softly, except Christina, who patted her mom on the shoulder. "Yes, you are, Mom."

Ecliptic Orbit around Howz, Aboard *Prometheus Minor*

"So," Nathan turned Beethlock's head so he could see what remained of his body, "we have your head and your body parts. And we have the option of putting you back together or spacing you and allowing all your parts to re-enter the planet's atmosphere, which would destroy all evidence."

"Huh." R'yhek scratched one of his mandibles. "That's both incredibly devious and very impressive, Nathan." He looked at the parts. "Who could find a body if it was nothing but burned atoms spread all over the atmosphere?"

"I thought so," Nathan agreed.

"What is it you want?" Beethlock finally spoke. "And why am I supposed to trust you will do what you promise?"

"Because between the two of us." Nathan nodded at Shi-tan, who had entered the large room and turned toward them when he noticed the alien parts on the tabletop, "I'm the only one who seems to keep his word."

Shi-tan picked up a hip, leg, and foot. "I wonder what happens—"

"Leave that alone!" Beethlock tried to shout. "Stop fucking with my parts!"

Shi-tan's eyes narrowed. He leaned over the table toward the head, "And you are who to give a Shrillexian orders?"

Beethlock stayed quiet.

Shi-tan nodded at the leg, and Nathan winked from behind Beethlock. Shi-tan gave the alien an evil grin, full of teeth. "I'll just go put these on my wall of trophies, Beethlock. You can negotiate with me for them." He picked up the parts and walked out of the room.

"WHAT?" Beethlock got out a shout this time. "That animal is leaving with my body!"

"That animal," Shi-tan called from the other side of the door, "heard you!"

The door cut off anything else Shi-tan might have said.

"Keep pissing off those in Bad Company," Nathan told him, "and I won't have much left of you to give back."

"Now," Nathan spoke loudly enough for the head to hear him as he walked five feet over to a wall that had a tool bench and lots of tools. He grabbed a foot-long half-inch-diameter rod which had a four-inch box on one side and a connector on the other. "I'm thinking you need to provide us with information for this negotiation." He picked up a connector and turned to face the table, eyeing a port he had found earlier on Beethlock's head. He turned and put the first connector back, then pulled out another and locked it onto the rod.

He stepped back to the table and palmed the head. "What are you doing?" Beethlock asked as he noticed his jack's door slide open.

"Making sure you keep your side of the bargain," Nathan answered as he jacked in the probe. He set the head and probe back down on the table. "For you to get your body back and get back down on Howz, you have to perform three tasks. The first is answer my questions, the second is apologize, and the third is take an oath to your new criminal boss."

"Who's that?"

"I was hoping you'd ask," Nathan grinned and walked around to where Beethlock could see him. "Welcome to Bad Company, you little pissant."

Inside Beethlock's head, his half-organic and half-electronic brain screamed in fear.

WHO ARE YOU? he asked, realizing that something had insinuated itself through his firewalls while Nathan had been talking to him.

My name is Prometheus, the entity answered, *and you are now my bitch.*

Nathan smiled as a green light clicked on and Beethlock's eye dimmed.

"He will be conversing for a while with Prometheus, R'yhek." Nathan called to the door, "And you can come on back in, Shi-tan."

The door opened, and the Shrillexian walked back in with the body parts under his arm. "This would have been kind of funny to put on a wall," he grumped as he placed the chunk of body back on the table.

"Yeah, true." Nathan clapped him on the shoulder. "Pepsi time?"

"Oh yeah," R'yhek agreed and started for the door himself. "I got dibs," he called over his shoulder as he went through the doorway.

"I wonder if he knows the ladies got into the stash after their spa?" Shi-tan asked Nathan as the two men left the room. A few moments later, the room darkened as the EI shut down unnecessary lights.

If one had exceptional hearing, one just might have been able to hear Beethlock's scream as he gibbered in fear, the EI reviewing his criminal life right inside his own brain.

CHAPTER ELEVEN

<u>Noel-ni Mother Planet Dorasei</u>

>>If that missile explodes it will harm at least seventy-two percent of the people within thirty feet, Bethany Anne.<<

Guess we'll just have to play catch, she told him.

"Guys, I'll be right back."

"Why?" John asked as he continued to monitor the situation while holding the young Yollin in his arms. He trotted back toward the vehicle Bethany Anne had been using.

The Bitches saw Bethany Anne put out an arm toward the incoming rocket, and it slammed into her location. Those around her screamed as both Bethany Anne and the missile disappeared.

"Someone shoot that ass!" John bitched. "I've got my hands full!"

Down the street, the Noel-ni policeman stared at the place where the Empress had disappeared in confusion until he noticed three of the alien guards staring straight at him.

"Oh—" he got out before two of them, arms blurring, shot him. He crashed back into the street, moaning.

"DAMMIT!" Noel-ni Officer-in-Charge Co'mins screamed into his radio. "Who gave Tellek a damned rocket? And where did the Empress go?"

"Sir," someone reported, "they've shot Tellek!"

"Good!" Co'mins snapped back. "It saves me from doing it!"

"But, sir—" Someone else wanted to argue, but Co'mins had heard enough.

"Listen to me." His voice went cold as he hissed, "If we don't maintain a healthy Empress, we might find a shit-ton of rocks laying waste to our finricken *planet!*" He saw someone holding up another radio and mouthing, "President." Co'mins wanted to start slapping the idiots around him who weren't paying attention to those they were supposed to be protecting and watching out for.

"Last time I checked, the empress of a powerful starfaring race doesn't randomly kill people. Help her people find out who she hit before she disappeared. Co'mins out!"

He slammed his radio down, cracking it. "Someone get me a new finricken radio!"

He put a hand out. "Channel?" he asked. He was handed a headset and told the number. He switched the channel and hit the connect button.

"Co'mins here, President Aerlix."

Bethany Anne reached out to where she calculated the tip of the missile should strike. As it drew near, she started twisting her body, pulling her hand away from the missile, and as it slid by her, she moved herself and the metal-based missile into the Etheric.

It made it about twelve feet before it exploded in the whiteness of the Etheric, pelting her with a few pieces of its casing and the strong surge of energy that was its real payload.

Most police tried to use non-deadly weapons.

Bethany Anne wasn't outside the range of the energy that was designed to electrocute its targets, driving dysfunction through their neurosystems.

Her armor intercepted it and used it to power up, which was a good thing since Bethany Anne had collapsed to the ground from her effort.

>>That took a bit out of you.<<

Fucking metal shit. She rolled onto her back. *I've got to figure out how to move metal into the Etheric better than I do.*

Well, TOM cut in, **now that I can see what happened, we can work on it. However, I can't promise anything. Our understanding never involved moving large amounts of metal. My tribe worked to move organic bodies. Anything we know about metal travel and the Etheric is more accidental than planned.**

Noted. Bethany Anne grunted and turned over, pushing herself up off of the ground. *Okay, guys, let me juice back up for a minute, then we will go back like a blazing inferno.*

"Incoming on your six," Darryl's voice declared in John's ear. "Looks like a worried mom."

John placed the Yollin girl in the car and turned around. He put up a hand and spoke in Yollin as the mom crossed the distance at a healthy pace. "She's fine, so slow down."

The mom, her mandibles clacking in fear, looked at the armored alien and then tried to see around him. He stepped away from the vehicle and pointed inside. "Get in with her. When the Empress gets back, I imagine we will cut this short."

"In?" D'leck asked him. His accent was a little strange.

"Yes, in," John confirmed. He looked up and drew D'leck's attention to the sky.

D'leck stopped just outside of the vehicle after seeing Sis'tael was okay and looked up, her mouth open.

There was a monster spaceship coming out of the clouds, and it looked deadly.

The president was not happy.

"I have a Yollin superdreadnought coming through my atmosphere right now, Co'mins. I'm sure you've seen the same video I have, where our police officer shot at the empress of the alien race?"

Co'mins glanced to the side, his aide mouthing "officer stunned, not killed," and he shook his head.

"Before those aliens shot our police officer!"

"Stunned him," Co'mins replied.

"What?"

"I'm being told that they stunned him, they didn't kill him."

"Well, thanks for small favors. Perhaps our people aren't going to war...if we can find their Empress."

The monitors around the van Co'mins was using as a mobile Ops Center started displaying the giant warship parting the clouds as it flamed through the sky, burning the atmosphere like the Chariot of Death itself.

Co'mins felt the first few drops of sweat leaking down his forehead. "Sir, the Navy—"

"Will be unable to fire inside our atmosphere, as we don't have Naval units that large. Also, our systems have been locked. I've got citizens screaming at me right now. So get your people on the ball, find that Empress and..."

The president's voice dropped off, obviously seeing the same thing Co'mins saw.

The Empress was back, and she was on fire.

Jhrex tried to move his muscles, but his body just kept spasming. The crowd around him had already been moving away when the aliens yelled in his language to "get back on pain—"

They never declared what the pain would be, and frankly, Jhrex wasn't too interested in finding out.

His friend had tried to help him, but with one look, the alien had caused him to jump back.

Then she disappeared.

He was busy trying to get feeling back in his arms when she reappeared, and Jhrex hoped that maybe she could reverse whatever it was she had shot him with.

But then he saw her blazing face and the lines of bright red breaking through her skin. Her helmet was off, and red balls of energy blazed in her hands before she threw them into the air.

"BRING ME THE ONE WHO HURT MY SUBJECT!" she screamed, her bright red eyes staring at Jhrex.

For once in his life, Jhrex wished he hadn't pranked someone, and at this point, he wasn't sure if his father could get him out of this trouble...

Or not.

Darryl walked toward the Noel-ni and clicked a command in his HUD as he touched the Noel-ni's spasming body. He waited while his armor siphoned off the energy. The convulsions of the youth, if Darryl had figured his age correctly, started to slow down.

"You are in a world of hurt," Darryl whispered to the alien, "so stand up and take your punishment like an adult."

An alien came over and put a hand on Jhrex. His spasms slowed, and the alien grabbed his arm, helped him to stand, and started marching him toward the Empress.

Jhrex looked to his left, noticing six police officers coming from a block away.

"Don't even *think* about it." The fiery woman reached for him.

Seconds later, none of the aliens were on the ground, since the Empress had disappeared and the vehicle she had been riding in went straight up into the air. That left the police officers with no one to deal with except those who had been on the side of the street moments before.

The president terminated the latest phone call, his lips twitching. The Empress' ship could apparently operate just fine inside the atmosphere, and she was traveling toward the capital.

Even now, that massive ship didn't look friendly. Worse, her ships in space were arrayed above her, and their navy didn't give a damn for the instructions his people had offered. When he had tried to get a direct connection to the Empress after she reappeared, he found himself talking to someone who looked just like her.

But wasn't.

She called herself ArchAngel, and she informed him that the Empress would be there in moments.

And so she was.

The Noel-ni had arranged a large podium and stage where they had been expecting to meet with the Empress after she completed her parade and arrived here in the main area of the city.

She was going to be early.

President Aerlix stood up from his desk and strode out of his office. His guard swung in behind him as he strode out of his wing of the Capitol building, practically flying down the two stories' worth of stairs two steps at a time and then down the main corridor into the bright afternoon sun.

Aerlix was very aware of his people's focus on themselves, how insular their society was. When he was young, he had traveled to multiple other planets. He had been trying to explain to his own people that to play on the larger stage, they would need to be less judgmental of others.

Now it might be too late.

He shook off the offer from a few to help cover him from the sunlight bearing down on him. He was sweating, but he doubted it was from the heat.

Rather, he could see the shape in the distance coming over the horizon. Clouds parted in front of it as the massive nose of the ship pierced the sky, ignoring the laws of the gods and gravity as it floated through the atmosphere.

The *ArchAngel II* had arrived.

His eyes flicked away from the alien's ship as he saw his Air Force's jets at its sides. He appreciated that the massive starship didn't just swat them like the little insects they probably were to it.

It was doubtful if any of their bombs would do anything to the shield that ship could produce. Ten minutes earlier, the Air Force had decided to play chicken with the ship.

And lost.

The warning had been clear, but the distance the Air Force was told to maintain had been breached.

The fighter that had been tasked with accidentally coming too close had been halted in mid-air by some sort of tractor beam. The video had captured the pilot trying to eject.

He made it a full three planes' distance into the air before he too was caught in the tractor beam and pulled into the ship.

So far, the Etheric Empire had been rather patient with his people, for all the good he felt it was going to do.

The ship's shadow began to cross his city. He could see it travel down the street in front of him, its darkness creating the illusion of a monster consuming the buildings to the left and right.

Then she was simply *there* in the street two blocks away. She had four guards around her, and she seemed rather irritated.

If he was any judge of her physiology.

President Aerlix stepped up to the microphone and tapped it, making sure it was on. "Empress Bethany Anne, our sincere apologies for the mess-up."

No one expected the apology to accomplish much, so Aerlix was surprised when the Empress' eyes started fading back to normal, and her face ceased to radiate fire.

She stopped about twenty feet from the podium, hands on her hips as she eyed the president. "Well, that's a lot better response than I expected, President Aerlix, considering my experience just a little while ago." She looked around at the video cameras from the news agencies and a few people who had arrived hours ahead of schedule to get good seats before returning her gaze to the president.

"Perhaps we might have a better discussion inside? I'm not really up to a speech today."

President Aerlix reached down to his microphones and started pulling them off. Unclipping the last one, he dropped all the electronics on the podium and walked toward the steps leading to the street.

Two of his guards looked at him, then at each other, and realized he was going with or without them, so they quickly caught up and went down the stairs alongside him.

"I hope it would not be amiss..." the president began. She had on armor, and he noticed weapons on her suit. He continued, "If we have the conversations on your ship? Perhaps it would be a bit safer."

Apparently, the videos hadn't been manufactured. She really was the Warrior Empress. The Boogeyman, they called her.

"For me?" she asked, amusement written in her eyes.

"No," he admitted, "for my people." He looked around. "I would hope that if I were on the ship, they won't be so quick to shoot."

Bethany Anne could hear the guards speaking into their microphones, warning the others of the president's plans.

"Request accepted," she told him and stepped forward to grasp his hand. Her Guards closed in, and the eight of them disappeared.

In bars across the planet, the televisions were turned to the news. Patrons watched, talked, and ordered drinks even though their last drinks were still on the table, full.

They forgot to drink.

The alien had grabbed their president and his guards and disappeared. There were some who wanted to attack the massive ship above the capital.

Even when the military pundits explained it would rip apart the city and kill untold millions in the capital, they could not be dissuaded.

They relished the opportunity to attack those different from them, no matter the cost to those who lived in the blast zone.

Their gods were mayhem, destruction, and death, not necessarily in that order.

Many of the less inebriated told them to shut the hell up. The stupid little fucker deserved what he got.

By then, the pundits watching the many videos of the

Empress' parade and the altercation had been able to pinpoint what had actually happened and who had started the problem.

It was clearly the teen Jhrex. His stabbing of the young Yollin had caused her to push people over in the crowd ahead of the Empress.

While the Noel-ni were not fond of aliens, they weren't fond of their own people stepping out of line either. Therefore, the general consensus was that he needed to be punished.

However, his punishment, the video wags suggested, shouldn't include being eaten by an alien, either.

Bethany Anne knew all this since ADAM had been watching the multiple channels, translating and pulling together the common threads from the news reports.

"I don't eat kids," Bethany Anne growled to John Grimes when the two of them were alone—the president was being shown around *ArchAngel*. She walked over to the machine that could give her some coffee. She didn't need it for the pump of caffeine; she needed it to feel human again.

"Boss," John called to Bethany Anne, then nodded to one of the ship's crew who had stepped into the small eating area. When he saw the Empress' expression, he decided that maybe he could get a snack from one of the other areas on the ship. "What do you expect, exactly?"

John walked over and accepted the cup of coffee Bethany Anne had pulled for him. "Well, not being called a cannibal would be nice."

"Can you be a cannibal if you aren't eating your own kind?" John asked, then took a sip of his coffee.

She looked at him. "Really? I'm all upset because they think I might eat their children, and you want to know the etiology... Wait, is that the right word?"

"Don't know, what are you going for?" John asked.

"The history of a word as much as the definition," she clarified.

>>You are looking for "Etymology." <<

Thanks!

"Okay, I meant etymology," Bethany Anne corrected herself.

John walked over and stuck his head out of the little kitchen area, then pulled it back in. "Must be nice having a speaking dictionary with you at all times."

"It has its benefits, that's for sure," she agreed, "but occasionally, there is a downside."

"Like what?" John asked.

>>Like what?<< ADAM echoed.

"ADAM is a best friend who never sleeps and never forgets unless I specifically command him to forget something, in which case he will delete the knowledge from his storage. For an encore, he now is best friends with an alien who can make the most frustrating comments at times."

"How much storage does he have?" John wondered aloud.

ADAM's voice came over the speaker in the room. "Let's just say the old libraries don't hold a candle to my memory stack, Mr. Grimes."

John chuckled. "Occasionally I forget I could just ask him myself."

"Pretty much," Bethany Anne agreed. "And that is the last thing. My two friends are with me twenty-four seven by three-sixty-five."

You would miss us, TOM claimed.

I would eventually, that's true, she agreed.

>>How long do you think it would take?<<

Longer than both of you would believe, but way shorter than I would believe.

>>I've done the calculations, Bethany Anne.<<

Of course you have, she butted in, but ADAM ignored her.

>>We have never been out of communication, not including sleep time, for more than four hours and sixteen minutes. In any instances longer than three hours and forty-

seven minutes, it was you who instigated the communication. <<

Huh. She thought about that a moment. *That is way shorter than I would have thought. I'll have to see if there is a subconscious need on my part to check in, or if you guys are just that needy and I'm trying to make sure you are okay.*

>>How can an AI be needy?<<

You're a guy. Guys are always needy.

>>That doesn't even make sense.<<

Actually, I might have to agree with her on that one. Even Kurtherian males can be needy at times.

>>Well,<< ADAM made a sniffing noise on their connection, >>*I am not needy.*<<

Suit yourself, she told him. She could feel the two of them talking as she disengaged.

John continued their conversation. "Given that we're on a 'hearts and minds' mission, can I say you pretty much suck at it?"

"That's what I was trying to explain to Cheryl Lynn," she grumbled before downing the rest of her coffee. She tossed the recyclable cup into the proper chute. "I'm not the right person to place in front of others, considering my previous methods of negotiation."

John took a sip, eyeing her a moment before commenting, "You mean if you aren't able to just slap them around for being stupid."

Bethany Anne didn't answer him for a moment. "I have a short temper." She pulled a chair out from the table.

"I wouldn't sit there if I were you," John told her.

She raised her eyebrows in confusion, looking at the chair and back at John. "What am I missing?"

"Weight?" John asked. "Remember three weeks ago when you sat in one of the chairs on the *Meredith Reynolds?*"

"And squished it," TOM added through the speakers.

Bethany Anne looked at the speaker and zapped her friend mentally. *Don't ever suggest a woman is heavy!*

She turned to John. "I took care of that."

But, TOM asked, **you are wearing armor. It isn't like I'm saying you're fat.**

And you had better not, or we will have a discussion that will make you wish for the days you were in the doghouse.

Strangely enough, TOM was silent for a few moments.

Bethany Anne sat down, and the chair didn't bow in the slightest. "I asked ADAM to pay attention and adjust my weight to normal me if I was about to do something stupid like sitting on a chair or table that wasn't rated for my armored weight."

John just shrugged and turned around, sticking his head back out the door, "Incoming, president and his posse."

Bethany Anne stood back up. "Be right back." She sidestepped and disappeared. A moment later, she returned, holding the Noel-ni teenager. She pointed to the chair and in his language, told him, "Take a seat."

The youth, face wet with tears and eyes full of fright, nodded and sat down. Bethany Anne observed that he didn't even move when the president walked in and noticed him sitting there.

She spoke first. "I have someone from your world I believe you would like back. He has purposely hurt one of my people. However, I would consider releasing him if you provide me one of mine in exchange."

Aerlix's eye only twitched slightly when he saw the youth. "Oh? Who would that be?" If he could get back to the world with the youth unhurt, it would go a long way toward shutting down his detractors. Some, he was sure, were calling on everyone to toss the Empress off their world right now.

Sometimes trying to govern an insular society into the future could be a challenge. Aerlix had come into his position thinking he would be able to help change his people's parochial focus, but he'd had little success so far. The damned Insularists called for more and more military, but frankly, his people needed more infrastructure, not more bombs.

But fear was what drove them, so fear was what he had to deal with. Elections were just two seasons away, and he doubted he would be able to pull off a second term. Sometimes what you thought was best wasn't what the rest of your people believed should be.

He had wanted to give peace a chance, but what could one do? This Empress had just shown his people how pitifully weak they were. The Etheric Empire had upped the game.

This meant that the neighborhood had just gotten more dangerous, as everyone would be trying to catch up. The Etheric Empire might be focusing on the Kurtherians, but they had—unwittingly or not—just changed the dynamics of the political groups in this area of space.

If he leaned that way, Aerlix could build a military supply company and ride the wave of investment that was bound to happen when another group came into power.

Until that happened, however, he needed to make peace with the Empress. Creating a group of people that felt strong enough to shake lasers at the Etheric Empire would have to be the role of some other government after him.

Two days later, the Etheric Empire left the Noel-ni capital.

Their consulate on the planet had been hit with a hundred and eighty-two requests to repatriate Yollins back to Yoll if the Empress would help them.

She commanded one of her ships to stay behind and gave everyone forty-eight hours to make it to the shuttles for liftoff.

It would take that long for D'leck's husband to be returned from the prison planet. Whether D'leck wished him back in the future or not, Bethany Anne refused to allow him to waste away.

Perhaps, like Bethany Anne, Sis'tael would appreciate a closer relationship with her father sometime in the future.

Even old hardheads, Bethany Anne had come to understand, could learn something about being wrong.

The Noel-ni Congress had wanted to play hardball until they understood that Bethany Anne would retrieve the father whether Congress approved or not.

And no.

Bethany Anne would have no problem dropping a rock, a really big rock, right on top of their building.

If they wanted to continue painting her as a child-eating alien bitch, then by God, she would play that bitch for all it was worth.

There wasn't anything the aliens had called her, she realized, that her own people back on Earth hadn't called her in the past.

This time though, she didn't shed any tears in the night with only TOM to console her.

Fuck them all!

CHAPTER TWELVE

QBBS _Meredith Reynolds_, Team BMW's Official Office Area

The drone was small, barely large enough to have the four legs it used for movement. It was as small as an aphid and could hide in the tiniest of crevices.

Three of them had finally made their way to the designated target's door.

In a booth in a bar near All Guns Blazing on the second floor, an Ixtali casually drank a human beverage he enjoyed. It was something called "root beer." It had none of the alcohol of beer and was sweet. With the straws the bar supplied, X'telent could sip the beverage and swipe through the tablet, whiling away time after he had held strategy sessions with others who utilized the safety of the Empire's personal meeting rooms.

A splendid cover for his covert efforts.

With the useless council working with the Etheric Empress, it had seemed X'telent's abilities would go unused.

Until now.

Now he was an open resource, his talents for sale to the highest bidder. Why the idiots didn't worry that someone might use the fact that their own space station was a safety zone against them, X'telent couldn't understand.

But that wasn't *his* problem.

He had been hired to find out about the R&D technology. He had been smart enough to figure out that the obvious location for research and development, the well-known Dukes Lab, was too well protected.

Even he wasn't surprised when his nanos got zapped far away from the inner sanctum. Further, he couldn't figure a way into the lab through the walls. He just didn't have the technology to drill through the rock walls into the core.

However, the beer-drinking researchers were something else entirely. It took him less than a week of his spybots listening in All Guns Blazing to figure out they were the ones who had come up with the powerful blast of energy that kept this base safe.

Once he had figured out the location—nicely hidden behind the bar—X'telent had set his most advanced spybots loose. Actually, he had set three teams of spybots loose.

One went in fast and had been fried immediately. X'telent did further testing and found out that would have been the normal result, no matter where he loosed the bots.

His second team of bots fared better. They got within thirty human feet of the security door before they were found and killed.

But his final team, the ones which plodded along, had passed the last zone of destruction yesterday morning. They would enter as soon as one of the members went into the sanctum.

Which would happen after lunch.

One or more of them always went back there, and his spybots had watched them pass each time.

He reached for his drink, mandibles clicking in anticipation.

Kitchen Area, All Guns Blazing

Inside William's ear, his name was called. "William, this is Meredith."

William inhaled deeply and let out his breath. He subvocalized, "Do I have to be the one?"

"Yes."

"Why?" he asked.

"It's your regular day," she replied.

William shook all over and slapped his arms. "But it makes me itch to even think that some microscopic little metal bugs are jumping on me," he muttered.

It was a moment before Meredith replied, "Bobcat says that if you don't hurry up, he will have to do it."

"Well, that's fine by—"

"And the whole time he is doing it, he is going to tell the story about your trip to New Orleans back in '08… No, he changed it to '09."

"That…*fucker*." William turned his head, looking to where he knew Bobcat would be at the bar behind the kitchen walls.

If he could only zap lasers from his eyes.

He had asked John once if the Bitches could do that, but John had laughed and said no. However, it was rumored that Bethany Anne had wanted that capability, but TOM had told her she couldn't have it.

Plus, if she did, what would she do while her eyes were healing all the time?

"Fine." He started moving toward the back. It really was his day to check out the offices at lunchtime. Figures the little spy bastard would choose his day to do this.

William walked out the back door of the bar and looked around to make sure no one was in the hall. He walked to one of the white panels on the wall. "I need in, Meredith."

There was a *click* and he pushed open the door that had looked like a normal part of the wall a moment before. He closed it behind him, entering the hallway that was about thirty feet long and allowed for multiple scans to confirm who he was as he walked toward the end.

Outwardly he looked fine. Inwardly he felt little mechanical crawlies all over his body.

God, he wanted to shiver, then take a bath in something that would kill the little guys. He came up to the door and pressed his hand against a panel. "It's me, Meredith, open up."

Meredith's voice, colored with humor, replied, "That has never been, nor will it ever be, the request for permission, William."

Forgetting himself for a second, William smiled. "I'm just shitting you, Meredith." He tried again. "Hey, Meredith, it's William. Do you have enough of my voice to verify identity?"

"Yes, that's better," she replied, and the door cycled open. William stepped inside and the door closed behind him. There was a pause before the other door opened and William stepped into the official office of Team BMW.

Official fake.

The whole office was nothing but a honey trap for those who believed they had figured out a suitable location to spy on the vaunted Etheric Empire. So far they had captured two previous spies trying to get inside the place.

Meredith had informed them days back that they had another contestant trying to abscond with their technology. Marcus had argued to allow them to get in, steal the data, and leave.

They would determine who the guilty party was when their planet exploded from the doctored data.

Bethany Anne had merely looked at the scientist. He sniffed under her glare and admitted, "We can be a bit annoyed with fellows stealing our hard work."

"You don't say?" Bethany Anne replied. "While I admire the concept, blowing up a planet of innocents isn't my idea of just rewards." She had brought Ashur with her that trip, so she summoned him back and before they left, she called to Marcus, "Clean up your data. I don't want planets going boom."

A moment later she added, "Unless we do it on purpose."

William walked over to the main computers and sat down. The computers in this area were on their own network and full of reams of useless data. ADAM's massive data pull from before TQB Enterprises had left Earth came in handy.

Instead of Earth's history, they had raided the data from multiple fake histories including George R. R. Martin's *Game of Thrones* universe for European History and *Second Life* for what day-to-day life had been like when TQB left the world.

Then, for shits and giggles, Bobcat and William had decided to add in midi-chlorians as a description of how some humans were able to exhibit amazing "Jedi powers." By the end of the night, just a little inebriated, Marcus had added some data from Laurence E. Dahners' Ell Donsaii series on traveling through the nth dimension by entrapping and using entanglement.

William had wondered if that was a smart idea.

"Why?" Marcus asked, then hiccupped.

"What if it were possible?" he had replied. "Wouldn't we be giving them the idea of how it works?"

Marcus had just stared at William, his eyes a little bloodshot, before smiling. "One moment!"

He got a vacant look like he did when he was using their internal communications abilities to talk with TOM, and then started placing math symbols in the extra documentation.

Marcus had then rolled back from the computer. "Now, that should give them just enough of the truth to send them down a rabbit hole for ten thousand years."

William had shrugged. "You really like to fuck over other scientists."

"No matter the species, cheating is not tolerated," Marcus had told him.

William went through the motions they always did, checking

data, pulling up spreadsheets, and running the latest reports for the fabricated data.

He scratched his chin and mumbled, "That doesn't look right." He pushed off the floor with his feet, rolling back to another desk, and hit another keyboard to turn on another monitor.

He liked to keep his input old-school.

He had been working for ten minutes when Meredith whispered in his ear, "What are you doing?"

"Checking the data for the ESD," he muttered. "Something isn't right. The original calculations didn't show the ability to miniaturize the—"

Meredith interrupted, *You know this is fabricated, right?*

William blinked twice, staring at the screen.

"Well, fuck." His eyes narrowed. "That's too damned random." He asked Meredith sub-vocally, "Take screenshots and video of this monitor until I stand up."

"Understood," came back.

William worked another ten minutes before getting up, stretching, and heading out of the room.

He went through the security process once more. Between the two doors, Meredith confirmed he had no spies on him anymore.

He wasn't even thinking about the spies. "Get me the guys."

"Are you including Tina?" she asked.

"What? Of course," William answered as he went through the security door and clicked it shut. "She's one of us, isn't she?"

"Yes, but she is female."

"Triviality," he replied. "She's one of us, ergo one of the guys." He opened the door to the back of the club and slid into the kitchen, then stepped over to the bar side, catching Bobcat's attention with a slight nod of his head.

Bobcat narrowed his eyes. He recognized that look on his friend. "Terry!" he called to the other guy behind the bar. "Take over, and call in help if you need it."

"Yeah, boss!" Terry answered. He was a Guardian and liked to work the bar when he wasn't on duty. They had another two days before the ladies and Stephen took over the bar full time.

Bobcat gave William his one-eyebrow rise of questioning, but William just shook his head. "Rounding up the group."

"Playhouse?" Bobcat asked, and William nodded.

Huh, Bobcat thought. *Something just got interesting.*

Maybe they would be handing over the bar early.

Gyada's team had been practicing together, and it *was* a team, although it was a weird team. She had practiced with Shun's team, and now she was working with a team of two female Weres who had three Guardian Marines backing them up.

When Peter and Todd had worked with twin Weres Brooklyn and Addison, they decided to try splitting the two girls up as well as putting them together.

It didn't take more than a few minutes to realize that together was better, which meant they had rethought the two-Guardian-Marine formation and changed it to three. Caden for left, Carter to focus on right, and Chris to deal with either back or forward.

Over the next two years, those five had become inseparable. Brooklyn was a five-foot five-inch-tall brunette with an olive complexion and a Marilyn Monroe mole that her sister would have killed to have.

Since she was blond.

"Mother loved you more than me!" she would fume when the two got into squabbles.

"How do you see that?" Brooklyn, the elder by three minutes, would ask.

"You got her mole," she would moan as she looked into the mirror.

Brooklyn would stare at her sister, who would be looking at her perfect face and hair so blonde it often looked white, and try to kick her brain back into gear. "Your complexion is perfect, and what you bitch about is my mole?"

Addison turned to look at her sister. "Guys aren't interested in perfect, they want character!"

Brooklyn *humphed*. "They want tits and ass. Whatever else you provide is a plus, unless it's intelligence."

The argument would continue down a common road from there.

Addison turned back to the mirror. "Stop picking guys who are six feet tall and little Greek gods, and you might get a guy who appreciates your intellect."

"Is that why your picks always look like Greek gods?" Brooklyn shot back, grabbing a brush to pull it through her wavy hair. "Hell, I could grate cheese on their abs, they are so cut."

"I never said I wanted stimulating conversation," Addison answered. "Give me size, girth, muscles, endurance, and the ability to shut the fuck up at the right times, and I'm happy." She took the offered brush from Brooklyn. "Make my eyes pop out and have to regrow, and I'll consider it all the conversation I need."

Brooklyn shook her head and smirked. Addison wasn't focused on long-term relationships. She just lived for the moment and, by God, if you didn't appreciate that about her, well, you needed to go find some other girl to cry your little bitch-ass emotions to.

Cuz she was all about the next guy once that weekend was over.

For all of that, she was quicker to ask how their friends were doing and bring soup if someone got sick than Brooklyn. Or she would stick around and help one of the guys in the team if they had been jilted by a girlfriend.

Addison was great with their team, but she ran through other guys like they were full-sized Ken dolls she could window-shop, buy, and then take back when the fun was gone. Most of the Weres loved that about her.

The only Were guy who was impervious to Addison's cute-ass smile was Peter. Brooklyn understood Addison's reason for never even trying to hit on the captain. Not only was it because he *was* the captain, but she figured Addison knew that Peter wasn't a typical Were guy.

At least, not anymore. They all knew his early story, and Addison didn't want to suffer the pain of being shot down.

"Well, maybe I want character," Addison admitted.

Brooklyn looked at her sideways. "Who are you, and what have you done with my sister?"

"Funny ha-ha." Addison tossed the hairbrush into the bag they used to hold their hair-care stuff. She walked out of the bathroom and continued the conversation after sitting down on her bed. "I think I'm getting tired of floozing about."

Brooklyn's eyes narrowed, and she put down the clips she was using to restrain her hair. She looked out the door toward her sister. "Now you're just scaring me."

Addison shrugged. "I think I have the hots for Caden."

"Okay, now, I don't think..." Brooklyn walked out of the bathroom to sit on her bed. They shared quarters with a single bed and a bathroom, a desk, and a wardrobe each. "You can't fraternize with the team, Addy."

Addison grabbed a pillow and pulled her legs up onto her bed, sitting cross-legged. She put the pillow in her lap and hugged it. "I was talking with him last night."

"Uh-huh, you do that all the time. What girlfriend left him?"

"Monica," Addison mumbled.

"That girl had no right to do Caden wrong. Nothing on Caden, but she shouldn't have been the one to get out of any relationship with that face."

"You'd think, but no," Addison agreed. "Seems she used Caden to get Jered interested in her."

"*Bitch.*"

"Skankasaurus, yeah."

"That's not usually something that bugs you," Brooklyn pointed out. "So, give! What's happened?"

Brooklyn watched as her sister's eyes went vacant, looking at something she couldn't see, but she did notice one thing. Addison's lips curled into a smile.

Ohhhhh, fuck. She's fallen for him!

"Have you ever noticed his smile?" Addison asked.

Brooklyn wanted to put her head into her hands and scream. Instead she replied, "Why, yes. I point it out to you at times, and you nod your head."

Addison focused back on Brooklyn, "That's because I accept that my teammate is happy again." She pushed herself backward on her bed and rested her back against the wall. "The problem this time was I didn't want to just help him as a friend. I wanted to hug him and make his worries about that swamp-donkey go away for the last time."

"Um, before this situation, I had thought you *liked* Monica."

"Jaw-monkey can kiss my ass. She used my teammate for her own personal reasons."

"Uh-oh. Tell me you won't let that—" Addison shot a glare at Brooklyn, who put up her hands. "Okay, okay. Next time we spar, I won't stop you from kicking her ass. Just know Peter is going to kick yours."

She nodded. "I'll own it," Addison confirmed. "But Giggle Tits is going to know she's been cunt-punted when I finish with her."

Brooklyn just looked at her sister. *Cunt-punted?*

Addison watched Brooklyn's face. "I'd kick ass and chew gum, but I'm all out of gum."

"Oh," Brooklyn nodded. "Got it." She grabbed her own pillow. "Where did you hear that?"

Addison looked up a moment, thinking. "Uhh, Chris, Carter, Caden and I were eating over at AGB when Bobcat and William started laughing about someone's lame-ass way of saying they were going to kick someone's ass."

"And?" Brooklyn asked. "You can't set up a comment about Bobcat and William like that and not tell me more!"

"More of their comments?" Addison asked.

Brooklyn considered tossing her pillow. She lifted it up behind her head.

"Whoa!" Addison snickered. She put her hands up to catch the offending weapon if her sister tossed it. "Give me a second to remember!"

"You got five," Brooklyn answered, leaving the pillow in the cocked position. "You damn near have an eidetic memory for curse words."

"That reminds me," Addison smiled, "the Empress came into our workout space about three weeks ago."

"Three seconds," Brooklyn warned her.

"Okay. There was a cunt-kicking carnival and an ass-kicking circus, some names they claimed came from Earth."

"Like?" Brooklyn asked.

"Chuck Norris, Jean-Claude van Damme Slam, Chris Brown your ass, Stone Cold Steve Austin."

"How do you use a name?"

"Well, if I told you I would have to go all Peter Pricolici."

"Never mind."

"Can I continue?" Addison asked.

Brooklyn eyed her. "Have I lowered the pillow?"

"So," she thought about it again, "there was 'natural selection,' 'Geronimo bunga,' *veni vidi vici*,' 'open a big can of whup-ass,' 'beat someone like they were their daddy.'" She looked over. "And a personal favorite, 'break off my foot in your ass.'"

"Always," Brooklyn nodded, "but that is one I know."

"Well, a few more were," she leaned forward, "and I doubt I have even a portion of them, 'we got bro-snowed,' 'chippenfuckyouup,' 'ass harassment,' 'skinnybitchectomy,' 'asskickginormous,' and 'a rear-end alignment.'"

"Damn!" Brooklyn lowered the pillow. "Just how many did they come up with?"

"I think someone stopped counting at eighty-three, then the next one was by William, who tossed out 'go medieval on your white honky ass,' and Bobcat popped up with 'fuck you in the juggahoe with a rear-package slam.'"

"Those two guys are so damned weird," Brooklyn whispered. "I'm glad Yelena took one for the girl's team."

Addison tossed her pillow to the side and slid off her bunk. "Thanks, Sis, I needed to be talked off the ledge."

Brooklyn watched Addison walk back into the bathroom. "What are you going to do?"

"Nothing," she called back, "because you don't screw your teammates." She turned on the water and murmured at a volume to be easily heard by Brooklyn, "And you never, ever, *ever* let them know you fell in love with them."

Brooklyn shook her head. For the last five years, she had been wondering if her sister would ever get over having to leave their parents in Russia and decide that loving someone was okay.

Now she wished her sister still wanted to fuck around. Helping Addison through this was *so* going to suck.

Especially since they had to continue their training with Gyada starting in the morning for fourteen straight days.

CHAPTER THIRTEEN

QBBS _Meredith Reynolds_

X'telent sipped his drink, mentally cheering his success at breaking through to the inner sanctum of Team BMW's headquarters.

Apparently all it took was brains, luck, and months of patience to break through the humans' security without getting caught.

X'telent motioned to the waiter. He wanted to savor one more drink before he went back to his rented room to enjoy his triumph. Fortunately, he thought, he had an abundance of all three attributes.

Especially brains and patience. He had been successful at each task he had been set. Now he just needed to successfully acquire the information, or enough information of value anyway, and exit safely.

Once he had the information his spybots had accessed, he'd move it to his ship separately from himself. That way, if anyone stopped him before he boarded, he would be clean. He didn't want to risk moving from his ship to another inside their space. From what he had learned, they had a special way of detecting communications in Etheric Empire space, and he didn't want to chance making them suspicious.

He glanced up when a shadow passed through the door. He kept his mandibles very still as he returned his eyes to the tablet in front of him.

Two humans had entered. One was a young male, and the other was the one they called Ranger One. Barnabas.

The young man was asking him questions, and the Ranger was smiling and nodding in agreement.

"I can have something?" Johnny asked Barnabas, looking at the menu the lady behind the bar had provided him.

"Yes, provided it isn't illegal or inadvisable for you to eat."

"What about a shake?" Johnny asked, looking at Barnabas where he sat on a barstool from the corner of his eye.

"That's fine," Barnabas answered.

"With Coke," Johnny added.

"Okay," Barnabas agreed.

"And chocolate."

"That's just disgusting." Barnabas frowned at the child.

Johnny paused, a look of concentration on his face. "Um, does that mean it is inadvisabubble?"

"Inadvisable," Barnabas corrected. "And no, but it *should* be illegal. It's a lot of sugar, and your mother will tear a strip from my skin for allowing you to eat so much it will make you bounce off the walls."

Johnny ordered his Coke float before turning back to Barnabas. "She wouldn't say anything ugly to you."

Barnabas smiled. "Maybe not around you, but I'd get one of those looks that tells me I messed up, and maybe next time I offered to take you out, she wouldn't let us go."

"Oh." Johnny frowned. "Sorry, I won't ask for chocolate next time."

"See that you don't," Barnabas answered.

———

X'telent watched the two of them until the child finished the treat the Ranger had ordered him. Barnabas had his back to X'telent the whole time and didn't seem to care who was in the establishment.

The two finished, and Barnabas paid and they left. Moments later, X'telent settled his own bill, exited the bar, and turned in the opposite direction. He would go back to his rooms via a circuitous route.

———

"Hi, Mom!" Johnny waved to his mother and dashed past her as she looked up from her desk, which faced the seventh level of the open court.

She turned to see only his back as he ran down their little hall. She slowly turned to look at Barnabas, who was smiling at her.

"How'd it go?"

"You should be proud." He nodded at Sarah. "He acted exactly as he needed to."

"So, like a young boy getting a treat from his idol?"

"No, like a young Ranger on his first adventure," Barnabas answered, face deadpan before winking at her. "Exactly like a young boy getting a Coke float."

Sarah blinked at Barnabas a moment before her eyes opened in concern. "You didn't!"

He nodded, affirming that he had indeed.

"Oh, God!" Sarah got up. "You owe me!" she called over her

shoulder as she raced down the hall to see what Johnny was up to.

A few minutes later, after admonishing Johnny that he couldn't use colors and draw on his tablet, she found a hand-written note on her monitor, asking if Barnabas could make it up to her by taking her to dinner the night after next.

Sarah smiled and took the note off as she whispered, "You rat bastard."

Three floors farther down, Barnabas walked along the concourse, subvocalizing to ADAM, "No, I don't know what information he extracted. What? Because the spy himself doesn't know," Barnabas clarified. "He doesn't review stolen data to limit the possibility of getting caught sniffing data packets."

A few moments later, Barnabas nodded. "Yes, I'll take that task on personally. I'll 'tag and bag him,' as Tabitha would say. I'm going to switch over to Meredith and find out where he is at this moment."

X'telent took a left turn at the next intersection and walked toward his rented abode. As he got close, he glanced at the door frame and saw that the little hair he had put there when he left was still in place.

The old ways to make sure no one had been in your room still worked. He pressed the tips of his fingers against the plate to the left of his door and provided a word in his own language that was a conglomeration of three words that didn't work together.

The door slid open and he glanced around the space, then entered far enough that the door closed behind him.

He locked the door and glanced at the furnishings, a long

piece they called a "couch" and a narrow place to sit called a "chair." He walked into the bedroom and pulled off his outside robe, choosing to go without a drape inside his own domicile.

Grabbing his tablet, he returned to the outer room and his four legs took him over to the couch, one of them reaching down to grab the edge of what the humans called a "coffee table." Using it as a brace, he settled straight down to compose himself.

He was logging into his tablet when everything went dark for a moment. He suddenly felt as if he had just woken up and his mind was trying to make sense of where he was. Fear rushed through him when he realized he couldn't move anything below his neck.

Turning his head, he clacked his mandibles.

"Hello," the figure sitting on his chair greeted him. "I know you know who I am, X'telent. However, since we have never been formally introduced, I should tell you my name is Barnabas. You are hereby detained for spying on the Etheric Empire. You are a prisoner of war, not a criminal."

"You're a Ranger!" X'telent spoke up. "That's police business."

"Oh, I'm a Ranger most of the time," Barnabas agreed. "However—" He was interrupted when the door opened and another human male walked in. "Oh, good." Barnabas nodded to the new person. "Let me introduce Stephen. He is the one I'm currently working for."

"Hello, X'telent." Stephen nodded. "I'm in charge of miscellaneous projects for the Empress, including counter-spying." His eyes glowed red. "Let's see what you know, shall we?" His hands reached for X'telent's skull. "Sorry, I can't guarantee this isn't going to hurt."

X'telent was frozen, unable to move, his mind racing with the realization that the humans would be able to read his thoughts.

"A lot," Stephen finished.

X'telent's mental scream seemed to go on forever.

．　．　．

QBBS *Meredith Reynolds*, Military-side Airlocks

"All aboard who's going aboard," Bobcat called over his shoulder before he turned and kissed Yelena. "We will be back in three days."

"See that you are," she replied, then kissed him back and bit his lower lip. "Or Momma is going to be upset."

"Momma?" Bobcat asked, a squeak in his voice.

"It's a figure of speech, you big scary-cat!" She laughed. "I know how to keep the bread from rising, worrywart."

"Well, I've heard the stories from Eric. You'd think he was a regular human again. Those twins are killing him! And it's 'scaredy,' not 'scary.'"

"Eric's just working it for sympathy, and good—scary didn't make much sense to me either," she admitted. "My first batch of Bitch's Pale Lager is going to uncork in two nights."

He kissed her one more time. "Good luck."

She shook her head as William walked by the two of them. Slapping Bobcat on the back, William laughed. "You two need to get over it. It's only for three days."

Yelena leaned around Bobcat and called after William, "Doing who knows what!"

"That's the point." Marcus headed for the Pod. "Don't know anything, can't share anything, and everyone knows you and Bobcat…" his voice trailed off as Tina went by.

"Are you doing the boom-boom?" she asked them.

"That the best you got?" Bobcat asked, turning to watch Tina enter the twelve-seat Executive Pod.

She raised an eyebrow in challenge.

Bobcat smiled. "Go for it, young Padawan."

Marcus stuck his head around the door. "Oh, I got to hear this."

William stepped around Marcus. "Go Tina, go Tina, *go!*"

"You got this!" Marcus encouraged her.

"No less than twenty," Bobcat warned.

Tina's eyes narrowed.

"And no help." He touched the side of his head. "That's cheating."

"*Hmphh*, wouldn't have done that. I know the rules," she answered, and jerked a thumb behind her.

"Okay, give it your best shot," Bobcat encouraged.

"What're the stakes?" she asked.

"First brew choice to the winner."

"Okay, I can live with that." She sucked in a deep breath and spat out her best. "Aggressive cuddling, bam-bam in the ham, balling, bandicooting, four-legged foxtrot, jerking it while she's twerking it, nailing, naffling, nobbling, plooking, plonking, pole-varnishing, shampooing the wookie—"

Marcus turned his head to William. "Oh, that's a good one." William nodded in agreement.

"Sinking the pink, tube-snake boogie—"

"A little ZZ Top," William commented. "I play that all the time."

Bobcat had already lifted through ten fingers, closed both hands again, and now had one fist of fingers open, indicating Tina had five more to go.

"Mingling limbs, humping," her eyes narrowed when he didn't give her credit for that offering, "gland-to-gland combat, going balls deep with one's Twinkie in the bearded clam."

Bobcat gave her two fingers' worth of credit as she squeaked out the last one, her voice about spent. "Tromboning!"

Bobcat looked at William and Marcus, a question on his face. "No cheating, Marcus!" he called. "I'm waffling on tromboning. That's a very common—"

"Nope." William shook his head as Marcus looked back at him. "Not for someone her age, so it counts."

Marcus turned back to Bobcat and pointed at William. "What he said."

"Yeah," Bobcat scratched his chin, "good point." He turned and kissed Yelena one last time before stepping toward the ship. "C'mon, rookie." Bobcat passed her on the stairs. "You get first beer choice at our new research digs."

Waving to Yelena, Tina turned and boarded the Pod. She was moving toward her destiny as the newest member of Team BMW.

Ahz Sector, Deep Space, Gerrand's Asteroid, Krollin's Restaurant

Kraaz walked into the restaurant after pausing in the reception area to allow his eyes to adjust. He saw that four other tables were occupied, and raised an eyebrow when he noticed a lone Shrillexian in a booth at the opposite end of the restaurant from his leader and the Leath he was meeting.

He would keep an eye on that one. He didn't have any obvious scars on his face or arms, so he was probably untrained in real combat. Maybe he'd talk to him after the leader's conversation.

He finished his sweep and clicked the transmitter attached to his belt. A moment later the leader of their mercenary company strode in, and Kraaz preceded him to the meeting.

P'kert, a Tulet, was stationed behind them and would cover any attacks from the rear. Once they arrived at the table, Kraaz stepped aside and allowed the leader to take over. Their leader, another Tulet named Bocklans, ran Darkness for Hire. It wasn't a very good company name, Kraaz thought, but they had a reputation both for being successful and taking high-risk assignments.

And since *they* had been contacted for this gig, it was pretty much guaranteed to be dangerous.

Bocklans pulled his hand away from his belt when the Leath kept both hands on the table. Since they had called the meeting he didn't expect a double-cross, but one needed to be careful. Darkness for Hire hadn't taken any assignments against the Leath so far as he knew. Hell, practically no one had taken any action against the Leath.

They just weren't around much.

It was only since the news about the war between the Etheric Empire and the Leath got out that the Leath started sending more groups out to the core systems.

And the rumor was, most of the contacts had twice as many meetings with those on the dark side as with the official political representatives.

Interesting times indeed.

The Leath opened his tusked mouth. "Greetings, Leader Bocklans." He turned and got the attention of a waiter. "Drink?"

"Of course, provided you are paying." Bocklans chuckled. "This is a more expensive restaurant than I normally frequent, you understand."

The waiter came over and took their orders. "Of course," the Leath agreed, "but I understand this location prides itself on keeping private conversations private."

Bocklans made a motion with his arm. "Perhaps," he answered. "But I wouldn't trust it too much unless I had support."

"And do you?" The Leath asked.

"A moment," Bocklans answered and turned his head. "Kraaz?" The Shrillexian looked at his boss. "Give me a distorter."

Kraaz reached into a pouch attached to his belt and handed a small electronic device to Bocklans.

"Appreciated," he replied and placed the unit in the middle of the table. "This will distort our communication outside the table area. Are we in agreement? Can I turn it on?"

After receiving permission, Bocklans turned the device on.

Bocklans called again, "Kraaz?"

The Shrillexian didn't turn back to the table.

Bocklans smiled. "I believe we can speak now."

"My name is irrelevant, but my rank is high in our intelligence branch. I have been sent on a…purchasing and talent-acquisition mission. What assurance can you provide that our request will be kept confidential?"

"I would be surprised if you haven't researched Darkness for Hire, and not in a good way," Bocklans replied.

"I have, but I am asking for additional assurance so that I understand your methods. It is hard to fathom how you keep secrets." There was a pause. "Given your organization…type."

"What you mean is, as a group for hire you do not respect." Bocklans put up a hand. "I don't care about your opinion of us. In our long history, we have had to kill only two leaders who leaked information that we as a group felt was detrimental to our company. You need to understand, this isn't *my* mercenary group. I've been elected leader, and I could be fired or quit. If I were fired I wouldn't know, since I'd be dead. If I were to quit, I would have to undergo the surgical insertion of a device that monitors if I am revealing company secrets."

"Why would you do this to yourself?" the Leath asked.

"Why do we do anything? For the challenge, of course. Many of us don't expect to live to old age. Only two of our leaders have retired. One committed suicide in a bar brawl he started with some thugs from a mercenary group he hated. The other lived another twenty turns in his own solar system. The rest of us die on assignment."

"Why do *you* take assignments?"

"We have a system. For each job we accept, we throw the dice during the operational planning meeting. If the dice come up red, the leader must be a part of the forward deployment during the planned op; that way all operations have the chance of being headed by the leader. If we make bad calls on jobs, eventually we get killed."

"It seems," the Leath scratched the base of one of his tusks inside his mouth, "that stupidity would get one killed eventually anyway."

"It does, but leaders don't necessarily survive even good planning."

"Is this how it works for all mercenary companies?"

"Some, but not all," Bocklans admitted. "Others have various methods. Some mercenary companies are truly businesses with owners. We happen to function as more of a cooperative model."

There was a pause before the Leath asked, "Why choose that model?"

"Income," Bocklans answered. "No sharing with upper management."

After this pronouncement, they waited in silence until the drinks had been delivered and the server left.

"Is there anything you would not do in relation to the Etheric Empire?" the Leath asked.

"Straight to the point. That is nice in a business relationship," Bocklans answered. "We will not attack their asteroid base or do any jobs inside it. Also, nothing on Yoll. Missions on other planets in the Empire will be determined by the job and the location."

"We are going to be suggesting that the Noel-ni planet Sertjal host a peace accord meeting for fifty of our people and fifty of theirs. During this meeting, we wish for it to be attacked, killing everyone at the event."

"Including the Leath participants?" Bocklans asked in surprise.

"Yes." He shrugged. "They will be killed for the greater benefit of the Leath race. They will not know this, of course." He picked up his drink and took a sip.

"Weapons?"

"We request minimum armament." The Leath put down his glass. "Nothing heavy. Besides, the location is a floating hotel."

"I'm familiar with those," Bocklans answered. "If an attack destroyed the engines, the whole thing would come crashing down." He nodded. "Elegant."

"Unfortunately, the attack has to take place after those who are attending the meeting go through a rigorous search, so unless you can hide something in advance, you will have to make it happen with whatever you are allowed to bring in after the event is underway."

Bocklans took a sip of his drink, thinking. "How are we going to gain access to the hotel?"

"There will be over a thousand people in its buildings at the time of the planned meeting, plus I'm sure there will be reporters. Figure it out."

The Tulet pursed his lips. "Won't the Empress just bolt? I would imagine her ships would just come down and get her."

"We will succeed. And we plan on spinning the news our way since we are getting killed in the public relations arena." Bocklans raised his eyebrows. "Don't be so surprised that we are aware of what is said in the news," the Leath told him. "Where do you think all the negative reports about her being a monster originated?"

Bocklans smiled. "That's...good to know," he admitted. "I was wondering how you were going to use the fact that your own people were going to perish."

"Easy," the Leath answered. "The Etheric Empire was willing to kill their own people to take out the highest-level officer in the Leath military."

Bocklans shuddered at the cold manner in which this Leath—who had yet to give him a name—had just told him they were going to kill their highest-ranking military officer.

Prime Intelligence Two clasped his hood to his face and exited the restaurant. He had walked down the sidewalk for only fifty paces before an enclosed four-person hovercar whisked up. He opened the door to the back seat and slid in.

Once inside, he found Second Line Prime Commander Tehrle on the seat next to him. "How did your meeting go?"

Prime Intelligence Two took off his hood and turned to his old friend. "Well enough. Mercenaries honor themselves and their reputations. They have taken the job." The car was speeding toward the spaceport. "Yours?"

Tehrle turned to look out the window. "The gods willed that they should also accept the job."

"Assassins to clean up any loose ends," Two mused. "Now we just have to implement the plan." He noticed his friend's jaw clenching. "First Line Prime Commander Ch'lockteck is either going to be removed from the military with all honors erased, or he will die valiantly for his people. Which end to his career do you believe he would rather have?"

Tehrle made a fist, then opened it, spreading his fingers out. "Ch'lockteck would rather go down fighting. At least this way he will have a chance to redeem his continued mistakes with the gods."

"And," Two answered, directing his gaze toward the front of the car, "so he shall."

CHAPTER FOURTEEN

Kraaz watched the Leath slip out of the booth and nod in his direction before heading out of the restaurant. He turned to Bocklans. "Job?"

"Yes," the leader answered, "but it isn't going to be easy." He thought about it. "We need to hire outside help; high-quality, low-risk grunt killers."

"Cannon fodder?" Kraaz asked. "Anything I should know?"

Bocklans shook his head. "They just need to know which way to point their weapons and who's on our side."

"Typical member-initiation job," Kraaz answered. "How many spots?"

Bocklans considered his answer. The Darkness for Hire mercenary group had over three hundred members at present, and at best, he would need forty down-and-dirty and a hellacious number of killers. He knew enough about both sides to believe it wouldn't go down very easily, even if none of the peacekeeping team had decent weapons to return fire.

Plus, he needed a group to go after the engines.

"Call it twenty for our engineering demolition team, with a

special pickup plan, and another hundred shooters," Bocklans answered.

Kraaz eyed Bocklans. "Special pickup plan?"

Bocklans turned and smiled at the large Shrillexian. "Yes. They need to exit the floating hotel, fall a significant distance, and successfully not go splat on the ground. We will be there to pick them up."

"Oh." Kraaz thought about it. "Wing suits?"

"Huh." Bocklans pondered the option. "That's damned smart." He slid out of the booth. "Got any ideas for new recruits?"

Kraaz nodded at the far booth, and Bocklans noted the other Shrillexian. "Fine with me. Catch up."

Bocklans met up with P'kert, and both Tulets exited the restaurant as Kraaz walked over to the other occupant. He was fully aware the other Shrillexian knew he was there, but he knocked on the tabletop to officially get his attention.

Kraaz greeted him while at the same time, elevating his opinion. This one's eyes and simple movements didn't speak of lack of practice. "May I sit?"

"Sure." The seated Shrillexian nodded to the other side of the booth. "North Continent?"

"Yes," Kraaz admitted. "Terrel mountains."

"Went by there once; a small village, good swimming."

"Probably Chr'stylx, maybe two hundred inhabitants," Kraaz sat down, "if you count the farm animals."

"Good enough." The other chuckled.

"My name is Kraaz, and I'm wondering if you are serving or committed?"

The Shrillexian nodded. "Name's Shi-tan, and committed."

Kraaz tried to remember where he'd heard that name. "Mercenary or commercial?"

"Commercial," Shi-tan told him. "New group."

"You seem out of practice," Kraaz remarked, but Shi-tan shut him down by laughing.

"Not hardly. In fact, I'm in more practice than I've been in years." He pointed to his face. "If you are asking about the lack of scars, my company has a really good medical plan."

"All right." Kraaz reached into a belt pouch. "I've got a few cards. If you meet someone who wants to join a mercenary group, we are initiating."

Shi-tan nodded his understanding. It was going to be a rough job, but if you made it, you were in the company. He grabbed the cards Kraaz held out. "Timeframe?"

Kraaz thought about that. "Two weeks max to call me. The rest will probably be travel time and practice. They need their own equipment; we don't want complete newbies."

Shi-tan nodded. "Understood."

Kraaz slid out of the booth. "Practice?"

Shi-tan looked up from his seat with a small smile playing on his lips. "You sure you've got time to heal before your job?"

Kraaz smirked. He liked this Shrillexian. "You and what posse?"

"Oh, just me." He reached into his belt, grabbed some local currency, counted out enough for the meal plus a tip, and then added some more on top. "I'll pay for your food." He called the waiter over. "Kraaz here is going to be back to pick up a meal to help his stomach settle in about five minutes. I'm leaving enough here to cover it plus a tip, got me?"

The waiter turned to Kraaz. "Sir?"

"Oh, what the hell." Kraaz grunted. "It'll be my celebratory ass-kicking sandwich."

Shi-tan stood up, and up, and *up*. Kraaz hadn't realized the Shrillexian was as tall as he was, but he didn't seem to be as well-muscled.

The two exited the restaurant and turned right. "About a block away," Shi-tan commented, "there is a field and some fencing that hides most of it."

"Worried about someone seeing you getting pounded down?" Kraaz needled. Shi-tan remained quiet.

The two made it down the block to the field, then each turned sideways to slide between chunks of the fence, Shi-tan going first.

On the other side, both took off their belts and pouches. Shi-tan twisted his neck, popping his vertebrae.

"Get ready for a proper Darkness-for-Hire ass-kicking." Kraaz ran at Shi-tan, thinking to catch him off-guard.

On Shrillex, as long as both fighters had dropped their belts, it was officially permitted to attack. Normally that wasn't what happened, but Kraaz had been out in the field too long to worry about what was normal versus what was prudent.

What was prudent was getting in the first—

The sledgehammer that punched him in the gut came out of nowhere and sent him stumbling back five steps before he lost his footing and fell. He allowed the momentum to throw him into a somersault and got back up, his hands ready to punch. And was surprised.

Shi-tan had barely stepped forward and was moving his fists in patterns he hadn't seen before.

"The problem," Shi-tan told him, "is that we Shrillexians are often too obvious in our need to fight."

"Yessss." Kraaz exhaled the word, allowing his healing to catch up with his breath. "I'd say I appreciate the chance to catch my breath, but I think I need to punch you so you don't talk me into suicide."

Shi-tan chuckled. "Doubt that."

"No," Kraaz stepped forward on the balls of his feet, "I think —" He jumped at Shi-tan, smashing his right fist into flesh. Pain exploded in his fist, and his knees buckled. He could hear the bones in his hand crack.

Shi-tan had caught Kraaz's hand and was squeezing it. Kraaz looked up just in time to see Shi-tan's fist slam down.

Kraaz hit the ground, blood pouring from a cut on his cheek. His bony spikes started to emerge from his face, and he had to concentrate to pull them back in. It was considered beyond cheating to use them in a friendly fight.

Or a friendly ass-kicking, especially if it was you who was on the receiving end.

Kraaz rolled sideways and pushed himself off the ground.

"Are you ready?" Shi-tan asked, and Kraaz grinned. It was one thing to fight, but it was an honor to fight someone so much better than you that they used it as a training exercise.

"Only if you think—" Kraaz had started to answer as his opponent attacked, his right elbow aiming for the mercenary. Kraaz moved his own arm to block it, but Shi-tan had already pivoted clockwise on his forward foot, raising his right arm as his body gained speed. His elbow slammed against Kraaz's skull, sending him staggering to his left.

Kraaz tried to set himself into a defensive position, but Shi-tan was already inside his guard. "My boss calls this a gimme," Shi-tan stated conversationally as he slapped Kraaz' left block out of the way and smashed his knuckles into Kraaz's nose, breaking it.

Kraaz tried to back up, but this just allowed Shi-tan to set one leg and lash out with the other, kicking him in the chest. The impact jetted him ten feet backward, where he crashed to the ground with the air knocked out of him.

"The problem..." his opponent continued as Kraaz tried to remember which side Shi-tan was coming from so he could roll the opposite way. Too late. Shi-tan grabbed Kraaz by the throat. "Is that sometimes a lack of scars just means that your opponent has truly incredible medical care."

Kraaz felt his feet leave the ground as Shi-tan lifted him into the air. He ritually popped Shi-tan's forearm twice and was let go to land on his feet.

Shi-tan helped him stand while he got his breath back. "I

think," Kraaz coughed, trying to encourage his neck to heal as he stood there, "I'll go eat my ass-kicked sandwich."

Shi-tan laughed a moment. "That would be good—the food will help you heal. But you will need to wipe off the blood before you get back to your ship."

Kraaz shook his head. "No, let them know I got my own ass kicked. It will help some of them realize there is always someone out there who can hand your ass back with change if they want." He looked at Shi-tan. "I misjudged you. My mistake."

Shi-tan shrugged. "It happens." He clapped Kraaz on the shoulder as he walked past him. "I've got to get back to my *family*, so take care of yourself."

Kraaz turned to watch his fellow Shrillexian stride away. "Any words of wisdom?" he called. It was customary, if a fellow beat you soundly, to ask for advice to help you improve your fighting.

Shi-tan turned and eyed Kraaz a moment, considering his words before speaking.

"Anyone can bring death, but if you want to know *true* death? Well, she dresses in armor, and her eyes glow red. When Death comes for you, ask forgiveness." He pursed his lips. "She just might have pity."

He finished speaking, turned sideways, and slipped back through the fence.

QBBS Asteroid *R2D2*

"I can't believe you got Bethany Anne's approval to call this R2D2." Tina glanced outside the Executive Pod as they headed toward four large asteroids. These had been pulled from the orbit of the sixth planet in the Yollin system, a planet named Yellek that was a particularly ghastly shade of green.

It had taken the team four months to stabilize the four asteroids in a decent orbit in the Quarantined Zone.

So far, no ships had entered the areas the QBS *ArchAngel II* and the QBS *Reynolds* would Gate into. It wasn't entirely because they could Gate right in on anything in that system (which was true), but also because the broadcast warning was, "We shoot trespassers."

Which was to say that as they entered the system, all ships were shown the areas that were "no go-no way-no how" as the documents and videos explained it.

Basically, they were given a map of the system and images of ships being blown apart as they crossed the lines into the restricted areas. There had been plenty of jokes about the rather blunt message, but so far, there hadn't been any incidents due to miscommunication.

You cross the line, we kill you dead.

The little Executive Pod slid into the virtually roped-off space and approached the asteroids.

"Easy enough," Marcus answered. "I told her I wanted to name them Right One and Two and Designate One and Two. I can't help it if she didn't think about what would happen if we shortened the names to just their initials."

"Or," Tina turned to look at Marcus, "she knew exactly what you were doing and didn't care because George Lucas isn't going to sue her out here in the middle of nowhere?"

"Well, technically—" Marcus started before Tina interrupted.

"Yes, we are in the Yollin system, but I don't think that Earth trademark laws apply this many light-years away."

Bobcat snorted. "I'd love to see the look on Bethany Anne's face if a lawyer tried to serve her."

William chuckled. "Hello, my name is...*oh, my God, your face is on fire! You're a demon, aren't you?*" He pushed both arms out. "Right before she pushed him into the Etheric."

"Wow, you don't like lawyers much, do you?" Tina asked.

"It's been much easier since ADAM, Meredith, and Bethany Anne started handling this sort of thing rather than lawyers," Bobcat told her.

"Does anything get to Bethany Anne?" Tina asked, forgetting to watch as the Executive Pod slowed down and an area in the deep shadow of the asteroid opened.

"Nothing anymore," William answered her question. "Last time she got pissed off at an inane question, she read their thoughts, and both were sent to prison asteroids."

"For pissing her off?" Tina asked. "That seems a bit harsh."

"Not really," Marcus answered. "One was trying to steal the intellectual property of the other. And the second one was guilty of something back on Earth that pissed her off so badly she contemplated killing him."

"But she didn't?" Tina asked. "I mean, obviously not right then, but she usually doesn't withhold the stick, so to speak."

"I think he had been punished before," Bobcat looked up, trying to remember, "back on Earth, but she found out he wasn't penitent or something. She made sure he wouldn't have the opportunity to do it again."

"Anyway," William took back the conversation, "no one wants the Empress digging around in their mind for old shit, so they allow the courts to deal with it."

The shadow caught Tina's attention as they ducked under the overhang and slid into the bay inside the asteroid. Behind them, the stars shone brightly.

Tina was the first to exit the Pod, followed by Bobcat, William, and then Marcus, who made sure the Pod was locked.

"Why do you do that?" Tina asked. "Who is going to steal one of our Pods out here?"

"Probably no one," Marcus admitted, walking around her to exit the bay, "but I like to practice safe Podding."

There was a groan from William and an "I'm working on it!" from Marcus ahead of her. Tina just shook her head and started walking as the guys went through the exit. The door slid closed behind them all.

It was her first visit to the new Research and Development Asteroid for Team BMW, and she'd be damned if she'd get lost.

She went through the door and lost it. There were four hallways that went every which way, and she couldn't see the guys. "Fuck!" she hissed, her frustration plain on her face.

"Tina!" She whirled to see Marcus down a hallway, his head sticking out from a second hallway. "This way." He ducked back.

She double-timed it to the hallway and jogged just a bit to catch up with him.

"R2!" William called as Tina entered the room and stopped short. The roof was at least ten meters high, and the room was a large domed circle. In the middle were four tables, each with a computer and tablet, and she could see table-based holographic units for personal work and a central unit she imagined would be used for group efforts.

There were also old-school whiteboards on casters around the tables.

"Yes, William?" A voice sounded from the room's speakers. The closer Tina walked to the middle tables, the better she could hear the EI's voice. She also noticed that the voice started with a little chirp, slightly reminiscent of the chirp from that old science fiction movie.

"That affectation," Bobcat sat at his table to turn on his computer, "is going to drive me to drink."

"You don't need a reason to drink," Marcus pointed out, "and you can tell R2 to stop it anytime."

"I'm just preparing you for the future," Bobcat commented, his computer booting as he got up and walked to William's table. "What do you have for us?"

"This." He threw his fist out, and his hologram sprang to life.

Marcus looked up as Tina walked toward the two guys and glanced at William's display before putting his head back down.

Seconds later, Marcus' head jerked back up. "That's not possible."

"That's what I said," William told him as he pointed to the hologram. "R2, highlight and enlarge Section Three-three." A large component of the electronics of the ESD beam technology appeared in the hologram.

Tina stood back and watched.

Marcus got up. "The..." he started, then got lost in thought again.

Bobcat rubbed his chin. "Where did you get this?"

"Random bullshit from our computers in the monkey's paw offices."

"R2," Marcus requested, "let me speak with Reynolds, please."

"Space station or ship?"

"Oh, yeah," William muttered. "Whoever thought allowing Reynolds to keep his name when he was chosen to also helm the next superdreadnought was an—"

"It was Bethany Anne," Bobcat told him.

"Goddamned genius," William finished. "Obviously thinking ahead... If an attack was launched, the two EI's could work closely together to protect the battle station and the superdreadnought. It was a fucking *epiphany*."

"Nice save," Tina told him.

"Why, thank you," William answered as he launched some design programs they had used to build the original Eat-Shit-and-Die Beam. "What caused me to think it might happen is the—'

A deep, gruff voice spoke from the speakers. "This is Reynolds."

"Hey, dawg," William greeted. "Take a look at what we got here, would you?"

Tina looked around, wondering where Reynolds' cameras

were. Or was he just reading William's computer and hologram directly? She thought about it and realized it would logically be both.

"The plans for the ESD beam," Reynolds told them. "This is section QQV2272, used for changing the Etheric energy into—"

Suddenly there was silence.

"What happened?" Tina asked.

"Give him a second," Bobcat answered. "Reynolds is tracking something down. He doesn't like to pontificate on what-ifs. If he knows we've seen something, he would rather go down a few thousand rabbit holes while we have our virtual thumbs up our asses than provide an incomplete answer."

"I think," Reynolds came back on, "there is potential here, William. My first pass at the calculations suggests the change is feasible."

"How many?" Tina asked, looking at Marcus.

Reynolds answered. "Two million, six hundred and seventy-two thousand, four hundred and twelve permutations."

"And that was?" Tina asked, annoyed.

"The number of different ways I could see to accomplish miniaturization of the components in the ESD beam that William has highlighted. Further, it includes all the downstream modifications we have installed since actually firing the beam."

Tina grabbed a chair from Bobcat's table and pulled it closer to him and William. "I feel like I'm behind."

"As well you should be!" Marcus answered, running a hand through his hair. "The ESD beam was one of our most secret projects. We never got a chance to fire it until the fickle finger of fate forced Bethany Anne's hand during the Yollin insurgency. We've been number crunching on those—" He stopped and looked at William. "Oh, shit. That's some of the data we used to seed the monkey's paw trap."

William grinned and snapped his fingers, then pointed to

Marcus. "I tell Bobcat all the time that you occasionally hold up your end of the job."

Marcus flipped William off while directing his attention to Tina. "That's how this stroke of genius occurred. Now we need to see if we can actually miniaturize the most powerful beam we have ever produced."

There was a loud *pop*, and the three of them turned to see Bobcat holding a bottle, quickly trying to suck off the foam that was spewing out the top. A moment later, he got it under control and turned to the rest of them, smiling as he lifted the bottle in their direction with a question on his face.

"Another round of research?" he asked.

QBBS _Meredith Reynolds_, Empress Bethany Anne's Meeting Room

"Are you shitting me?" Bethany Anne looked at Cheryl Lynn, who shook her head. "Those bastards want to talk peace?" she confirmed as she sat down at the meeting table and rubbed Ashur's head. Cheryl Lynn took the chair next to her.

This time Cheryl Lynn nodded in agreement. Her face was studiously blank, giving away nothing as Bethany Anne stared, her eyes narrowing as she absorbed what Cheryl Lynn had just related to her.

Bethany Anne stopped petting Ashur as she considered the ramifications. A moment later, her attention was drawn back to Ashur as he bumped her hand a couple of times. "You know, Ashur," Bethany Anne told him, "you really do focus on what's most important to yourself."

"Are you sure he isn't trying to keep you from going ballistic over this request?" Cheryl Lynn asked.

Ashur chuffed at her, and Cheryl Lynn replied. "No, I'm not trying to give away any secrets. However, you generally try to get Bethany Anne to pet you whenever she's upset."

Ashur chuffed again.

Bethany Anne chuckled. "Well, yeah. I suppose for you it *is* always a good time to get a head scratch, you old goat." She reached down and scratched Ashur's ribs. "Okay, lie down while I figure out how the Leath are trying to screw us."

Ashur chuffed, and when Bethany Anne sat back in the chair, walked toward the door and laid down next to it.

"We were just in the Noel-ni system two weeks ago." Bethany Anne blew out a breath and looked at Cheryl Lynn. "You aren't saying anything to me here."

"That's because I don't know if you want my professional take, or need me to listen to you bitch for a while."

Bethany Anne glared at her. "I went to a bunch of planets to prove I didn't eat babies and look where that got me."

"It proved you didn't eat babies," Cheryl Lynn pointed out. "We got some good PR from your support of the Yollin teenager."

"And I was accused of practically eating the Noel-ni kid," Bethany Anne shot back. "He wasn't thick enough to have made a good sandwich."

Cheryl Lynn stared at Bethany Anne, then put a hand across her mouth.

"That's not going to work." Bethany Anne looked at her. "I see the laughter in your eyes!"

Cheryl Lynn mumbled between her fingers, "That's because it's so wrong it's funny!" She shook her head, hand still clamped over her mouth. "But so, *so* wrong!"

Ashur chuffed, and Bethany Anne looked at him. "I know, right? I could have fricasseed—"

"Oh, my God, *stop*!" Cheryl Lynn took her hand off her mouth, but instead of a smile, there was a horrified gape. "Do you know what would happen if you ever joked like that around a microphone?"

"Of course." Bethany Anne smiled and leaned forward. "I'm ego-maniacal, not stupid."

Cheryl Lynn blinked a couple times. "Oh."

For a few seconds, neither of the women spoke, but finally Cheryl Lynn broke the silence. "Your feelings are hurt."

"Hell, yes, they're hurt!" Bethany Anne replied, a flash of red in her eyes. "Do you have any idea what it feels like to have billions of aliens wonder if you're an evil lunatic?" Bethany Anne leaned back in her chair. "I can't go to a planet without them shrinking from me or wanting to test me or trying to trip me up."

She pushed her hair out of her eyes. "I'm in a goddamned gilded cage surrounded by weapons of mass destruction, and half the fucking galaxy worries I may come after their world to spread catastrophe, carnage, and chaos."

Cheryl Lynn shook her head. "Nice alliteration."

"Thank you, I rather liked the whole catastrophe, carnage, and chaos thing." Bethany Anne glanced at her friend. "However nice it was, it's still true," She finished, daring Cheryl Lynn to argue the point.

Cheryl Lynn's eyes narrowed as she thought about it. "Boss, what's the worst that could happen?"

"Those fuckers actually want peace," Bethany Anne answered without hesitation.

"Wait." Cheryl Lynn shook her head as if to dislodge something in her ear. "What? Say that again."

"Huh?" Bethany Anne frowned. "Don't you get it? I'll never agree to peace with the Leath. They are ruled by a Kurtherian group we are going to take down. Period fucking dot." She shook her head slowly. "No way, no how, *never* are we going to have peace."

"Uh," Cheryl Lynn frowned, "okay. So what do you want to do about this peace accord request?"

"Oh, that's easy," Bethany Anne smiled. "We are going to attend so I can kick some ass."

CHAPTER FIFTEEN

Bethany Anne was in her suite on *ArchAngel II* when John knocked on the door. She called to him to come in.

John cracked the door and stuck his head in. "You wanted me?"

"Yes," Bethany Anne replied. "What are you guys taking into the meeting?"

"Well," John stepped into her room carrying a box, leaving the door to the outer suite open, "they have banned armor and major weapons."

"Uh-huh," Bethany Anne replied, "and if you say this hotel doesn't have a shit-ton of weapons all over it, you're lying."

"Oh, no doubt," John agreed. "The thing is," he held up his hand, fingers closed before he put up one finger. "They prohibit all forms of chemical propellant." He put up a second finger. "All forms of laser or beam energy," he put up a third finger, "and various and sundry slug-throwing devices." He put up a fourth finger. "Any form of body armor you wear like clothes and," he put up the last finger, "gloves."

"So, the Leath are big motherfuckers, but all any of us can have is a blade or some other personal weapon that can't deliver death at a distance."

"Well, what they don't know—" John started and Bethany Anne smiled.

"Won't hurt us," she finished. "However, tell me the good news —what's Jean got for us?"

"You remember the fight back on Earth where we were attacked at the hotel?" he asked, and handed her the box he had brought in with him.

She took it.

"Yeah." Bethany Anne smiled, her eyes losing focus for just a moment. "Damn! Good times, good times." John snorted. "Hey! Those *were* good times, personally speaking, of course." She walked over to a wall that had a door, but no handle. "ArchAngel, open my weapons room."

There was an audible click and the eight-inch-thick door swung away from the wall. Bethany Anne went inside as John walked to the doorway, peeked in, and whistled. "When did you get those KRISS Super Vs?" he asked and stepped in to pull one of the submachine guns off the wall. "Damn, you have been holding out on me!"

"Well, actually..." she began. John ignored the sound of her stripping and opening the box behind him as he studied the submachine gun.

"God, these are wonderful. Take out just a couple of pins." He turned to his left, where there was a little table for working on the weapons. He grinned when Bethany Anne pulled out the stick-on armor design that went under their clothes and...

"*Gott Verdammt*, that's cold!" she bitched behind him. "Ranting bollock experiment... Oooooh, damn." There were a few more choice words as John took apart the .45 caliber gun, checking to make sure there were no rounds inside. "These were designed using concepts from the Kalashnikov," John told Bethany Anne. "Large pieces that wouldn't fuck up in the field. Easy to disassemble and clean."

"Uh-huh," she agreed. "Wow, she even gave my woohoo some protection."

John stopped looking at the gun and glanced up at the ceiling, trying to assimilate what he had just heard, and realized what she was doing. "I'm not going to ask."

Bethany Anne ignored him. "Wow, hope you don't have a hairy sasquatch when you rip this shit back off."

"*La la la,*" John intoned. "More information than I wanted to know about my Empress," he told her, carefully not looking.

"I mean really," Bethany Anne gasped a second later, "a minute on a lady's lower lips…"

Bethany Anne grinned when John launched into his own version of super-speed to put the submachine back together, place it back on the wall, and step out of her weapons room. She imagined how red his face must have been and snickered.

Once she had the armor in place, she grabbed her stretchy fabric two-piece and put it on, then donned her leather gear. Ball gowns were for princesses, and *she* wasn't a princess.

She was the *Queen Bitch.*

A few moments later, she stepped out of her weapons closet and walked over to John, who was busy with his tablet. She placed her two swords on the bed and held up the KRISS. "Hey, big guy." He turned to her, one eyebrow up. "This was supposed to be a gift to you on our anniversary. Sorry," she told him and held the gun out to him.

John's eyes narrowed. "Damn, how many years has it been," he asked as he accepted the submachine gun from Bethany Anne, "since you saved me in the Everglades?" He turned the gun over and continued the inspection he had cut short back in the weapons room.

"Too damned long, and yet just yesterday," she answered. John didn't see her surreptitiously wiping a small tear out of her right eye as she enjoyed his delight at receiving the gun.

Her guys really liked to shoot the old stuff.

"It's a shame we can't bring this," He looked up, a question in his eyes. "We can't bring this, right?"

"Not exactly," she agreed, "but we can chat about it with the others before we go down to the hotel."

"So," Bethany Anne grabbed her swords and walked out of her bedroom, "what did Jean give you guys? Cod protection?"

"Not funny, BA," John groused.

"C'mon Ashur, c'mon Matrix," Bethany Anne called out, and the two German Shepherds came out of their room. Ashur's totally white fur contrasted starkly with Matrix's black body and four white-stockinged feet. Matrix was two inches shorter at the shoulder than his dad. "Make sure you both wear your armor as well."

I hate armor! Matrix sent. *It's constricting.*

"No armor, no go," Bethany Anne told him. "No choice."

This sucks planetarium piss, Matrix grumbled and jogged past Bethany Anne into the hallway beyond.

Bethany Anne shook her head and smiled as she heard Darryl singing just outside her front door. *"I've got the biggest codpiece of all!"*

Noel-ni Planet Sertjal, Floating Hotel

"This is Giannini Oviedo outside the Unpronounceable Purple Hotel—"

"Stop!" Sia lifted her drone HUD glasses and gave her friend *the look.* "Seriously? The unpronounceable purple hotel?"

"No." Giannini shook her head. "*I* said the name with capital letters, like a proper name. *You* did not."

"How am I supposed to know the difference between capitalized and uncapitalized generic names?" Sia asked.

"I'm a professional, so you have to listen closely." Giannini smiled. "It's all in the inflection."

"I'll inflect you! Now say the name right," Sia told her friend and slid the glasses back down on her face, covering her eyes. "In three, two, one..." Sia pointed to Giannini.

"This is Giannini Oviedo outside of the XerpresciechCoth Hotel, which is the largest floating hotel on the Noel-ni Planet Sertjal. This," she waved behind her at its three buildings, the swimming pool that spanned them all, and the varied landscaping, "is the location at which the Noel-ni have suggested the two starfaring combatants hold discussions related to their war. The Etheric Empire has accepted the Karillian into their coalition, thus providing them protection. The Leath, on the other hand, consider the Empire's efforts to stop the final acquisition of the Karillians' planet as a further justification of the war which, they warn, could affect multiple species and systems in this part of space."

Sia changed the view to a drone flying above the pool. "As you can see, this hotel is full of tourists and vacationers from all over space. There are over a thousand support personnel just for this hotel, and additional personnel have been brought in for the VIPs."

Sia cut back to Giannini.

"Empress Bethany Anne will be meeting with Leath First Line Prime Commander Ch'lockteck, who is responsible for the military endeavors of the Leath." Giannini pursed her lips. "Strict weapons constraints have been placed on both sides; no weapons are permitted. The assumption is that the talks should at least be safe, if not exactly quiet. One presumes the Noel-ni have seen the videos of John Grimes, as they have also demanded that no armored suits be allowed. All attendees of both parties to the accord will be inspected before being allowed to leave their respective ships. I'm told Empress Bethany Anne has brought all five Queen's Bitches as her personal guard."

She paused a moment before continuing, "We are sure our viewers will join us in wishing these peace talks all success. As we make our way inside to talk with those who have arrived, this is Giannini Oviedo reporting from Noel-ni planet Sertjal."

Noel-ni Planet Sertjal, XerprescriechCoth Hotel, Three Days Later

Matrix was mentally bitching to TOM as he wandered through the hallways and backrooms surrounding the main conference area for the peace talks. The talks had been going on for two days and the back and forth on petty issues had driven Matrix nuts, so he volunteered to go do something else.

They stuck him on outer perimeter guard duty.

This is just stupid! he sent to TOM.

Oh, and why do you think that? TOM's voice came back over the communication chip embedded in Matrix' skull.

I'm just patrolling around and around, doing nothing important. These aliens are going to start wondering what I'm doing, especially if I find a door I can't open. I'll just have to turn around. Before you ask, it's annoying because it's embarrassing.

You are still worried about how others perceive you, little one.

Bigger than you.

And that means what exactly, Matrix? Do you believe your physical characteristics somehow make you superior to others? Is this why the occasional door you can't open upsets you so much?

Matrix went silent, pondering what he'd said as TOM continued his side of the conversation.

You wanted to see the cosmos with me, and to understand math. Neither of those activities requires you to be a massive specimen of your kind. It's enough that you have sharp mental characteristics and a willingness to travel. So tell me again, why are you upset about the physical issues?

I'm getting my ass handed to me during workouts with the Guardians. They change to their wolf form and are so fast I can barely think quick enough to get away, much less attack.

Matrix stopped in the hallway, and the door in front of him slid open. He entered the large public area and padded through it, passing two restaurants and a small store before he found another unmarked door. After he waited in front of it for a second, it slid open, and he jogged through it.

And the armor?

Matrix could feel the armor grow tighter as TOM mentioned it.

I hate it. It keeps bunching up the fur on my back near my legs. Occasionally it pulls a hair.

How often is occasionally? TOM asked, wondering if Jean had somehow missed a design flaw.

Maybe once a week, Matrix admitted.

I think you will survive, TOM replied. **You are allowing your irritation with the armor in general to color your opinion about all the small annoyances right now**.

It's just so damned constricting, Matrix shot back. The scent hit him as he was finishing his thought. *You can't... One second.*

Matrix sniffed again and recognized the odor as something he smelled when Darryl and Scott had been doing...

Target practice!

Two doors ahead of him opened and six aliens stepped out. He turned around and saw another two doors opening behind him. His eyes opened wide in alarm.

One of the aliens aimed a weapon at him. *TOM!* he screamed mentally. *WE ARE UNDER ATTACK!*

Matrix tried to run, but a bullet slammed into his body, throwing him down the hallway to crash into the wall. He lost consciousness as feet trooped by him. The last one in the group lashed out, kicking Matrix in the head.

CHAPTER SIXTEEN

There are assassins, Che'al thought, *and then there is me.*

The Noel-ni glanced down at the timepiece she wore on her wrist. It provided a visual representation of the time until her strike, allotted time to accomplish her task, and finally her time to exit the vicinity, all according to plan.

Che'al had been planning this hit since she was hired. It had taken her seven trips to bring all the parts she needed. None of them by themselves amounted to much, but once she took them out of their hiding places and reassembled them, she had one of the most powerful weapons a person might acquire for precise efforts such as hers.

Death was her business, and business had unfortunately been rather sparse, which was why this job had been such a godsend. Her contact had provided a significant portion of precious metals to fund the beginning of the job without any arguments.

It was always nice to work with other professionals.

She had pegged the client as military, based on the precise directions and information provided. She figured the contact was much more familiar with Leath than the Empire since their information about the Leath group was more complete.

However, the dossier on the Etheric Empire primary had been decent.

Her own resources had provided little more. The Etheric Empire's effort to keep sensitive information under wraps had suffered when the Empress had visited the Noel-ni some time back. Some of the Empress' abilities, or at least her armor's capabilities, had leaked. It was universally presumed the armor she wore provided the ability to fire the balls of power.

Che'al was stationed just inside a small air-handling box on the south side of the large room where the peace talks were being held. She had been listening to them arguing, and she was just shy of thinking she might end her own life if she had to listen to more of this.

The Leath were being obstinate and illogical, and the humans were being protective and unyielding. It didn't take a genius to understand these two would never achieve peace. This would be, Che'al decided, a mercy killing; these two factions wouldn't have to work any longer on a lost cause.

She was counting down the final few moments before she connected the power source to her rifle. She didn't know if the security below did active searches for unexpected power, but she'd rather be careful. If the options were not getting her hit set up in time or being found out, she would choose to fail her shot.

The other could get her captured, and capture would be the end of the line. Failure to make a hit was a black mark but did not ensure a grisly death.

Her timepiece started thumping on her wrist, letting her know it was time to power up. She reached for the battery and slowly pushed it into her laser carbine; the little snick when it seated was all the noise it made. She lifted the rifle to her shoulder, looking into the room through the metal grate before placing her eye to the scope.

The gentle thump, thump, thump of the countdown on her wrist let her know it was almost time.

On the last thump, she squeezed the trigger.

Ch'lockteck looked very good in his uniform. His upthrust tusks weren't very long, which was helpful for speaking but horrible for impressing the females of his species. He had been told to make these peace talks last for five days before he left in a righteous huff.

For the first day and part of the second, he had almost convinced himself the gods had decreed he would die at the alien's hand.

He had an intelligence report on those across the table from him, and while Ch'lockteck was formidable, the guards around the woman knew their business when it came to killing. He didn't doubt they would be deadly, even without their armor.

He just had two more days of this mind-numbing bullshit to go through before he could slam his fist on the table, declare these talks useless, and get back to attacking the very people he was staring at.

Perhaps he should study them further, get into their minds...

His eyes narrowed as he considered what questions he should ask. He felt rather stupid, not having thought about this before now.

Well, stupid or not, he would make up for lost time.

Bethany Anne watched the Leath across the table narrow his eyes in thought. For such a different species, they had similar mannerisms and physical tells she could—

TOM! What the fuck? she screamed mentally when her body was violently thrown to the side.

Then, her mind amped to vampiric speed, she heard the sizzle of melting plastic and twisted her head as her right hand protected her from slamming to the ground.

The back of her chair was melting, and John was twisting and grabbing his leg. The smell of burning fabric reached her nose from the burn hole in his clothes.

She hoped his armor had stopped it.

She hit the ground, turned her fall into a roll, and worked to pop up.

ALL MY PEOPLE! She sent out a mental shout. *WE ARE UNDER ATTACK!*

ADAM! she yelled, glancing at the hole in her chair and John's leg and following the line of sight to where she thought the sniper must be hiding.

Ch'lockteck's eyes opened in surprise as the Empress dove off her chair. He saw the beam hole in her guard's leg as Ch'lockteck twisted to the side and pushed away from the table, but was not able to do much more.

A second beam hit Ch'lockteck in the back of the head, and his brain was instantly heated to well over a thousand degrees. As his brain cooked its moisture turned to steam, building up pressure in his skull until it exploded a mere few microseconds later. His body rolled forward as the chair continued rolling backward and his corpse hit the floor with a thud.

Che'al stroked the trigger of her rifle as she refined her aim, targeting the base of the Leath military leader's neck. She ended up hitting him square in the back of his skull since he reacted a bit faster than she had calculated.

Not that it mattered; she had allowed for some movement.

Her ears picked up the screams just starting in the room as she pulled her eye from her scope to see what she had done to her first target.

That was when she realized she'd made the last mistake of her life.

>> I have reviewed the schematics. There is an air filtration system box large enough to hold an assassin twelve feet to the left and three up from where you are presently looking.<<

Bethany Anne flung her empty hand back like a pitcher at a baseball game. When her hand was all the way behind her, a red ball of Etheric energy popped into existence and she flung it toward the location ADAM had described. The energy streaked across the room to slam through the metal, causing something behind the grate to explode. Parts of a body were expelled, raining down on the crowd below.

Bethany Anne realized she was hearing weapons fire. Her face crackled with energy, the red lines etching into it, eyes blazing and hair flying on a wind of her own as she sought the location of those attacking.

While she might not have a weapon, they did.

And soon her people would be armed as well, with weapons taken from the corpses of those stupid enough to fire on them.

Especially since they had been warned by Nathan's team months ago. "It's about damned time!" Bethany Anne yelled, glancing quickly at John. He had a bad burn on his leg, and it looked like the beam had made it into muscle. She was sure it was healing, but it probably still hurt like a son of a bitch.

Two attackers came through the main doors holding what looked like some kind of submachine guns. She focused on the guns and pushed energy to heat them. The mercenaries dropped their weapons, screaming in pain and frustration as a couple of their friends bumped into them from behind.

One had bad trigger control and ripped a few rounds off right into his buddy's back.

They must be newbs. She grabbed the swords that had lain on the table and yelled over her shoulder. "Scott!"

The erstwhile New York policeman turned toward her, seeing the sheathed sword already halfway to him in the air. He reached up with his left hand, caught the sheath, and pulled out the katana with his right as he twisted. He continued his spin, swinging the sword to slice off the arm of a mercenary who had come through a side door.

Scott kicked the screaming Noel-ni back through the door, shattering it as he bent down to grab the attacker's pistol.

"Behind you!" Darryl called.

Scott flipped the sword and jabbed it backward while keeping his head low, and he felt the sword hit flesh. He turned to see a Leath, who had decided to jump into the fight. "Hold this a moment," he told the Leath, who was staring in confusion at the sword through his body.

Scott pulled the fingers and hand off the recovered pistol and dropped the severed arm, gripping the pistol in his right hand. With his left, he grabbed the hilt of the sword. "Thank you, I'll take this back now," he told the Leath, and lashed out with his boot, kicking the Leath off the sword.

He smiled in glee. Now he was doubly armed!

He looked around to make sure Bethany Anne was safe and found Darryl fighting to her right, blazing away with two pistols. "You greedy ass!" Scott shouted. "How did you get two?"

Scott heard John to his left and turned to see what the commotion was, then ducked the body flying over him.

"Don't kick the *Gott Verdammt* leg!" John was yelling at the alien, who landed in a five-foot-diameter potted plant as he spoke. The vase cracked, and so did the alien's skull. "It fucking hurts!" he finished.

Scott raised the pistol and shot three times through the small side door, then turned and ran toward Bethany Anne.

>>**Bethany Anne, there have been a number of distress calls from the engine deck.**<<

"What the hell does a hotel need with an engine deck?" she asked, casually shooting two more mercenaries who poked their heads into the room. She looked at Darryl. "That's fourteen and fifteen!"

"Seventeen!" Darryl answered, grinning from ear to ear. "You failed to kill this one!"

"What?" Bethany Anne asked.

>>**The hotel floats using the power from the engine room.**<< ADAM reminded her.

"Oh, shit! These cock-juggling root-juice-loving fart-box tongue-punchers are trying to drop the hotel," she bitched as she shot another enemy.

She looked to her left. "Eric! Keep it safe here with John. I'm taking Scott and Darryl for a little R and R."

He nodded.

"Oh, fuck a duck," Scott kicked a pistol lying on the floor toward his team. "Reconnaissance and Retribution tasking, here we come." While he was making his smartass comment, he and Darryl had hot-footed it over to Bethany Anne, who grabbed them both and disappeared.

The three mercenaries who had seen the three humans disappear gawked. One immediately died from a slug through the skull. It blew out the back of his head, which splattered one of the female hotel staff who had been standing frozen near the wall with the others.

She fainted, slumping to the floor.

John noted that some of the Leath who had realized the humans weren't the cause of the commotion were busy killing mercenaries. Like Bethany Anne, he appreciated that the mercenaries had finally attacked so they could be done with the charade.

He hadn't appreciated the assassin. That person had done well, hiding herself. As long as the effort to drop the hotel didn't work, they would be okay. Bad Company had provided good information, but it seemed they had been short on a few important details.

The beam had been ablated by the armor he had wrapped around his legs, but it hadn't been enough to reflect or stop it.

His leg got cooked, and frankly, he didn't have time to deal with the mess healing was going to make of the armor right now. Getting that shit out of his skin was going to require a trip to the Pod-doc.

Better than no leg, he mused as he shot another mercenary. That's when Peter decided to join the party with four of his Guardians, and the Leath realized they weren't the only aliens who could roar.

Peter got the message regarding the assault in time to palm two knives and notify his team, who had been tasked with stopping any attacking force from coming into the hotel.

The first two mercenaries with unveiled weapons were gifted with diamond-tipped throwing blades to their skulls.

They had barely hit the ground when Todd, who had refused to be left behind even though he couldn't use guns, went to their bodies and grabbed both weapons. "God!" He cycled one of the weapons and made sure he understood how it worked. "Now I don't feel so—"

"Downnn!" Peter yelled, and Todd ducked, another blade flying over him to hit an alien disguised as a waiter in the gut. The mercenary dropped his weapon to grab the hilt of the knife, but his head snapped back when Todd drilled him through the skull.

"Wow, aims high," Todd commented as he swept the area, one knee on the ground, looking for those not screaming their heads off. Tourists and guests were escaping outside. Todd pointed the loud weapon into the air. "Get down!" he screamed and squeezed the trigger twice to emphasize his command.

He wasn't sure what the aliens heard when he screamed in English, but a substantial number hit the deck and the humans were able to fire at those wielding weapons.

Something slammed Todd's chest, throwing him off his balance and causing him to roll as he cursed up a storm.

Peter was next to him in a moment, one hand checking his friend, the other grabbing the extra pistol. "Stop laying down on the job!" Peter grunted and lifted his friend.

"Takes a punch and keeps on ticking," Todd gasped.

"Timex?" Peter asked, firing two shots, not sure where the round that had hit Todd came from.

"No, my heart," Todd answered. "That shit packs a wallop!"

"I don't see any more. Let's join the crew inside," Peter directed, and Todd shouted for the team to pull back while he sent the command over their comms as well.

Once they knew the mercenary group had been hired, Bethany Anne's team had requested a VIP tour of the facilities. They had purchased rooms dispersed around the hotel's various structures so that if Bethany Anne needed a rapid reaction force, she could grab someone and leave.

And she had.

They hadn't really expected the mercenaries to go after the engines, but they had developed a plan for that eventuality.

It involved Bethany Anne, a couple Bitches, and a massive

amount of mayhem, especially since the team had secreted weapons in a room near the engines. There wasn't going to be any opportunity to get past them. And, as her father liked to say...

If you weren't cheating, you weren't trying.

CHAPTER SEVENTEEN

Noel-ni Planet Sertjal, XerpresciechCoth Hotel

Kraaz and the team slipped through the back hallways, which were used for monitoring and supporting the infrastructure of the massive hotel away from the eyes of the customers.

Reaching their third crossing, he stopped and looked around the corner, then pulled his head back. He held up a hand and put up two fingers.

Behind him, P'kert flicked his weapon to stun, took two steps around Kraaz, and shot both of the hotel support staff. Their general goal was still to kill everyone, but they were stunning the staff down here in case they happened upon someone from Engineering and needed them alive for knowledge or passwords.

They would kill them later.

Bethany Anne, Scott, and Darryl appeared in the middle of the cheapest room in the hotel. Cheap because it was on the lower decks near all the equipment and noisy. Perfect for her people.

All three went to the weapons cases, popping the locks and opening them. They slipped on the armored jackets and donned the HUD helmets, locking them down to the jackets. They pulled out the Jean Dukes pistols and holsters, sliding their arms through the straps and seating the equipment, and lastly reached for Jean Dukes' version of submachine guns. These still used standard gravitic power, but their slugs were bigger and made of a softer material, so they had punch but wouldn't go through too many pipes or walls. They didn't want to bring the hotel down unnecessarily in a random firefight by destroying the very equipment they were trying to save.

All three lids slammed shut at the same time. Darryl flicked his eyes to the display that provided him access to the camera they had placed outside the door.

The hallway was clear.

Darryl exited first and took a right outside the door, then Bethany Anne and finally Scott left the room. All three ran down the hallway and did a quick jog through an "employees only" room to come out in a service hallway.

"Left!" Bethany Anne called. She was connected to ADAM, who was monitoring the mercenary team through the hotel's video and other security infrastructure. "Right, then two hallways and we'll be in front of them!"

The three raced through the concrete halls.

Kraaz felt the difference in the air and put up a fist to halt his team. He looked behind him, then down the hallway in front.

Something didn't feel right.

"We got trouble?" P'kert asked from behind him.

Kraaz nodded. "I don't know what it is, but something is ahead of us."

"Shock?"

"No." Kraaz shook his head. "Trouble, and we'll need to go through it."

"That's why we are paid the big bucks," P'kert commented, sliding his pistol into a holster and pulling out a larger beam weapon. It was a twenty-shot Kellen D3, and it could drill through walls and make organic life wish it had never been born.

He loved this gun.

Kraaz chuckled. "I'm pretty sure we're being paid the big bucks because we have to jump out of a falling hotel and successfully not die at the end of the fall."

"That's just a bonus," P'kert told him. "Now get your Shrillexian ass moving."

Kraaz just nodded and flipped his own pistol's safety off.

Sia was tucked behind a large potted plant, completely focused on the different video intakes from her four drones…

Scratch that, three drones now. Someone took offense at one of them and shot it down.

Still, she was giving all her attention to the video she was capturing in three different locations. One outside, and two here inside the hotel. She could feel Giannini's body somewhere above her, protecting her this time as Sia captured as much good footage as possible.

Sia could hear Giannini commentating, mumbling stuff—Sia didn't know what, but it would be relevant when they put the video of this attack together and reported it.

Provided they lived.

P'kert was damned handy with his Kellen D3. It wasn't so much he saw something down the hall as the reflexes honed over multiple battles that told him he needed to fire. Kraaz had already confirmed he thought something was ahead of him.

So P'kert stroked the trigger. He thought he saw a body come around the corner only to get tossed backward before a large red ball of energy streaked toward him. He spun to the side and tried to dive out of the way, but it was too late.

Half of his body was ripped apart when the energy slammed into him, ending his life immediately.

Behind him, Kraaz and the others dropped to the ground when two more flaming orbs of power came shooting down the hallway. One went past, exploding some thirty paces behind him, and the other caught Chr'stepf in the head, melting it immediately, his body convulsing.

Kraaz was firing down the hallway when the floor and walls started exploding. He wasn't sure what was being used, but the amount of destruction suggested some sort of tripod-mounted devices.

Kraaz's shoulder exploded in gore as something blew his arm apart, his weapon going who-knew-where as his pharmacope injected painkillers into his system so he could keep his wits and his focus.

In the haze of his pain, he looked at his group and realized that every one of his men had been either killed or substantially wounded like himself. His enhanced healing couldn't force a non-existent arm to regrow.

"Control," he snapped. There was no way his team was going to be successful. It was up to Bocklans to figure out what the team needed to do next.

This operation was a bust.

"There is no more Control," a voice called to him.

Kraaz slowly turned his head back around. The silence in the hallway after all the destruction sounded deafening to him and his heartbeat was louder in his ears than the hissing of the pipes spewing liquids somewhere behind him.

Kraaz's eyes opened as he fought through the pain to see a dark human, his chest a rumpled mess where P'kert's beam had hit him, come out of the smoke first, before another figure came into view behind him.

He saw the red glowing in the smoke and swallowed in understanding.

Her eyes flamed red, her hair floating as energy crackled around her, and streaks of power were etched on her face. She wore a red armored jacket on her shoulders and held a helmet in her hand.

Death had come, and he hadn't even known who she was when he'd watched the Etheric Empire's Empress for those three days.

Death had been sitting there weaving a spell of confusion, just as she had sung a song of attraction to those who had courted her their whole lives.

Now Death had come to reap their souls.

"Forgive me," Kraaz mumbled. "Forgive me, Death, for I knew not who I fought."

The Empress of Death stared at him as he lay on the ground bleeding from the shoulder where his arm had been blown off. Death's voice was deep, without pity and without anger as she spoke to him in his own tongue.

"Sleep," Death commanded, and a blue ball of energy formed in her hand.

Then Kraaz knew only darkness.

Across the systems, a second battle was being fought. This time it wasn't with guns and explosives; it was with words and video, accusations, lies, and press releases.

It was a war for the hearts and minds of the empires who did not have a stake in the fight between the Etheric Empire and the

Leath. In short, it was a fight to spin the truth of the battle on Sertjal and bring sympathy, or at least antipathy, to the conversations.

The Noel-ni wanted to blame someone, *anyone* other than themselves for failing to provide the security they had promised. They accused unknown assailants even though they had the same proof in their possession as the Etheric Empire and the Leath did —the attack had been executed by a hired mercenary group.

Leath reporters blamed the Etheric Empire for hiring the mercenary group that had successfully killed their highest ranking military officer after their own primary had mysteriously and miraculously dodged the assassin's beam headed in her own direction.

They pointed to the fact that the humans had been armored and had quickly acquired weapons during the fight and killed the mercenaries they had hired as proof that the Etheric Empire had engaged Darkness for Hire.

The Leath had made a big production of the First Line Prime Commander's funeral, sending video to nearby systems of the massive expense and respect they afforded their fallen hero. He had been a Leath of action but had died trying to promote peace.

While the Leath as a group hadn't been much of a known factor before, they were now rapidly creating connections with news systems and businesses and courting relationships with high-ranking politicos in systems large and small.

The Etheric Empire was busy distributing their video of the attacks, tracking back the proof, forcing the Noel-ni government to confirm their findings, and sharing video from the hotel's own security cameras to counter the Leath's "lies, lies and more lies," as the reporters quoted some of the Etheric Empire's people.

The Leath accused the Etheric Empire of kidnapping their people when almost twenty of their delegates went missing.

The Etheric Empire representatives had shrugged their shoulders and asked how they could misplace their own people.

In secret, the Etheric Empire had accepted anyone from the Leath system who wished to seek asylum for political reasons, not trusting their own government.

The others went back to their planet—those who lived.

Yollin System, Almost Three Years after the Noel-ni Peace Accord Debacle

Admiral Thomas watched the stars from the two-story window in the upper room of All Guns Blazing as he puffed on a cigar.

He was drinking a whisky made from a barley-type grain that was easily grown on one of the more underutilized Yollin land areas. The bar was branching out into manufacturing their own alcohol and brews, some of them directed at the different alien species. Yelena, Cheryl Lynn, and Stephen were diversifying the bar's business.

Bad Company was the exclusive wholesaler of their alcohol throughout the different systems. So far, the venture had provided a nice profit, but nothing that would allow them to grow substantially.

Yelena and Cheryl Lynn were often accompanied by Stephen and various members of Bad Company when they visited different worlds, finding out what crops they grew, and what crops were cheap or underutilized.

Hell, on one world, they had found a weed that produced a very mellow drink the Shrillexians found pleasant. It gave them a gentle buzz that didn't cause them to lose situational awareness. Shi-tan started mixing it in his Pepsi at times.

Nathan tested him: Shi-tan would drink ten of the concoctions, and then they would spar. Shi-tan felt he was mentally tracking, and the tests confirmed he was fighting at about ninety percent of his top form.

Plus, the buzz had worn off during the first two minutes of fighting.

It wasn't until the third week after Shi-tan had started consuming the drink that Bastek noticed he wasn't as aggressive as normal.

To test that theory, Bastek had Shi-tan drink the brew every time he felt like fighting. And almost every time, it had caused Shi-tan to mellow out and overcome the desire to fight.

Now Shi-tan and Bastek wanted to negotiate with Bad Company for the rights to an extract. Bastek wanted to produce the product because it would allow the Shrillexian people a chance to stop sending their people off to fight. They had done this for generations, their people often coming back maimed or worse.

Admiral Thomas heard the *clop clop clop* of a Yollin coming up the stairs. It was the middle of the third shift, and there should only be one Yollin coming up now. He glanced to the side and nodded.

"You humans," Kael-ven waved a hand in the air to bat the smoke aside, "still confuse me with your desire to pollute the air around you with burned dried vegetable matter."

"Normally," the Admiral turned and stubbed the cigar out in the ashtray he had brought up for the purpose, "I'd agree with you, but these are made of a sweet plant from God-knows-where on Straiphus." He turned back and held out a hand to the previous Planetary president. "How are you doing now that you're retired?"

"Huh," Kael-ven grunted as he walked to the other side of the tall bar table the Admiral was using. He shook Admiral Thomas' hand and looked at the drink on the tabletop. "This for me?"

"Of course." The Admiral nodded. "You see any other Yollins in here? You think I'd have a Yollin-designed mug filled with your favorite beverage ready for someone else?"

Kael-ven stopped lifting the mug to his mouth, his mandibles frozen in the open position. He slowly closed them. "Admiral, tell me this drink won't mess up my thinking processes when you hit me with the big job?"

"I'm that transparent?" Admiral Thomas laughed. "And of course not. If I wanted to do something like that, I'd ask Bethany Anne to speak with you."

"She wouldn't need to put anything funny in the drink," Kael-ven told him, then took a sip of the beer. "Dark. I like it."

"That's what Yelena said. Says you are one of the few Yollins she knows that really enjoys the dark stuff."

"Might be the reason I like it." Kael-ven took another sip. "I don't have to worry about sharing the personal stash at my house with anyone else."

Thomas chuckled. "I understand," he glanced at Kael-ven's mug, "and there is no way I would take your beer."

"Of course not," Kael-ven agreed. "You are a discerning man, but you have yet to ask your question. Once you get your answer, *then* I will worry about you taking my drink away."

The Admiral looked at Kael-ven, a small smile playing on his lips. "Actually, I have a keg waiting for you downstairs for your return trip."

"Okay, now you are scaring me," Kael-ven admitted. "I won't be able to enjoy this beer or the view," he pointed to the window, "if you don't alleviate my concern about whatever you are going to ask. How bad is it?"

Thomas turned and grabbed his whisky, swirling it. "Depends on how much you enjoy ground-pounding." He took a sip of his drink, his eyes observing Kael-ven's mannerisms, watching him for any hint about his thoughts.

Unfortunately for Admiral Thomas, multiple years as the Yollin in charge of the planet had trained Kael-ven to show nothing of his thoughts. "And if I am happy on the ground?" he asked.

"I'll give you *two* kegs of beer, but both of them will be on a ship you have to visit to retrieve them." He let Kael-ven think about that for a moment before adding, "One at a time."

"And if this," Kael-ven pointed to the stars outside the window, "appeals to me, what then?"

"Then," Admiral Thomas smiled, "I buy up the remaining kegs of dark, we ship your household lock, stock, and barrel—well, *barrels*—up here, and you join the Etheric Empire's navy, where," Thomas looked sternly at Kael-ven, "you have always belonged anyway."

Kael-ven's eyes narrowed. "How many kegs are available at the moment?"

Thomas grunted. "None for you. I'll buy them just so you can't take them and go back to the planet."

Kael-ven's mandibles tapped twice. "Smart, but not my question. I really want to know how many kegs we are talking about. Do they only have three, or are there more?"

"Twelve dark, fifteen stout," Thomas replied.

"What's the job?" Kael-ven asked.

"I want you to work on building up the navy and the armed troops. Engage with the fighting captains and those who are going to be stationed on the ground. Plus, we have new destroyers that need personal attention to figure out who gets what ship."

Kael-ven laughed, his "heh heh heh" both soft and raspy at the same time. "E'kolorn is wanting a big group?"

"He wants them *all*," Thomas told him.

Kael-ven threw a hand out. "That's because he figures that's the place to start the negotiation. He probably has ample reasons why he needs them and sixteen different attack runs the enemy might use, and can tell you how those ships are the only way..." Kael-ven noticed the Admiral's narrowed eyes. "What?"

"It just so happens," Thomas tapped the tabletop, "that E'kolorn had *exactly* sixteen different scenarios."

Kael-ven grabbed his glass. "Oh." He lifted his drink close to his mouth. "Imagine that," he added before he took a drink.

There was silence while Kael-ven finished his drink and put it down. "Good stuff, Admiral." He looked out the window. "How many of the destroyers are online?"

"Probably the exact amount E'kolorn told you when you helped him figure out his strategy."

Kael-ven clicked his mandibles in humor once more. "I can't help it if friends ask me for my opinion. You didn't get there first."

"You helped make it a pain in the ass for me." Thomas nodded. "So, you in?"

Kael-ven shrugged. "Of course, but I want all twenty-seven kegs."

"Done," the Admiral agreed.

"When do you want me to start?" Kael-ven asked as he watched the Admiral bend over and reach for something at his feet.

Admiral Thomas lifted a leather satchel with a lock on the outside. "That lock will be opened as soon as you communicate with ADAM, and the answer is 'right now.' The kegs are ready to load on your ship."

Kael-ven reached for the pouch, and the lock clicked open. Admiral Thomas was pleased Kael-ven didn't balk at getting started. "Have them shipped to my personal warehouse here on *Meredith Reynolds*. It maintains the right temperature, and I keep my other kegs there as well." He opened the briefing and started reading the overview. "I'm surprised you printed this stuff out."

"Old-school, your eyes only, blah blah blah. Plus, as soon as you touched it, you agreed to the job."

Kael-ven nodded absently, still scanning the paperwork. Then his eyes opened wide. "This says my first project is to tell E'kolorn why he only gets twenty percent of the destroyers." He looked at the human across the table from him.

Admiral Thomas smiled. "Why, yes! Yes, it does. Imagine how pleased I am that you are already familiar with E'kolorn's arguments and are *so* practiced with the politics."

"Twenty-seven kegs," Kael-ven muttered, looking at the rest of the tasks he had been assigned, "was not enough."

"Too bad, and welcome to the navy. It's good to have you here."

Kael-ven looked up, a twinkle in his eye. "If I'd had to spend another three months dirtside, I would have joined the navy as a raw recruit. This way, I'm twenty-seven kegs richer and have a better job." He reached over to shake Thomas' hand. "It's damned good to be back where I belong."

Kael-ven kept looking through the document as the Admiral took a few more moments to enjoy the view. When Kael-ven's eyes grew large once again and he looked up at him, Thomas sent a special message and waited for Kael-ven's next question with amusement on his face.

Kael-ven pointed to the document. "It says here I'm going to have a co-member to whip the Marines we have coming into shape. Who is it? If I have to kick the ass of another hard-headed ground-pounder like Kiel, I may space myself."

Thomas chuckled. "That is a bit melodramatic."

"Says you!" Kael-ven shook his head. "They can be more obstinate than Bethany Anne."

This time it was Thomas who grunted, "Okay, I may decide to space *myself* if that's the case. However, I think you might be okay with our pick. He's a bit of a pain in the ass, I'll grant you, but he only very recently retired, and he is coming up here now for you to interview."

At that moment, Kael-ven heard a Yollin coming up the stairs. When the Yollin entered the room, his eyes showed surprise, then elation, and finally confusion. "Kiel?" He walked toward the Yollin mercenary. "I thought you would never quit the Empress' force." He reached out to shake hands human-style with his old friend. "What happened?"

"Who says I had a choice?" Kiel laughed, tossing a nod to the Admiral. "Bethany Anne called me two hours ago and asked if I might wish to work with the navy. I told her my oath was to her."

Kael-ven tilted his head slightly to the left and asked, "So what happened?"

"She fired me on the spot." Kiel made a slashing motion with his hand. "Told me to move my shit and come over here to interview for a position she needed me in."

Kael-ven looked at the Admiral. "Does he not know?" Thomas shook his head. Kael-ven turned back and pointed to Kiel, then to himself. "It seems the Empress wants you and me to build a Yollin fleet. Me on the ships, you on the Marines."

Kiel snapped into attention, his smile wide. "Reporting for duty, sir!"

Kael-ven's smile was open and honest, excitement alight in his eyes. He started to say something but stopped, then just shrugged. "I've missed you."

Thomas lifted his whisky and sloshed it around in the glass, whispering to himself as the two friends caught up for a few moments, "Those Leath don't have a fucking clue what it feels like to have a Yollin foot so far up their ass that Yollin toes will tickle their tonsils," he took a sip, "but they will." He blinked twice before looking out the window into space and asked himself, "Do Leath even have tonsils?"

CHAPTER EIGHTEEN

Planet Shrillex, North Continent, Terrel Mountains

The Shrillexian fumbled with the food bowl, grabbing it with his one hand and pulling on the sealed top. "Damned pain in the ass," he grunted as he considered just ripping it off.

Unfortunately, he already knew what would happen if he succumbed to his frustration. The result would be food all over the countertop and the floor, and just last night he had noticed the piece of vegetable that had gotten stuck in the corner of the ceiling and dried there. He had bitched about that piece for a full five minutes since he had to find his little ladder and unfold it with his one arm to remove it.

But he was alive.

Death had come for him. Kraaz had replayed both his original fight with his Shrillexian contact and the ruinous, aborted attack on the hotel. Bocklans had been killed later for his part in the project, and the remaining mercenaries had decided to fold the company.

It was rumored that the Etheric Empire still intended to track the mercenary company through the different systems it had scattered to, and Kraaz wouldn't put it past them. Those aliens didn't seem like the live-and-let-live type to him.

Except…he was alive.

He exhaled and stepped to the side to pull out a drawer and grab eating utensils.

It was plain to him that the Shrillexian he had met on Gerrand's Asteroid had been working with the Etheric Empire. That he had given Kraaz a warning was enough to provide the clues he needed, but nothing he would understand until after the fact.

Now he was armless, company-less, and damned near without any family.

Oh, he had a twice-distant cousin somewhere in the South Continent, but their two groups had always ignored each other at family reunions, and Kraaz didn't care to display his infirmity anyway.

Once the company had been dissolved he didn't have a place to go, so he had just returned to the family homestead. The house had been locked up by his younger brother before he left for space, after their mom passed away. The key had been hidden in the hole in the old tree. Kraaz hadn't even needed to ask where his brother Mih'took had placed it.

It was the same place Kraaz had hidden toys from his brother so many years ago.

There was a short *beep* from the alarm system. Kraaz looked at the monitor, but it showed nothing. Still, there might be a few who would wish him truly dead after the fights his company had been a part of.

He pushed the bowl of vegetables away and looked up as the light receded. It was as if clouds had just covered the sun, but it had been a completely cloudless day so far.

He noticed vibrations shaking the surface of his drink and a very hard-to-hear hum.

He opened a drawer to his right and, reaching underneath it, he touched a button. A piece of the wall to his left opened, revealing two blasters and a rifle. He grabbed a pistol. Flicking through the settings one-handed, he thumbed it off safe and walked to the kitchen door leading to the porch.

His homestead was on a large plot of land on the side of the mountain. They had a goodly amount of grass a couple hundred steps away that was flat, and they had used it to winter the herbivores before taking them down into the valley to fatten up.

He squinted in worry as he stepped onto the porch. It was entirely too dark. His eyes searched the tree line, but he felt nothing there. He stepped off the porch and looked up.

His mouth opened in surprise. There was a massive ship blocking the sun, so damned close it looked like he could touch it. He could certainly shoot it if he had half a mind to be a complete idiot, but he was armless, not bistok-shit crazy.

At least, not yet.

He turned to the back of the ship and realized that while it was a good size, it looked bigger because it was so close.

The ship moved sideways, and Kraaz saw an open hatch. Inside the hatch was a figure, Shrillexian if he had to guess, in some sort of black armor. He had nothing in his hands, one of which was holding onto the side of the hatch.

The bastard jumped out of the hatch and fell toward the ground, but about halfway down, he slowed. By the time he reached the ground, he was moving slowly enough that he just walked toward Kraaz, who was squinting at his uninvited guest.

"You know," the helmeted and armored person walked up close enough and then stopped, "my boss would appreciate it if you would holster the weapon before I take off this helmet."

Kraaz eyed the suited interloper. "Do I need to shoot you?"

"No."

"On your honor?" Kraaz asked.

"On my personal honor, I will not offer you harm unless I am protecting myself," he told him, "or my *family*."

Kraaz turned his head, recognizing that inflection, "Shi-tan?" he asked, as his thumb reached to put the pistol's safety on. He turned and stepped back onto the porch, placing the pistol on a chair. "I'm not sure if I should hate you or damn you."

Shi-tan took off his helmet. "Sorry, boss' orders. He figured you might be a little upset by how life had turned out."

"Yeah, she was Death, all right," Kraaz admitted. He stepped straight up to Shi-tan and put his hand out in recognition of a fellow countryman. Shi-tan responded in kind, and the two walked toward the porch. Kraaz went up first and pointed to another chair, leaving the chair with the pistol unoccupied.

Shi-tan leaned back against one of the rock posts that held up the porch's overhang. "Oh, Bethany Anne isn't my boss. Nathan is, but she's Nathan's direct boss."

"Well, she is some scary bistok shit. She and her two guards went through our people like they were made of cloth." Kraaz unconsciously scratched his arm's stub. "When she looked down at me after blowing my arm off, I didn't even flinch. Just remembered your words and figured I was done."

"What happened next?" Shi-tan asked. "I fought her once, but she wasn't using any of her major powers."

"You fought her?" Kraaz asked, surprised.

"Well, all I remember is working to get hit fewer times, but I woke up the next morning in my ship, ass so thoroughly beaten I didn't remember much of anything, and there was a document indicating I'd signed up with her."

Kraaz grunted. "For a non-Shrillexian, it was amazing how my blood sang when she walked down that hall." He shrugged. "It was a shame I was on the other team, but we gave our word, and word is blood."

Shi-tan looked from the front yard to the valley below, then at the mountain peak in the distance. "What happened to your mercenary company?"

"You don't know?" Kraaz asked, but Shi-tan continued gazing into the distance. "Leader Bocklans, a Tulet, was fired for such a monumental screw-up, and the few of us who finally got back to the meeting place a month later voted to break up the company. Some figured if we stayed together, the Etheric Empire would put a price on our heads."

"Well," Shi-tan turned back to look at Kraaz, "it wouldn't have been a price on your heads. She would have sent the Guardians, or a Bitch or two. Either way, the mercenary company would have been dissolved."

"She's that way? That isn't right." Kraaz thought about it. "Mercenary companies wouldn't come after her."

"She doesn't care. It's a message that might makes right. For the longest time, no one came after mercenary companies because other mercs would aid them in a fight, and who would want a bunch of mercenary companies pursuing them?"

"Well, apparently she doesn't care."

"She is after much bigger fish. She is a live-and-let-live type of person. You choose to not let-live and she returns the favor."

Kraaz eyed Shi-tan. "How did she beat the assassins?"

"One almost got her, but she was warned by a guard just before he was hit."

"Taken out by us?" Kraaz asked.

"Not out—he healed in the hospital. But he is now a believer in armor. He happened to trip across one of your teams just as you started the operation. It was just enough to have her friends take action."

Shi-tan understood Kraaz's need to know how things had gone so wrong, so he continued explaining a few after-action items. "The first assassin was killed by Bethany Anne. They didn't trip the second assassin until some of her Guardians had changed forms. One of the Guardians, Peter, smelled and heard the second assassin. He punched through some metal, grabbed the assassin who was hiding inside, and ripped him back out. The assassin punched two slugs into Peter's gut and got his head ripped off for his efforts."

"Peter died?" Kraaz asked.

"No, he's a Pricolici," Shi-tan replied. "They heal fast. I'm told he bitched for a while because the shots put him on the ground with his guts everywhere. The armor stopped it from being worse, but it's hard to protect against a blast when the barrel is at point-blank range."

"I have no idea what a Pricolici is, but healing fast would be nice." Kraaz took a moment to look around. "I wouldn't have listened to your warning if you had told me straight out, so I can't bitch when I'm here without an arm."

"Too many of our people wouldn't be here at all. You had to eat your pride to do it," Shi-tan pointed out.

Kraaz looked at Shi-tan, "Have you seen her when she is *Death*, coming for you?" Shi-tan shook his head, and it was Kraaz's turn to look at the mountain in the distance. "Well, let me tell you, fear is plentiful. It was like she was pushing it ahead of her. It made it very difficult to think, much less return fire."

There was a pause as both Shrillexians were lost in their own thoughts. "Regrets?" Shi-tan asked finally.

"It took a few weeks," Kraaz admitted, "but now I don't have any. We were outmanned, outplayed, and frankly outclassed. The Leath have got some damned good PR people spinning it like crazy, that they aren't the ones who hired the whole hit in the first place." His eyes narrowed. "Why hasn't the Etheric Empire pointed their fingers at the Leath?"

"I'm not part of that group," Shi-tan admitted, "so I don't have a clue. What are you planning to do next?"

Kraaz narrowed his eyes. "I'm not staying here. I'm not fit to be a rancher or a farmer, or frankly to stay here at all." He nodded to the ship above them. "I don't know who might want me, but I'll get fitted for an arm and I'll do something. I'm too young to die here on our planet. Just, next time I'll make sure to vet the company I'm with a little better." He chuckled for a moment, a little glint of humor in his eyes. "Make sure they have the right attitude when it comes to taking on Death."

Shi-tan smiled, then nodded to himself when he got the command in his ear's receiver. "So, about that... I know a company that might want to interview you."

Kraaz looked at him. "Is it a good company?"

Shi-tan chuckled. "Oh, it's a very *Bad* Company. But," he nodded to him, "it is the best *family* you will ever join. I personally guarantee that, on my family's honor."

Kraaz looked around, taking in the sights: his family's home, the valley, and the trees. He looked back at Shi-tan. "On your family's honor?"

"My personal honor," Shi-tan confirmed. "My boss is on a bit of a Shrillexian hiring spree."

"But you said it is a bad company," Kraaz returned, eyes inquiring.

"That's actually the name of the company. Bad Company. Consider us good guys who wear black."

Kraaz stared at him blankly for a moment.

Shi-tan sighed, "Apparently I need to show you a few of the human movies they call Westerns before that will make any sense to you. We're the good guys, but the laws are a bit nebulous for us at times."

Kraaz started to smile. "Like spying on secret meetings?" He reached up and rubbed his jaw with his hand. "How did you get that knowledge?"

"Well," Shi-tan grinned, "that's the bad part. It's what we did with it that makes it good."

"Action?" Kraaz asked.

"How often do you want your ass kicked?" Shi-tan queried in return.

Kraaz stood up and walked over to the pistol. "Give me a few minutes to lock this place down. I haven't had a good ass-kicking since…"

Kraaz opened the door, his voice floating back from inside the house, "Death blew my arm off."

While Kraaz was inside the house, Shi-tan stepped off the porch and looked around his planet. It was damned beautiful in these mountains. Then he looked at the ship floating above him.

But the planet wasn't home, and it didn't have family waiting for him to come back to them.

QBBS *Meredith Reynolds*, All Guns Blazing

Stephen walked past the long line of people waiting to get into the bar and nodded to the bouncer they had stationed up front. He didn't really enjoy coming through the front, but when he walked through without waiting, those who asked "who the special one was" would find out he worked with the Empress.

Directly.

That would generally cause people in the line to start whispering about his importance, and it helped business. Stephen walked through the bar, stopping a couple of times to speak to people he recognized as being regulars and congratulating a few, dropping a few things he knew or remembered about them.

On one occasion, he had noticed an upset young female who normally would have been surrounded by friends. He glanced into her mind and realized she was lovesick over a male on her team. She was a Were, he was a Guardian Marine, and apparently her heart had gone in a direction her mind had never expected.

He felt for her, but having your heart ripped out was part of growing up. Sometimes love didn't care about the rules, but the rules didn't get changed to fit your heart. Stephen had sent a message to Yelena to find another female Were to come say "hi" and hopefully help her.

This time there weren't any problems, just congratulations on a new child to be offered to one regular who was drinking with friends to celebrate.

He finally made it to the kitchen, and from there into the small meeting room where Cheryl Lynn and Yelena were waiting for him. He smiled at both and sat down.

"This has to be quick," Cheryl Lynn started. "Bethany Anne isn't happy the Leath are so quiet, and we have proof they are moving ships around. They are up to something, but we don't know what." She touched a button on her tablet. "Baghdad Bob is due to be on again in two hours, so I have to be there to refute his latest lies."

"Sorry," Yelena asked, "Baghdad Bob?"

"Um." Cheryl Lynn explained. "That's right, he was probably more of an American thing. Way back when the US was after Saddam Hussein, his Information Minister Saeed al-Sahaf would come on TV and say stuff so hilariously inaccurate that other countries accused then-President George W. Bush of hiring the guy during the war. He would say stuff like 'the Americans are on the run,' and yet you could see American tanks in the background of the video being shown to back his claims." She shrugged. "So now, anytime you have a mouthpiece for a government or company who is lying outrageously, we tend to call them Baghdad Bobs after Saeed al-Sahaf and his lies."

"You remember his name?" Yelena asked.

"Only because I had to look it up to tell Peter the story two days ago," she answered. "So, getting back on track, the plans are looking good."

Stephen nodded. "Team BMW is going to be stuck in R&D for at least a decade or more." Yelena grimaced, and he turned to his left to face her. "It's true. They are working on two projects, and neither one is a cake-walk."

"I know." Her shoulders relaxed. "I get him for the weekends mostly, or I can go over there, but occasionally I'd like a big man-chest to rest my head on, and he isn't available."

"So, what do you do?" Cheryl Lynn asked.

"Bellatrix has to suffice," Yelena answered. "Or I start thinking about a new beer recipe and tease him via video."

"Does it work?"

"Only once," she admitted. "But I think he only told me it did and was really here for something else."

"No, I'm aware of that story," Stephen replied. "He was here for you and made up the reason to come get the part."

"Awww," the two ladies cooed at the same time.

"So," Stephen got them back to business, "new bars?"

"Yes." Yelena nodded. "But do we franchise, or..." She saw Cheryl Lynn's face. "Okay, we stick with our own people."

"I get that you are thinking profit," Cheryl Lynn replied, "but we can't trust a franchise, even if they are vetted by us in advance. We want complete control, and no one should be able to question us."

"I'd suggest a profit-sharing plan as well," Stephen added. "Further, we need to figure out something as amazing as the window into space for each bar."

"Ooohhh!" Yelena's eyes went distant. "Each bar is unique, one of a kind in that area of space."

"Yes. Determine the best things about this bar and replicate to the best of our ability," Stephen agreed.

"Keep them in the Etheric Empire for now," Cheryl Lynn added. "We don't want to be in the jurisdiction of another polity."

"Do we keep the All Guns Blazing name?" Yelena asked. "So we could have an All Guns Blazing Straiphus for example?"

"That brand is priceless," Cheryl Lynn told them. "Plus, we will sell clothing and merch. Further, I think we need to do some sort of challenge for our customers to try all the liquor, and if they do, they get a patch or something."

"You know how the merchant ship crews like their buttons and patches."

Stephen's eyes opened. "I like that," he exclaimed. "Imagine someone walking around on another space station with half their vest full of All Guns Blazing patches?"

"Walking marketing." Cheryl Lynn nodded. "The kind that pays *us* and then promotes us."

CHAPTER NINETEEN

QBBS *Meredith Reynolds,* **Empress' Suite**

Bethany Anne walked into the large closet and looked around. The room was about twenty feet by thirty feet and had all sorts of sections for clothes that were relevant to each role she played and even sorted by what species she had to meet with for an event.

She hated most of it.

She gnawed on her lip, her mind considering the ramifications of what she was considering. So far she had been pretty good at hiding her thoughts from her two tag-alongs.

Just then, Ashur padded into the room. *Matrix is finally going to his self-defense lessons without me having to pester him.*

Bethany Anne looked at the white German Shepherd standing just inside the doorway. "He should since he almost got his ass handed to him permanently."

Bellatrix was livid. I think she had a bit of a scare again. It took Yelena a while to calm her down.

"Mothers! Can't live with them if they worry... Okay, never." She continued her look around the closet. "How are you?"

It hurt when I thought he was dead, but we spoke about that. I used to hate the armor as much as he did, so I understood his annoyance. However, I've been better... What are you doing?

Restrict your questions to me only. I don't need Nosy Nancy One and Two to start asking questions before I understand what's on my mind.

Ashur walked a few more feet into her closet and dropped to the floor with his tongue hanging out. *We going somewhere we shouldn't?*

Maybe.

Good. I'm bored.

Maybe not. You are pretty hard to hide. Your damn picture has been spread across the systems. Hell, I understand there is actually a doll of you over in the Torcellan system.

Think again.

"Huh?" Bethany Anne caught the amusement in Ashur's mental voice and turned back to him. "How are you doing that?" she asked when she saw that Ashur had changed his coat to a light tan and his feet to black. She walked over to him and knelt, stroking his fur.

You can stop that sometime next week.

"Yeah, you are a glutton for punishment," she told him as she checked her hands. She grasped a few hairs and examined them in the light. "Wow, how do you do this?"

I worked with TOM. Apparently if you can control the nanocytes, you can modify your body structure. I've been working on changing my fur color for a little while. Bellatrix and I are going to go to the costume ball as each other if she can figure it out.

Bethany Anne dusted her hands to get off the hair and stood up. "That gives me an idea."

TOM?

Yes, Oh Most Wonderful of Wonderful Organic Vehicles? What are we doing in the closet?

ADAM?

>> Yes, ma'am?<<

Kiss-ass.

>>Wait until she can pull you out and stomp on your head, then you might have a little bit more respect.<<

She can already shock me, and we both know she won't kill us.

Are you two quite through having a conversation in my head?

Sure, for the moment, TOM agreed. Still curious why we are in the closet. I know for a fact you have nothing on your schedule for a week.

Exactly. Both of you are commanded to not divulge where I am until I allow you to state otherwise. And that means no hints either, ADAM.

Where are we going? TOM asked. She could almost sense him wanting to move her eyes so he could look around.

Have you read the story, The Prince and the Pauper?

>>Yes, as of a second ago. We have no Prince..ess.<<

No.

Bethany Anne wanted to roll her eyes as ADAM updated TOM.

>>There was a prince who wanted to go out of the castle, and he found a fellow who looked just like him. They switched places so each could experience the other's lot in life. Unfortunately for the prince, no one believed he *was* the prince when his father died on the throne while he was away. It was written by Mark Twain in America in 1881 as a parable to not judge a person by his appearance.<<

I highly doubt anyone is going to sit on Bethany Anne's throne while she is gone.

No one wants it, so that is why it's safe, Bethany Anne jumped in. *Make sure you guys are locked into whatever projects and have what you need.*

Who are you bringing along? TOM asked. When Bethany Anne didn't reply, TOM sighed.

Well, *shit!*

Bethany Anne went to one side of her closet near the back corner and pushed some dresses to the side. She grabbed a box and pulled it out, then walked toward her dressing table. Dropping the box on the table, she pulled off the top.

Folded neatly inside were some old leather pants, three Under Armour shirts, and some old holsters. Bethany Anne ran her hand over the leather and cracked a smile.

ADAM, send a message to Reynolds.

>> The space station *Reynolds*, or the superdreadnought?<<

Well, fuck, Bethany Anne mused. *Really didn't think that through too well.* The ship. Tell him to start powering up.

Why aren't you taking *ArchAngel*? TOM asked, curious.

Everyone expects the Empress to be on ArchAngel, *that's why.* Plus, Reynolds *has something I want.*

TOM connected to ADAM, and the two went through the manifest. So far, neither saw anything out of the ordinary.

What could she want?

Planet Leath, Main Continent, Leath Navy Department, R&D, Third Level Underground

First Line Prime Commander Tehrle nodded his head at the two second-line navy strategists he passed as he walked down the hall. For once, he didn't have five others dogging his steps as he went to his meeting.

It was refreshing, actually.

When the previous First had sacrificed himself for the greater good, Tehrle had been ready to step into the position and move forward with new plans. Unfortunately, he had to deal with some politics at the same time.

Then Prime Intelligence One got involved, and there were two sudden leaves of absence by the military's top brass. Tehrle's troubles settled down, allowing him to focus on beating the Etheric Empire.

Security checked him one more time before he walked to the final door—no window in it, just a vast amount of metal—which was opened by a guard. He strode through.

In this meeting he was going to find out what changes their ships needed before they could overpower the Etheric Empire.

Further, he was going to meet the Sixth of the Seven after this meeting to see what the gods could provide, beyond what the Leath had been able to figure out. Sometimes he wished the gods would just tell them what to do, not focus on allowing the Leath to come up with ideas in the first place.

But he was a military man, so he preferred to get to the point. His job wasn't to help nurture people to greater heights, and if he remembered anything from his time in school, the gods *were* here to nurture them, not give them handouts.

He sure hoped that nurturing was the right strategy. If it proved not to be, Terhle believed this Etheric Empire would eventually be on this planet, killing his people.

If he didn't do it to them first.

Tomorrow he would start the strategy sessions, and together his council would work on two major offenses to crush the Etheric Empire under their feet.

Now, if the Etheric Empire would just give them a few years to get set up, all would be perfect. He pursed his lips and realized he would need to sacrifice some ships over the next few seasons to keep the Etheric Empire focused on small battles and not the war.

QBBS *Meredith Reynolds*

"This is John Grimes," the Bitch announced over the speaker system in General Lance Reynolds' office. The General raised an eyebrow when the video came to life. "Have you seen Darryl, by any chance?" John asked, annoyed. "He hasn't shown up for his shift."

Lance's door opened and Cheryl Lynn stuck her head in. "Bethany Anne anywhere? No one knows where she is."

Lance's eyebrows started to come together. "Come on in, Cheryl Lynn, and close the door." He turned back to the video. "When was Darryl due?"

John's lips pressed together. "Two hours ago."

Lance looked at Cheryl Lynn. "One hour."

The door opened again, and Admiral Thomas and Kael-ven came into the general's office. "What the hell are *you* missing?" Lance asked the two gruffly.

Thomas, his face annoyed, slowly switched to thoughtful. "What are *you* missing?"

John spoke up from the video. "A Queen's Bitch."

Cheryl Lynn added, "The Empress."

"And a superdreadnought that had the missing Bitch on it," Thomas finished.

John spat a curse. "So, how did we lose Bethany Anne again?"

"She has a week off," Cheryl Lynn pointed out. "I bet if I look, there will be a request for vacation or some other note in my inbox."

Lance put his fingers up to his eyes and started massaging them. "She's going to give me a *Gott Verdammt* migraine." He looked at Admiral Thomas. "Yes, I know, I'll heal."

He looked at everyone in his office. "Okay, folks, back to business, but quietly start getting stuff prepared in case we have to stage a rescue."

"If?" John chuckled. "I mean, I assume you don't mean rescue Bethany Anne, but rather to rescue someone else *from* Bethany Anne."

"It was so much easier on Earth." Cheryl Lynn shrugged her shoulders when she saw Kael-ven look at her with a question on his face. "Back in the good ol' days. She might disappear for a few hours, then she would be back and happy again for a while. We would hear that this terrorist group or that terrorist camp had been destroyed, and no one would know why."

"She always got busted by the description of the sword cuts," John continued the explanation, able to see Kael-ven turn his head in his direction from his side of the video. "No one else on Earth had the strength to decapitate a bunch of men fighting in the dark. She said it was therapeutic."

"What we are sorely lacking," Admiral Thomas spoke up, "is a small group of extremists she can kill. What we *do* have are systems full of bad people who might take her a few years to decimate."

"She only has," Cheryl Lynn looked down at her tablet, "six days." She turned it to Lance. "Here's her vacation request."

Lance reached for a cigar, stuck it in his mouth unlit, and chewed on it for a moment before looking at the Admiral.

"Well, *shit.*"

QBS *Reynolds*

"I'm telling you, we are going to have to change your name," Bethany Anne was sitting in the chair behind the captain, speaking to the visage of her father on the screen.

"Because humans cannot ascertain which Reynolds you are speaking about from the context of the conversation?" Lance's gruff voice was appropriate, she thought.

"Hell, my own AI couldn't tell, because I gave him no context, so shut the hell up and start thinking about name changes. The Reynolds back there," she jerked a thumb over her shoulder, "has dibs on the name."

"But I *am* Reynolds," Lance's voice shot back.

"You are the son of Reynolds, basically," Bethany Anne told him. "So come up with a name, and we will tack on Reynoldsson at the end to denote your sire."

This time the EI was silent for a moment. "How about your father's middle name?"

"Alexander?" Bethany Anne thought about that a moment. "Okay, but just be ready to answer to Alex as well."

"I can certainly make that change to the programming."

"You are hereby christened 'Alexander,' or 'Alex.' Natalia?" Bethany Anne waited for the captain's chair to spin around enough that the captain could answer.

"Yes?" Captain Natalia Jakowski asked her Empress.

"Preference?"

"Let's stick with Alexander. It isn't often used, so it will be easier to call a person 'Alex' and the ship *Alexander*."

"Okay," Bethany Anne stood, "fine by me. Make the adjustments. I'm going to go speak with my annoyed protector." She turned to her left and walked off the bridge.

Outside the door, Darryl was standing guard. "Ready?" she asked him.

"I hope you know John is going to be pissed." Darryl started walking right beside her as they went down the hall.

"Of course. It will do him good." Bethany Anne turned left, and Darryl had to double-time his steps to catch up. "Actually, it will do me a lot of good, and him a little good."

"What is the plan?" Darryl asked.

"You, me, old clothes, a clunky ship that just happens to be in the hold of the *Alexander*—"

"*Alexander*?" Darryl asked.

"Sorry, I renamed the ship. Well, technically, he renamed himself. It was a pain in the ass to have a battle station named Reynolds and a superdreadnought called the same," she answered.

"A couple of us were wondering," Darryl admitted as they came to Bethany Anne's suite.

The single guard stepped aside and the two of them walked in, the door sliding shut behind them.

"Well, it's done now," she admitted, grabbing a box from her table. In this suite were couches, a large dining room-looking table where she held meetings, and some chairs. "I'm going to change, so go get into some civvies that make you look normal."

Darryl noticed Ashur to the side. "Uh, what happened to you?" he asked.

I changed the pigment in my hair. It is an advanced ability TOM says is rare. Tabitha has been trying to work on herself for a while with little success, Ashur replied.

"Well, you look different," Darryl answered, "but don't lose your white. It's a classic look," he called over his shoulder as he stepped out of the room.

Bethany Anne was bemused as she and Ashur watched Darryl load the small spaceship with boxes of weapons.

"Real armor for when we go into battle." He slid a box into the hold.

He picked up another case. "Four beam rifles and sixteen extra ammo cartridges for said rifles," he called and slid it in.

"Case of grenades."

"Two months' worth of nutrient pouches."

"We are only going to be gone four fucking *days*," Bethany Anne told him, looking at the pile of boxes behind Darryl. "It will take you four days to load all this shit on the ship."

"Case of Team BMW portable shields." He loaded it while Bethany Anne's head turned from right to left to right again.

"Case of Team BMW pucks, remote-guided."

"Small case of four Etheric energy boosts, usable by you, of course."

"Another case of Jean Dukes pistol rounds."

"Case of skin armor."

Bethany Anne rolled her eyes. "I'm going to get the ship

warmed up," she told him. "You act as if I'm going to start an interstellar war or something."

"I've got no idea, but I'm going to be like the Boy Scouts. I'm going to be prepared."

"Whatever," drifted back from inside the ship as she walked to the cockpit.

The QBS *Alexander* receded into the distance as Darryl confirmed what he could with the controls as he sat on Bethany Anne's right in the two-seat cockpit. "Why does everything look so old but work so well?" he asked.

"This is my little ship," Bethany Anne answered, flipping two switches to her left. "ADAM, take over for a bit."

ADAM's voice came over the system. "Which location did you wish to visit?"

"Do we have any info on which spaceport is the worst?" she asked.

"Port Sharn, Section T-772 in the borderlands is reputed to have a group of Darkness for Hire mercenaries reforming their group."

"Oh, that is *perfect*." Bethany Anne's eyes flashed red. "I warned them not to do that."

"I don't think they are worried," Darryl pointed out. "We are way more than a couple days' travel from there in this ship."

She whispered, "Oh, but there you are wrong, my friend."

"Yes." TOM's voice came over the speaker. "Welcome to the— so far *only*—small ship in the Etheric Empire which can Gate." There was a pause. "Please don't scratch the paint, Bethany Anne. We don't have another one."

"I imagine that if I scratch the paint," she replied as she belted in and gestured to Darryl to do the same, "neither one of us will be alive to care."

"Wait, what?" Darryl asked. "I didn't get a last kiss from Natalia."

Bethany Anne checked a couple of screens for TOM's sake and confirmed the last information. "Hope you got some last-minute nookie last night." She winked as she told ADAM, "Punch it!"

"We have come out approximately eleven hours from T-772," ADAM told them a few seconds after they reappeared. The stars were different than they had been a moment ago.

"Any chance someone is going to be able to tell we gated in?" Bethany Anne asked.

"Only if they were looking right here when it happened," TOM replied.

Darryl spoke up. "You mean it approaches a hundred percent, then?" He looked at his Empress and saw Bethany Anne gazing at him with a raised eyebrow. "What? If this was a movie or a book, then the one-in-a-billion chance that someone saw us would be a 'yes, they did, and they would have a battleship ready to pounce on us.'"

TOM snickered in her head as she turned to view the instrumentation. "You have a point, but I'm going to choose to believe the probability is infinitesimal." She unbuckled her belt. "You might as well make yourself comfortable. It will be a few hours until we get to the port, which is good. It's morning there now. By the time we arrive, it will be early in the evening."

"Perfect time for barhopping."

"Exactly."

"So, tell me something about yourself," she asked.

"Well, you know the basics," Darryl replied. "Special Forces, sandpit operations, on loan to Frank's group when all hell broke loose."

"Two siblings, brother and sister. Both parents passed away, right?"

He nodded.

"Why stick with me in Florida?" she pressed.

Darryl smiled, "All this time, and *this* is what you want to talk about?" He shook his head. "Sure, I guess it's time. Hell, Natalia is wearing me down."

"Should I put my fingers in my ears and go *la la la*?"

"Wear me down, not wear me out." He chuckled. "I've got the special nanocytes, so I don't ever have to worry about wearing myself out."

"LA LA LA LA LA!" Bethany Anne had her fingers in her ears as Darryl shook his head. She pulled the fingers out an inch and asked him, "Are you done yet?"

"Sure, sure." Darryl smirked. "My brother was an ass, really into himself, and he went down the wrong path. I sent money to my sister for ten years, until she finished college and got married. I gave her and her husband the money for a down payment on a nice home in an upper Chicago neighborhood, and the last I knew, they were popping out little nieces and nephews. Their plan was to have six babies."

"I'm sorry." Bethany Anne glanced down before looking at him, knowing they had most likely died. "They didn't want to come with us?"

"Bethany Anne, I never asked," Darryl admitted. "They were fairly liberal, and when the group of people they hung around with decided they were against the war, I got thrown out with their previous concepts of family. It wasn't but three weeks later I got asked to go on a very special assignment, one they had to admit had a high probability of dying for my country and so black that you might as well just have told your family you wouldn't *be* back."

"Frank's stuff?"

Darryl nodded. "Yes, Frank's stuff." His eyes went a little

vacant. "It was hell fighting across the US like we did, but in our group," he looked at her, "it wasn't about if you were white or black or red or whatever color you might be. It was *us* against *them*. Those we fought might have been fellow Americans before, but when we fought the Nosferatu we were protecting the rest of our country from something *truly* evil. It was the walking dead day after day after day. Our rest days were used to travel to the next outbreak, forever heading east across the country, until we hit Florida and the final showdown."

He sighed. "If I had died?" He shook his head slowly. "I would have died with *family*. My brothers, who had fought in hell right beside me, and this one scrawny little woman with a mouth that would embarrass sailors." He smiled, talking like she wasn't right next to him.

"I got to tell you, she was hell on wheels. You could feel her *passion*, her need to protect all of us. She was like a momma bear looking after her cubs, but shit, we cubs all towered over her."

He took a deep breath. "I'll never forget that day we chop-pered out of those Everglades and then set back down. None of us spoke about what we were going to do, but we didn't need to. By then, the four of us could read each other's minds. We stepped off that copter, and if anyone had wanted you, they were going to be coming *through* us."

He turned to gaze at her once more. "You got to remember, you were the boogeyman, the Baba Yaga, the vampire, the *enemy*. So when you came back for us, we were a little worried someone might try to off you right there at the end if you were too tired."

Bethany Anne reached out and put a hand on Darryl's shoulder. "I never knew that."

He shrugged. "You didn't need to know. You had our backs, we had yours."

He chuckled and shook his head, smiling to himself. "Baba Yaga. Maybe we should start using that as your code name."

Inside her mind, ADAM gave Bethany Anne an update on the

name and the Slavic mythology behind it. She snickered. "Okay, I like most of it except the old crone thing." She paused a moment, her eyes narrowing. "However, that gives me an idea."

She laid back in the pilot's chair, "If I scream or something, ignore it. It's just some pain I need to get through. TOM?" she called.

"Yes?"

"How long will this take? Don't want Darryl to worry."

"Probably at least two hours. He will see the changes, of course, if he wants to, and he can ask me anything while it is going on. However, I'm going to put you under so you don't feel the pain."

"Okay." She turned to Darryl. "Baba Yaga?" She nodded. "Baba Yaga indeed."

CHAPTER TWENTY

Planet Leath, Tienemehn, Defense Planning

"I've called you here in order to see if we have a shot at attacking the Etheric Empire directly." First Line Prime Commander Tehrle looked at his war council. It included four from the navy, four from Intelligence, and four from the army. "I'm aware that we have a contingent who are asking why we don't attack them and get it over with, and who think the Etheric Empire will be attacking us directly."

He paused a moment to look up, as if he were searching the skies above their location. "Which they won't." He returned his focus to the Leath at the long black table in front of him. "Now, I could give a few explanations, divulge previous reports from the honorable previous First Line Prime Commander, but I would rather give our intelligence group a chance to show footage of their base in action."

Prime Intelligence One stood and nodded to those in the room. "We have pulled together videos of Etheric Empire ships provided by others, plus some video from our own ships when we engaged with them over the planet Karillia." He touched a button on a remote he was holding. "This video is our ship-to-ship action over Karillia. You can tell that the humans and Yollins move their ships more independently than we do, yet they still seem to be able to protect each other. When our ships decide to do something independently…"

He pointed to a ship that had attacked one of the smaller Etheric ships, causing considerable damage. Everyone was excited by the destruction until the video advanced and their ship was blown to pieces. "The Etheric Empire takes every opportunity to destroy ships who stick their tusks too far out."

The previous excitement took a dip when the Leath ships started dying. "We are outclassed and outgunned on a ship-to-ship basis so far," he clicked another button, "but here is a video many of you have seen. I am bringing it back up in this meeting to set the context."

He pointed at the screen, his voice deep and his speech slow. "The main Etheric Empire ships were drawn into the Straiphus system due to a navy uprising by the Kolin and Chloret castes. The upper castes did not appreciate the new Empress' edict that all Yollins were created equal, and they revolted. I have to give them," he clicked a button and a multi-system map showed, "respect for coming up with a daring plan, and it worked at first." He clicked the button again, and the display showed a line going from system to system. "Most did not know the Yollin super-dreadnoughts could Gate themselves. It was a huge secret, so imagine the Etheric Empire's surprise when all their main ships were suddenly in another system."

This time the video showed one Yollin dreadnought and multiple offensive support vessels gating in. "Then these Yollin Navy vessels, crewed by the dissidents, showed up."

Audio came online, but it was in Yollin, so with a slight lag, an interpreter translated both sides of the conversation. "This is the Ministry of Defense warning the captain of the superdreadnought to back off."

Prime Intelligence One looked down the table. "He refused."

The intelligence officer didn't have to see what was happening on the screen; he could tell when a massive beam left the battle station and melted the opposing force.

"That," he pointed behind him to the screen, "is what awaits those who enter the system without permission. We don't know how many shots it can fire between cool-down periods, or if it can fire more than once a day. We could try to overwhelm the battle station's offensive ability by staggering our ships to come from multiple directions. There is no way the battle station can flip and attack all the ships in a sphere. However, then we are reduced to fighting a ship-to-ship strategy, and that strategy is not a good solution at this time."

"I thought those videos were propaganda?" Second Navy Line Commander Bok asked, nodding to the screen.

"No, this video was prepared by our spies in the Etheric Empire itself and verified by research. That weapon is real."

First Line Prime Commander Tehrle nodded to Prime Intelligence One. "Thank you for that presentation." He looked down the table at the rest of his council. "If any of you believe we can go running and gunning into the Yollin system and overcome them easily, then you need to reconsider, ask intelligent questions to explore your belief or give me your resignation letter. I'm not going to have someone with more stupidity than wisdom helping me overcome these non-believers. The gods have spoken, and the Etheric Empire is our next challenge."

Second Navy Line Commander Bok asked the question the Prime was waiting to hear. "What happens when we beat them?"

Tehrle's smile was genuine as he looked up and down the table, "The gods provide us access to the next level of technology."

Torik, Third of the Seven, adjusted his robes and pursed his lips as he looked at Var'ence, Sixth of the Seven, and commented, "Are we being smart by withholding the next level of technology?" He nodded to the video of the meeting they were watching. "The enemy seems to have advanced technology beyond what we have provided."

Var'ence was quiet for a few minutes, pondering the question. "Truth is still truth. It is not our place to change the path. They survive and mature, or they do not. It is the process a species goes through to confirm they are capable of handling the next stage of their evolution to greatness."

She shrugged. "It is the way of the Phraim-'Eh Clan. We are not the Reben or the M'nassa, who would shape their children against the truth."

Torik bowed his head to her wisdom and went back to watching the video.

Port Sharn, Section T-772, *Tramp Princess*

Darryl looked at his Empress and rubbed his jaw. "I don't want you to take this the wrong way..."

"Uh-huh?" Bethany Anne looked at her friend. Both of them were standing just inside the airlock as they listened to the cycling of the connections that would allow them to exit their ship.

"You are flat hideous," Darryl told her. "But you didn't do anything to your body, so my mind is fucked up."

Ashur barked his agreement.

"I refuse to walk around in an eighty-year-old body," Bethany Anne told him. Her hair was mostly gray, with streaks of darker gray that almost looked black. Her skin was wrinkled, including her hands, and had marks that looked like age spots. She lifted her hand. "Even seeing these hands bothers me. A girl has to have time to age gracefully." Their door started to open, and the two turned to look outside.

"And let me tell you, two hours isn't enough time," she finished. The large flat dirt expanse where over forty-plus spaceships rested was a very dark rust color. In the distance, there were a few mountains which had greens and blues up the slopes, but down here in the valley, there wasn't much but rocks and dust.

All three were wearing nose and mouth respirators. The atmosphere wasn't technically poisonous, but it wasn't very good for humans or canines, either. Their nanocytes could have helped them breathe, but that made no sense since they could use what Bobcat termed the "Bane Rebreather."

Plus, it helped hide their faces just a little more.

She walked down the steps to the ground. Darryl came down right behind her holding two backpacks, and he handed one to her. Ashur had jumped down and was looking around.

She noticed that his hair color was slowly changing to match the dirt.

Sliding the backpack over her shoulder, she made sure she had access to her pistols and pouches. She cinched up her backpack and had ADAM secure the ship.

If anyone comes near, take off, and we will regroup. This ship doesn't get captured.

>>**Understood.**<<

"So, what did you do on your vacation?" Darryl said out loud, then answered himself in a higher voice. "Nothing much. Went to a new spaceport, found horrible aliens, and killed them."

"You sure you weren't a Marine?" Bethany Anne asked as she walked past him, hands grasping the backpack straps.

"Hey!" Darryl caught up to her. "Special Forces. Watch your tongue."

Bethany Anne grinned. "Still have a bit of rivalry in you?"

"Always," Darryl admitted. "Doesn't matter how long it's been.

If your headgear is different than the other guy's, we have to see who jumps higher, runs faster, throws harder, or…"

Bethany Anne smirked. "Pisses farther?"

"Right, that," Darryl agreed quickly.

The two of them made their way across the landing zone, only seeing one vehicle in the distance moving a group of aliens to a ship that was sitting on legs. It looked like a Saturn V rocket ready for takeoff.

"Not much for worrying about people coming or going, are they?" Darryl asked, keeping an eye out around them. He had his hand near his Jean Dukes special, and it was already dialed up to eleven. There was no way he would allow anything to attack Bethany Anne without maximum response being directed back toward the other side.

"Nope," Bethany Anne agreed. "Just like I like it."

Darryl heard the change in her voice, and he felt the calm before the storm descend over him. In SF, he had been responsible for more than a few enemy disappearances in the night. Now, with this small planet's star receding into the distance and night falling, they were here to do it again.

Bethany Anne looked toward the fifteen blocks that made up the small spaceport. There were two avenues heading north to south, and four heading east to west. Some additional buildings huddled on the outskirts, but they were like the casinos outside Las Vegas that weren't either downtown or on the strip.

They weren't major players.

"Plans?" Darryl asked as the two of them followed a group of rowdy aliens down the middle of the street. Apparently only a few vehicles came down here, and those that did wove in and out between pedestrians.

"Find them, confirm them, kill them," Bethany Anne told him. "Baba Yaga is the Queen Bitch's Avatar, and she has been commanded to dispense her displeasure."

"Oh." Darryl grinned as the three of them walked down the street. "So, same shit, different planet?"

"Terrorists are terrorists," she replied. "I don't care if the payment is money or faith. You don't take jobs against the Etheric Empire and expect to survive."

Darryl looked around to see if he could find any hints about where they needed to go. "Kind of a zero-tolerance protocol."

"Very zero." Bethany Anne pointed toward a building a block away. "ADAM says there is a sign pointing to that building we need to check out."

"That's got to be helpful," Darryl mentioned as the two moved forward. "Kind of late asking, but what about money?"

"Gold. It's universal," she replied. "Almost every species has a use for it, and some fucktards have gone to planets, mined the shit out of them, and moved on." Both stepped to the side as a vehicle passed them on the left. "Did I tell you TOM verified that an alien species went to Earth eons ago, mined a shit-ton of our gold, and left?"

"Nope." Darryl lowered his left shoulder as another alien, this one looking like a blue quadrupedal fish, walked straight into him. The fish-alien bounced off, stumbled back, and tripped. It landed to Bethany Anne's right and started bitching up a storm.

"Baba Yaga," she kicked the alien's forehead and knocked it out, "doesn't *appreciate* your tone of voice." As the two passed it, she added, "Nor you trying to get in our way."

There was some laughing around them at the casually violent response, as if these aliens did it all the time.

"You!" a deep voice called, and the two turned to see a big Shrillexian in the street. "That was my friend!"

"You think it was his friend?" Darryl asked.

"Unlikely. Maybe shipmate." Bethany Anne shrugged. "You or me?"

Ashur chuffed, and both told him "no" at the same time.

"Oh, definitely me." Darryl swung off his backpack and

dropped it next to Bethany Anne. He moved toward the Shrillexian. "Got a name, dirt-nap?" he called.

"Oh, yes. And you will be singing 'Cosol' as I pound you into the dirt," Cosol told him, and spit into the dirt street.

"Doubt it, Cosol," Darryl replied and ramped up his speed. Cosol's snap-kick was blocked by Darryl's armored shin.

The Shrillexian pulled back his cracked foot and moved to his left as a few others walked over to watch.

Bethany Anne picked up Darryl's backpack. "Apparently Baba Yaga needs to explain the hierarchy of pack mules," she grumped. She slung it over her shoulder as she stepped closer to the fight. A brown eight-foot-tall walking mass of muscle was moving toward the same spot as Bethany Anne and gave her what she felt was an ugly face as he slotted himself into the circle, blocking her view and taking her place.

"Now, that was just rude." Bethany Anne lashed out with her right foot, knocking a leg out from under the alien and causing him to fall backward. He was quick, swinging his right appendage around to hit Bethany Anne as he twisted into the fall the kick had caused.

His fist met her forehead with a crack, breaking his fingers. She dodged, and he missed his grab and rolled into the dirt. Bethany Anne tossed the packs down. "Baba Yaga's spot, asshole," she spat in English.

He obviously didn't know the language. She said the same thing in Yollin, then Torcellan. He apparently understood the last. He roared and sprang at her from the ground, expecting to wrap her up and take her down to pound her.

Instead, she slammed her fist into his skull with her feet set on the ground, stopping his momentum cold. His body slumped straight to the dirt. "Baba Yaga is *not* pleased with your attitude," she told the comatose body.

"You think," Darryl called, and Bethany Anne turned to see

both him and the Shrillexian staring at her, as well as the rest in the circle, "that maybe Baba Yaga can stop taking my cool?"

"Baba Yaga was trying to watch you take out the Shrillexian when she was accosted," she called back. "She's too damned old for disrespect."

Ashur chuffed.

"Whatever," she told him, then picked up the backpacks and stepped into the opening in the circle. The aliens on either side moved half a step away and Ashur parked himself next to her.

Darryl turned back in time to catch a nasty right hook from the Shrillexian. He stepped back on his right foot, but that was all he did as he reached up and wiped the blood off his cracked lip.

Cosol noticed the alien's healing ability was faster than his own.

"That all you got?" Darryl asked. "Because I'm going to open up a ten-gallon can of whup-ass on you."

"I got that and a bit more," Cosol told him as Darryl's forward kick caught him squarely in the abdomen, picking him up and tossing him two body-lengths backward into three aliens who got too close. The move took all four of them down.

Darryl walked over to the four squirming beings and grabbed Cosol's foot. He pulled him out of the mess and heaved, throwing Cosol over his shoulder to fly back toward the ground. He landed so hard it made Bethany Anne wince.

"He still your friend?" Darryl asked the stunned Shrillexian. "Cause if he is, I'll just knock your ass—"

"Of course he is my friend." Cosol had moved his foot under him and he pushed off, driving his fist up toward the alien.

Who caught it, stopping his fist within inches. "Now this is more like it," Darryl commented as he slammed his knee right into Cosol's face, breaking his nose and sending him back onto his ass again.

"Baba Yaga is getting bored," the old lady called, and the animal next to her chuffed.

"You need practice," Darryl told him as he snap-kicked a shot to Cosol's forehead, knocking him out. He walked through the circle to Bethany Anne, who tossed him his backpack.

"Let's go," she told him. "That was a nice warmup, but I'm ready for the main event."

Waless Bar, Port Sharn, Section T-772

The Tulet pointed to a rectangular table near the bartender. "That group over there is the one you're asking about. Though," Farl caught the Tulet's attention, "you know who they are?"

The Tulet nodded. "Darkness for Hire—what's left of them. They disbanded for like three months because they tried to operate against the Leath and the Etheric Empire. The Leath haven't said anything about it, but the Etheric Empire has said they will go after the mercenary group if they ever find them again."

"Out here?" the Tulet asked.

"No, hope not," Farl answered. He drew a drink and gave it to a waitress before he continued, "Otherwise I wouldn't have them in my place. I don't think the Empies would come out here." He glanced over as the doors to his bar opened and two new aliens came in. His eyes narrowed. "Well, damn."

The Tulet turned around. "What?"

"Those are humans. Only humans I know of are Empies. I've no idea who that shorter one is, but she looks old for their type of people, so maybe this is a warning mission. The dark one looks like muscle."

Farl considered his next move as the two humans went straight for the back of the bar. He was reaching for a pistol he kept under the bar when a voice spoke in his head.

I am Baba Yaga. I am the nightmare in your dreams...

Which, the voice hissed, *you won't have any more of if you touch that weapon.*

Farl pulled his hand away from the gun and looked at her. The old human was staring at him, eyes glowing red.

"That makes thirty-three new recruits," Caster told the Tulet next to him. "I told you, make me leader, and we will come back from the dead. We had a setback, that was all."

Caster looked up to see two humans coming toward him. He reached for the pistol but stopped, his hand on the butt. The old human had her pistol pointed at him. "The Empress..." she began loudly, and the whole bar went quiet.

I've got behind you, Darryl sent to her.

Chuff, Ashur added, keeping watch on his side.

"...told Darkness for Hire she would not allow the mercenary group to survive after attacking her at the peace conference."

"It was a job," Caster spat. "We lost, we left."

"It was an attack," she shot back, "and the attack is not finished until the Empress says it is finished."

"What makes her think she is right?" Caster asked. "We have operated this way for generations. Mercenary companies stick together."

"Mercenary companies don't scare Baba Yaga," she told him. "The Empress told me to make sure Darkness for Hire was disbanded." She pulled the trigger and Caster's head exploded. She turned and shot his second, who was next to him, blowing his hand off at the wrist.

The one to Caster's right had already started bringing his gun up when Bethany Anne's next two shots entered his chest and blew his insides out his back. She turned and eyed the bar, "Now, those were the most recent leaders of Darkness for Hire, which had been warned to disband on pain of death. Hello," she nodded her head to the bar. "My name is Baba Yaga, and I'm Death. Who else is a member of this mercenary group?"

No bodies stirred. She casually placed her pistol back in her holster and crossed her arms. "Okay, now that I'm not holding a pistol, how many members do we have?"

Fourteen of those sitting in the bar started moving. Ashur took off, and Bethany Anne was slammed in the chest by someone who had palmed a pistol and shot her from underneath a table. His head exploded a microsecond later as Bethany Anne fell back against the table behind her.

Ashur ripped his arm half off when he jumped across a table, grabbing the wrist in his teeth and holding onto it as he landed on the other side. The hand spasmed, shooting the alien to his right in the leg.

Farl was considering going for his weapon when the mess degenerated quickly. The one who called herself Baba Yaga stood back up, gray hair floating, face on fire. She started throwing multiple streaks of red light, blowing bodies apart in her anger.

"The Empress said no Darkness, or you die." She walked toward the front of the bar, and as she was passing a table with three aliens with their hands on the table she casually back-handed one, the table breaking his face when it slammed into the surface. "That includes shooting Baba Yaga in the back. You try to shoot me or mine, I will kill you too."

"Clear," Darryl called, and a moment later, Ashur chuffed.

There were now eighteen dead on the bar's floor. The old human, her eyes returning to normal, addressed the barkeeper. "If Baba Yaga comes back, she burns your establishment to the ground. Understand?"

The barkeeper nodded.

"For the record," she spoke to the room as she started for the door, Darryl covering those left alive behind her and Ashur jogging ahead, "there is *no* safe distance from the Empress."

The door shut quietly behind the three of them.

Thus began the stories of Baba Yaga, the Etheric's Witch of the Night.

CHAPTER TWENTY-ONE

<u>**QBBS *Meredith Reynolds*, Military Meeting Room, One Year After Baba Yaga's Introduction**</u>

Bethany Anne tapped the table. "So, to sum up the last four weeks of effort on the planet Merrek: the Leath hit this world two months ago, we didn't respond because we didn't know, we have teams on the planet now, but the Leath are already dug in, and it has become a massive clusterfuck."

Admiral Thomas looked at Lance, Kael-ven, and Kiel before nodding. "Yes, that about sums it up. We knew they had left their system, but our hidden spy couldn't go with them. It wasn't until we searched the general area of space we suspected they had gated to that we found the planet and their ships in the system. It was based on the extrapolation of the location and angle of their Gate. Unfortunately, it has taken this long to safely acquire enough video."

Bethany Anne looked at the ceiling in thought for a moment before returning her gaze to those at the table. "Frankly, the Leath are probably as surprised as we are. They are surprised we found them this quickly, before they really got dug in, and we are surprised they outsmarted us."

"The Leath are bitching about us in the press again," Cheryl Lynn added. "Suggesting we are attacking their world and killing their harmless civilians."

"And the videos from our Guardians and Guardian Marines?" Bethany Anne asked.

"Prove it's a complete fabrication; lots of very impressive video," she replied. "When Dan is working with the teams on the ground, he tries to pull as much video as he can."

Bethany Anne shrugged, "Can't be helped. Just keep pumping out the truth and showing that the Leath are also killing the locals. And let's make it a priority to get the translation working properly." She looked around. "Where are Peter and Todd?"

Kiel spoke up. "I asked them to help train with the Second Yollin Battalion so we can get them on-planet as soon as possible. The Guardians are in a stalemate right now. We need to get more bodies on planet." He looked at his notes. "I have integrated three companies of Yollin Marines with the human groups on Merrek, and they are getting bloodied and having to learn on the job."

"Navy has stopped new ground support," Thomas admitted. "Just like us, the Leath can get small ships on- and off-planet, so the forces on the ground are not increasing by much on either side. They have some big bastards guarding their Gate in space, and we haven't been able to push them out yet. Every time we get new firepower, they add another. We subtract, and they do too. I'm pretty sure both of us are rearranging our ships in case someone tries a sneak attack in another location."

Lance grunted. "Neither group has been able to achieve a decided tactical advantage, so we both do what we can. They have more troops, but we have better equipment, mostly."

Bethany Anne nodded. "Okay, let's talk again in seventy-two hours unless something changes."

. . .

Planet Merrek, Minor Continent, Outside Zone 02-3433, Forty-Eight Hours Later

The female wolf ripped into the Leath's neck and twisted her teeth, and the nasty taste of Leath blood invaded her mouth.

Again.

Looking around, the wolf saw that the Marines on her team had decisively rebuffed the Leath effort to overwhelm their position.

Brooklyn changed back to human form and struggled over the muddy ground on this godforsaken alien planet to her team. "Join the Marines, see the universe, kill nasty Leath, and taste their blood," she grumbled as another wolf, legs caked with mud, trudged over to her. "It seemed so sexy in theory." A moment later her sister Addison was in front of her, weaving on her feet before unceremoniously dropping down on her ass in the mud.

"You look like shit," Brooklyn told her.

"Bite me," Addison replied. "It's a bad hair day."

Carter walked past the two of them, giving them a half-hearted smile. "Don't worry, this whole *planet* is a bad hair day."

"Yeah," Caden called over his shoulder from behind Brooklyn. "And for you fuzzy-wuzzies, it's a whole-body bad hair day!"

"If I didn't like him," Addison whispered under her breath, "I'd save the Leath the effort and kill him myself."

Brooklyn's eyes lit up. "I'll do it!" When Addison's eyes flickered yellow, Brooklyn just shook her head. "You still got it bad."

"Like a dog in heat," Addison grumped. She shrugged at Brooklyn's astonishment. "Well, the metaphor was appropriate."

"*Fuck!*" Chris yelled. The four humans and eight Yollins on their expanded team turned to look at him and Chris pulled off his goggles. "Fucking Leath destroyed our last eye-in-the-sky." He peeked over the small berm they had constructed and ducked back down to look at Brooklyn. "We won't have extra eagles for at least three hours, according to Command."

Brooklyn's mouth twisted in annoyance and she called, "Look

sharp, everyone! We need to be a little more vigilant now, that's all." She looked at Addison, "You okay going back to wolf?" She touched her nose. "I need the sensory support."

Addison raised a hand for Brooklyn to pull her up. When she was standing, she asked, "Anyplace in particular?"

Brooklyn turned to look in Caden's direction and spoke softly, "Out in front of Caden, if you can deal with it."

Addison flipped her sister off and turned toward the Marine in question. "It's not like I'm going to sniff his ass or anything."

Brooklyn snickered as her sister slogged through the mud, not looking very sexy. *Maybe that will help all the damn pheromones she's polluting the air with,* Brooklyn thought.

When the attack came, it came quickly. Battles are fluid: sometimes your side wins, sometimes it loses.

And you lose good people. People who had a life ahead of them. Perhaps even love ahead of them.

A future, kids, grandkids…

But no.

This time this battle went to the Leath. A small pocket of Etheric Guardians and Guardian Marines were overrun during the last hour they lacked overhead coverage, the Leath having destroyed their drones.

Just like the Etheric Empire took out Leath equipment any chance they could.

It was a fight to the end, Yollins protecting humans, humans protecting Yollins, as real teams do, no matter the species.

At the end of the battle, with dead friends' bodies spread throughout their defensive position, two Were sisters and one human male were still fighting. The male went down, his leg exploding, and the dark-haired sister took three shots to the chest, the barrage of rounds finally overcoming her armor.

Of the hundred and thirty-two Leath who overran the Etheric Empire's Guardians, barely forty were alive when the last female changed in front of their eyes. She stood like a human, but her features were animal.

That human took out twelve more Leath before she succumbed to the firepower ravaging her body from all directions. The Leath squeezed their triggers with abandon, their small hind-brains screaming in fear of the monstrosity in their midst.

She crawled back, bleeding, and changed back to human, then took the hands of her sister and the man who had been with them at the end. Her blond hair was coated with mud as the Leath surrounded her and her team, taking liberties with the bodies...

And filming it.

Planet Leath, Tienemehn, Defense Planning Headquarters

Prime Quarter Leader Conclek didn't bother taking off his armor as he trudged through the hallways of the lower levels. He had been pulled home from the front lines to answer to some back-line operational weenie's questions while his people were getting ripped up on Merrek.

All because of some jackasses who got lucky and decided to have a little fun.

Carrying his armor's helmet under his arm, he nodded to the two guards who checked his credentials. Once approved, he knocked on the door of the meeting room to which he had been ordered to report. He was told to come in, so he pushed the door open and entered.

It took him a half-second to realize these weren't back-line operational weenies, and he clicked his heels together and saluted smartly. Well, as smartly as his armor would allow.

The First Line Prime Commander was sitting at the table with two intelligence officers and an Ixtali.

"Sir! Prime Quarter Leader Conclek reporting as ordered."

First Line Prime Commander Tehrle nodded, allowing Conclek to drop his salute.

"I'll make this quick, Conclek," the First Line Prime Commander growled. "These are Prime Intelligence One and Two," he pointed to the other two Leath at the table, "and our deep-cover agent Ze'mek from the Ixtali undercover effort," indicating the Ixtali. The First Line Prime Commander nodded toward the second Leath at the table. "Two will be asking you questions."

"Prime Quarter Leader," Intelligence Two began, congenially enough. "I understand a group of your soldiers overran and killed an Etheric Empire Quarter some three days ago. Correct?"

"Correct." Conclek wasn't sure how much he should admit. What wasn't admitted might not be known.

Unfortunately, the First Line Prime Commander knew the rest. "And," he interrupted, "they were disrespectful to the bodies, took a video of it, and sent it to galactic *newsgroups?*"

"Well, yes." It wasn't the best situation, but it had helped the morale of his fighters to send that out to the universe. Those Etheric fighters were damned hard to kill, but apparently enough rounds would do the job.

It was a *great* training video if nothing else.

Prime Intelligence Two continued his questioning. "Do you know much about the Etheric Empress, Prime Quarter Leader?"

Being smart, Conclek left out his opinion of politicians and kept to what he knew. "She has a reputation for being unable to keep her anger in check."

"That is all?" he asked, his voice smooth.

"That is enough," Conclek replied. "I'm sorry, but leaders who can't control their emotions will eventually do something very stupid. We will be there to make her regret it."

"That's all," the Ixtali slowly stood up from the table, "I needed to hear." He nodded to the three sitting. "Contact me, should you need me again." Turning, he started toward the door, pausing briefly to stare at Conclek. "You should get your affairs in order." He opened the door and stepped out.

The door closed behind him with a gentle *click*.

Conclek looked back at the Leath still at the table, confused. "Am I being punished?"

"Not by us," First Line Prime Commander told him. "But you will be dead, nonetheless. I'm sending you back to Merrek to reap what your people have sown. We can't get any more troops to Merrek in time to make much of a difference, and our Intelligence knows the Empress has sent someone to the planet."

"Someone?" Conclek asked. "How can one person make much of a difference?"

Prime Intelligence One clarified, "It is a small group, maybe five to ten total. But it includes the one they call..."

The Ixtali Ze'mek started walking away from the door, not needing to hear more of the conversation. He was well aware of who was heading toward Merrek, and he wanted to be on the other end of the galaxy for a while.

QBBS *Meredith Reynolds*, Empress' Quarters

Bethany Anne caressed the wooden box, running her hand across its smooth sides before sliding it to the two clasps on the front.

Each opened with a *snap*.

Lifting the top back on its hinges, she enjoyed the caress of the low light on the silver blade inside for a moment. Then, gently, she pulled out the katana, turning it to the left and then to the right as she examined the cutting edge. Satisfied, she reached for the sheath and slid the blade home.

ADAM, is this suit fully charged, and do we have full connectivity for the sensor circuits?

>>Yes, Bethany Anne.<<

Backup armor?

>>Yes, Bethany Anne.<<

Plenty of ammo?

>>Yes, Bethany Anne.<<

Reaching forward, she grabbed her holsters and slid first her right arm, then her left through the holsters' loops and locked the rig in place. Reaching to the right, she grabbed first one, then the second of her two Jean Dukes Specials with their armor-piercing rounds.

After she'd locked them both in place, she touched a button on her right leg. The ridge along her leg opened and slid apart. A small hilt slid upward for Bethany Anne to grasp and remove. Lifting it, she sank her emotions into the Etheric and *pulled*.

The blade sprang into being, the red glow along its three-foot edge humming as if in anger. When she cut off the energy the blade disappeared, leaving her with only the hilt. She slapped it back on the clip and it slid back into the armor on her right leg, the ridge sealing again.

She looked over her shoulder. "John?"

"Yes, boss?" his somber voice replied.

"Do you have extra slots for grenades?"

John chuckled. "BA, I *always* have slots for my little friends."

"Good to know." She turned back to the armaments in front of her. Given the sheer weight the five of them could carry, it was effectively a toy store for grown boys and girls—and Bethany Anne was fully grown.

And mad as hell.

ADAM cut in.

>> **General Reynolds is asking what the target for this operation is?**<<

Tell him the planet Merrek.

>>**He says he knows that much. Where specifically?**<< ADAM asked after a moment.

Bethany Anne grabbed a gear bag and started filling it. That task completed, she stepped out of her weapons room.

Tell him the whole **Gott Verdammt** *planet.*

>>**Oh.**<<

CHAPTER TWENTY-TWO

There were black bands wrapped around the Guardians' and Guardian Marines' arms. Each had seen the video shared by the Leath with the multi-system news agencies, and anger burned in every human and Yollin in the units.

Practice time had doubled, and the fighting units' desire to get to Merrek was thick enough that Kiel could cut it with a dull knife.

The rumor was the Empress was sending her Avatar, Baba Yaga, to the planet, and all remaining Guardians would accompany her.

Kiel had told them to practice hard so they could get a bit of their own back, and they had.

Shipyard staff started signing up for double-shifts. Those on the planet sent gifts, wrote songs, and performed plays in cities all over the world. Those on the space stations wore black armbands in support and memory of those who had been disrespected on a foreign planet.

And all watched and waited for the Empress' response.

It was Yollins and humans... No, it was _Etherians_ who had

239

been disrespected, and the entire Empire was ready to provide the response.

With interest.

———

Bethany Anne looked in her mirror. *Do it, TOM.*

This is going to hurt like a sonofabitch.

DO. IT.

Not on the way to Merrek? We would have more time.

Which part of "DO IT" don't you understand?

The screaming part, he replied.

The pain hit. Torture rampaged throughout her body as TOM forced the modifications through her nanocytes, pulling raw power from the Etheric to make the changes she'd requested.

John checked on her when he heard the whimpers she couldn't hold in and watched in fascination as she changed. Her jet-black hair turned white—pure white. Her skin morphed to black leather, and her eyes were now white orbs with red irises.

She had told her people to suit up in black armor, not red.

Her hands grasped the countertop, squeezing hard to deflect her attention from the sheer hell moving through her body.

Then it was over.

Her body convulsed, bucking back and forth for a moment as she and TOM fought to keep her body upright.

"I got..." she croaked, her voice a rough whisper, "this."

She slowly straightened up. John stayed in place, but even he had to stop himself from taking an involuntary step back when she looked at him.

"I see the Queen Bitch has upgraded her look," he commented. "Or is this someone else?"

Her voice was deep, raspy; neither that of the Empress nor the Queen Bitch.

"The Queen Bitch is an angry Bethany Anne." She headed out

of the room toward the bedroom of her suite. "This is my alter ego Baba Yaga, the Witch of the Night."

She picked up her bag of weapons and the two people disappeared from her suite, her last comment drifting in the silence.

"Also known as Death."

QBBS *Meredith Reynolds*, Open Court

The anger roiling through the multiple stories was palpable. The *Meredith Reynolds* was almost over-full. There was a path that led from the hallway beside All Guns Blazing to the exit to the space docks.

First the news had been whispered, then the Guardians and Guardian Marines, black bands around their arms, had flooded into the bottom level, the Food Court, and made a lane.

Then others rarely seen in the outer docks strode into the open court. Yollins from the space stations, Yollins from the planet.

A few ships from Straiphus, and miners from the asteroids.

There was a whisper that *she* was going to be there. The rumor? The Witch—the one the Empress sent into the universe to strike for the Empire.

To scare those who thought fear was their personal weapon. She reclaimed it.

She had white hair, the stories said, and her eyes would glow like the Empress' own. Many said she was the sister of the Empress or a demon friend.

Some whispered it *was* the Empress—her darker half.

When asked, Empress Bethany Anne would only say that might didn't always make right, and even the mighty could fall to the Witch of the Night.

Baba Yaga.

But this person had never been seen, so the stories were just that.

Stories.

They said she had six who traveled with her, where the Empress had only four. Six who killed with and for her. The roster changed as to who would go, as the Empress commanded.

Baba Yaga and the Six Horsemen, one human had joked. But someone else had changed it to *Baba Yaga and the Shinigami*, and that had stuck.

A hush fell over the crowd, and then a strange feeling came over them. Their anger turned to caution as they looked at each other, not knowing what to expect as the Guardians locked arms below them.

John, Eric, Darryl, and Scott had their helmets on, and their black armor's matte finish drank in the light. Two more armor-clad men joined them. John nodded. "Stephen, Peter," he acknowledged through their suits' comms.

"Death." Peter's voice was light, playing off what the team had code-named John.

"Where is Baba?" Stephen asked, then shook his head. "Never mind."

No one needed to be told when Baba Yaga would arrive. The fear she was *pushing* had increased, and they could feel her coming closer. Bethany Anne had decided to play her role to the hilt. She had agreed that those outside the Empire couldn't know the Empress would be sucked away again, as she had been to support the Karillians.

So she had created a new version of herself, an avatar—one she was ready to christen with the sacrifices of those who defiled her fallen. Her people.

Her Guardians.

Stephen has been asked to stand in for Akio, Bethany Anne sent, her mental voice rough in their minds. *Let's go*, she told them, and started walking out of the hallway.

The six Shinigami swept into motion behind her, striding side by side.

Bethany Anne had told John that no one needed to protect Baba Yaga, but he itched to get ahead of her anyway. Not that it mattered; Reynolds was watching this event to make sure no one tried to attack Bethany Anne.

In the second row, behind those who formed the front line on the main floor, stood a younger Yollin male. He had signed up a few years ago and had been through Guardian training. He had been planet-side supporting the Guardians' recruitment efforts when the first hastily-pulled-together teams had been sent to Merrek, and it had pissed him off.

He needed to go, and *soon*. No one should treat the dead as his fellow Guardians had been treated, and he was ready to explain that clearly by shoving his rifle down the throat of a Leath and pulling the trigger. In solidarity, he linked arms with a human to his left and another Yollin to his right. He had hoped to see the Empress and John Grimes and the others on the floor, but the whisper was she was sending the Witch.

He snorted. He had seen the Empress' videos, so he wasn't sure if sending someone else was going to do much. He was still considering this when fear struck him. He noticed that his compatriots' muscles locked, as did his. He craned his neck to see Baba Yaga walk out of the hallway with the six Shinigami behind her.

Drk-vaen locked his limbs in place, but the sweat coming off his forehead betrayed the lie; he was afraid. A quick glance around the floor showed him he wasn't the only one.

Where the Empress was beautiful, Baba Yaga was hideous,

for a human. Where the Empress was fun and light unless she was angry, Baba Yaga was born of fear. The Empress had dark hair, but Baba Yaga's white filaments floated on the wind, making her appear as a vision of Death who walked in the light.

Where she shouldn't be.

The Shinigami behind her (not that Drk-vaen knew what the name meant, but he had been told it translated as "death gods," so he chose to believe it) radiated resolute death.

The Leath had angered the Empress, and now the Empress was sending her response. Baba Yaga didn't stop to speak as the Empress would. She swept across the floor, her black face surrounding sharp white teeth and white eyes with red irises and walked toward the...

"*Holy shit!*" the human beside Drk-vaen yelped.

Baba Yaga had disappeared, and so had the Shinigami. Collective breaths of surprise and relief when the fear disappeared swept the multiple levels of the open court.

Soon enough, thousands all over the court realized the pictures and videos of Baba Yaga and the Shinigami on their tablets had been corrupted. No one had a recording of any kind. The Witch of the Night remained only a story.

But this time, thousands of Etherians and others from multiple star systems all told the *same* story.

Baba Yaga was real, and she was Death.

Drk-vaen almost felt sorry for the Leath on that planet, but after he had watched the video one more time, he decided the Empress had made the right call. She had called upon Death and pointed her toward Merrek.

And the Leath were about to die.

Planet Merrek

"Confirming that all Etherians have been pulled from this

planet?" Bethany Anne asked as the *Tramp Princess* dove toward the planet.

In space, *ArchAngel* and the renamed *Alexander* were facing off against four of the Leath superdreadnoughts, with both sides having an assortment of other large ships on their flanks.

The Leath weren't sure what the humans were up to, but they had confirmed there were no troops on the planet now, to the best of their knowledge.

So they brought in upper-level politicians to create a message for their PR machine, which was being broadcast across the planet.

Then Darkness rolled over the planet, and a new video showed up. It spoke seven languages, one of them Leath.

The video featured a dark background with an even darker figure speaking, glints of her white hair appearing on the outer fringes. The voice was gravelly, but the message was clear.

In seven languages, it claimed it had arrived with the Darkness. Nothing would save them; they were cut off. Baba Yaga was here.

It was time they met their gods in the afterlife.

Planet Merrek, Minor Continent, Outside Zone 02-3433

"The weather is horrible," Se'zal grumped as he ate his food while sitting on a large rock. He turned to Chanto, who was picking up his own food. "You think that Bobo Yaha is going to dare show its face here?"

"What?" Chanto asked as he opened his pouch. "And it's Baba Yaga, and I wouldn't know. However," he pointed his eating utensil at his friend, "we are the ones who made the video, so if she's real, what do *you* think?"

"I think—" he began, and then stopped talking, his head having disappeared in a splash of color.

The Leath contingent had been reinforced from the twenty-eight survivors back up to a complement of sixty-four when Bethany Anne and the Shinigami surrounded them.

They had no clue. A total of five messages had been sent to Command saying they were under fire and taking casualties when suddenly all communications from their location ceased and Command could no longer raise them.

There were only seven moving bodies remaining, and all were human.

Images that could be matched to the videos sent to the news agencies were forwarded to ArchAngel. The *Shinigami* had been videoed, but you never saw the face of Baba Yaga. In one picture, you could make out her black leather-like hands, and in another, the back of her head with her floating white hair could be seen, but that was it.

The group finished their job, encircled the white-haired Witch, and disappeared. Above, the ship waiting for them turned toward the east and vanished.

Planet Merrek, Leath Command Center

Prime Quarter Leader Conclek ground his teeth, his tusks rubbing on his lips. "Are you telling me," he snarled, "that we have lost seventeen support outposts in six days?"

Conclek listened to the incoming report and took a few deep breaths before responding, "Well, pull the other twenty into five groups, increase the guards, and have everyone hunker down. We will make that Bitch Witch come to us." He closed the connection and turned to his aide. "Somebody get me a connection to those shits up in space!"

Bethany Anne watched as the Leath detachments started moving to centralized locations. She scratched her normal face, having decided that looking like Baba Yaga was a bit off-putting when she saw herself in the mirror. "ADAM," she called while she, Stephen, and Scott were working at the table that had been set up in the main room on her ship, "how are we doing on cracking their communications?"

"We're exactly nowhere," ADAM replied. She heard John walk down the hall and stop at the doorway. She assumed he was leaning against the wall and listening. "They are using high-quality technology, and we haven't been able to break it yet."

She tapped her lips, thinking. "Do we know for certain which location is the main base?"

"With eighty-seven percent accuracy, yes," ADAM answered.

"I hate guessing," she whispered. "How long before they finish their efforts to pull their people together?"

"Best guess," Stephen answered, "it will take up to a week."

"Can we attack the smaller groups?" she asked Stephen.

Stephen thought about it for a moment. "Well, we could always do that, but what they are doing is exactly what we hoped they would. It would take us a lot longer to go after individual locations, so they are hunkering down. Just be thankful they aren't trying to hide behind non-combatants."

"Probably don't think of them as protection," Scott commented. "They seemed pretty assured of their own importance."

"Well," Bethany Anne looked at the map once more, "let's hope they don't get that idea before we eradicate them."

John stepped into the room and stepped up next to the table, looking down at the map that had been projected.

It took a moment, enough time for Bethany Anne to look up to see if he was studying the map or what. She saw him point to the table, so she looked back down.

"What about staying *here* and seeing if anyone passes in the night?"

247

Bethany Anne considered the valley and shrugged. "I don't think it would be any better than waiting."

"No," John reached up and scratched his chin, where a beard was starting to grow in, "but if we got lucky, we could have some fun."

Bethany Anne's eyes flashed red. "I *like* fun."

"Stupid stupid stupid," Cor'rida commented as she humped her weapon and loaned armor through the forest, a branch popping back to hit her square in the face. "Dammit!" she called. "Remember there are others behind you."

Cor'rida had been in her assigned location working to create a viable government oversight office for a total of two days when her life had changed. She, like many others, went from important to so much dead weight in the estimation of the military. She was given a rifle, a suit of armor that almost fit, and a sum total of one short afternoon of practice with both.

Jum, the troop ahead of her, chuckled. "This is what we do every time a command comes down from either military or you political *zeenoobs*. Just, now you get to do it with us."

"What happened to pick-up by vehicles?" she asked, stepping over a large rock.

"Flights are shut down; we don't have the resources. That damned Baba Yaga destroyed our ships on-planet. They hit four air command locations simultaneously. I understand it was pretty damned bad for the soldiers stationed there, but even worse for the ships. Nothing was left."

"One Etherian did this?" she asked, grabbing the branch from Jum before he let it go, which saved her a smack in the face.

"Nah, there had to be at least four, or they couldn't have hit them at the same time," he answered, waving his hand around his face to shoo off some sort of insect. "Reports are, more than one location had two combatants, so probably about eight."

"We have over forty-four with us right now!" she grumped. "We can't take them out with how many of you guys? Are you all useless?" she asked, just as a rather large branch caught her in the face, sending her slamming backward into the muck. "YOU GROMBULD!" she screamed. She rolled over on the ground and stood up, reaching for her lip. She pulled it out; it was bleeding. "*Jum!*" she yelled and ducked under the branch, storming forward. She saw a body lying in the grass ahead. "Get off the ground!" she hissed and went over to him. "It's not like you can hide from me!"

Her voice dropped when she realized Jum was missing a large chunk of his head and bleeding from multiple locations in his chest.

She started to hyperventilate and turned around. Behind her was an alien with floating white hair and a weapon pointed at her.

Cor'rida put up her hands. "Hold! I'm not military!" she cried, only to fall into the dirt a second later, blood dripping from her lips.

The black-faced, white-eyed alien walked over to her. "I'm aware you aren't military, but all Leath on this planet have been condemned by the military's actions. The Kurtherians you call gods will pay for what you did to my people. If I have to track them for the rest of my long-assed life, I will find them and put them in a grave."

She turned around, holstering her pistol. "Perhaps your ancestors should have chosen different gods." She finished her speech to a Leath whose open eyes stared into the planet's atmosphere, her dead ears unable to hear anything the Witch had said.

CHAPTER TWENTY-THREE

QBBS Asteroid *R2D2*, R&D

"I'm thinking I should grab a large wrench and beat the box William is working on with it." Tina put her head down on the worktable in front of her as Marcus, five feet farther down the long rock table, looked at her.

"Um," he pulled his glasses off and used them to point at her, "that might be a catastrophically bad idea."

Tina turned her head to look at him, then reached up and moved her dark hair so she could see better. "We go *boom*? I'm kinda okay with that at the moment. This is so damned *frustrating*."

Marcus inhaled. "Yes... Yes, it is." He scratched his cheek. "Isn't that your personal project?"

"Yes," came a muffled reply from under her hair.

"How long have you been working on it?"

"Half my life," she told him.

Marcus chuckled, "Tina, we haven't been on this asteroid that long."

"Time is relative," she answered, reaching up to move her hair again. "Space, time, existence, gravity, energy. I bet I could stumble on a way to time-travel with all this math." She lifted her head off the table.

"Why isn't R2 helping you with it?" Marcus pulled his chair next to hers. She saw his eyes moving across the equations on her tablet. He reached forward, advanced the digital page to the next, and kept reading.

"Are you doing the math in your head?" she asked, curious if it was Marcus or one of the EI's or TOM or ADAM.

"Some of it," Marcus answered, his voice soft, his focus elsewhere as he tapped her tablet to change the page again. "Why didn't you ask for help with this?" he asked while his eyes scanned her work.

Tina's eyes narrowed. She probably knew Marcus better than anyone who wasn't presently on this asteroid, and his scientific curiosity was totally focused on her math in front of him. *"What are you seeing?"*

Marcus didn't answer. He just flipped another page, reading as his lips moved silently, and flipped again. After a couple of minutes, he reached the end of her notes and thoughts. He looked at her for a moment, his brain still partially in some other mental location, and leaned back from the table, chewing on the earpiece of his glasses. He finally answered her question.

"Genius," he told her. Then he looked up. "R2, please call Bobcat and William. Tell them we are holding an immediate mandatory meeting."

Merrek System, Outer Space

"We will bring the auxiliaries to this location." Prime Commander Mehnib of the Leath navy designated an area in 3D space. "From here we should be able to block the Etherians long enough to pull Prime Quarter Leader Conclek and anyone else left on the planet out."

"Casualties?" Commander Unt'er asked from his destroyer.

"Hopefully minimal," Commander Mehnib replied. "We can't just leave them there when we have a decent shot at retrieving them."

"Sir?" a voice called from outside the discussion tank. It took a second for Commander Mehnib to realize he was the target. He turned to look through the haze the holo caused in his vision. "Yes?"

"We are tracking two new Etherian ships, sir."

"Type?" Commander Mehnib asked. They maintained full awareness of the Etheric Empire's shipbuilding capacity, and they shouldn't have been able to field any new ships.

"They are *ArchAngel*-class superdreadnoughts, sir." The operator glanced at his screen, then back at the Prime Commander. "New designations, sir. We haven't tracked these before."

Commander Mehnib swore under his breath as his jaws grated together. The Etherians had been able to build ships somewhere they didn't know about.

They had just changed the spacescape. Commander Mehnib stepped out of the holo and walked toward Communications. "Get me a private line to Prime Quarter Leader Conclek."

Planet Merrek

Conclek listened to the voice on the other end of the comm and kept his face relaxed with an effort. "I understand, Prime Commander Mehnib. Don't worry, we will take care of this annoyance and finish our original task. We took out dozens, so I'm sure we can take out a handful of Etherians, no matter *how* scary they believe they are." Conclek nodded. "Yes, of course. We will be here."

Prime Quarter Leader Conclek closed the comm and snorted, thinking back to what the Ixtali spy had told him when he was on Leath. *"You should get your affairs in order,"* the spy had said before exiting the meeting room.

Perhaps he would die, and perhaps he would not. So far, this Baba Yaga had gone through three of his outposts, destroying each in turn. He had commanded the fourth to join him here at headquarters. This location had been dug into the ground, and the security doors were closed.

"Reminds me of China," the black-faced, white-haired woman remarked. Her harsh voice suited her visage as the seven Etherians looked at the last concentration of Leath on the planet.

"It's going to be a bit tough. Lots of places to get shot to hell," John commented. "We need to blow the door and get some spies into the place to give us some idea of what we're looking at. We don't even know how many levels deep this sumbitch dives."

"Well, we have *some* idea," ADAM told everyone. "I've dropped some explosives and measured the shock waves. My best calculation is we are looking at a minimum of five hundred levels on the low side, upper limit two thousand. We know four hundred troops just arrived from the last location."

"Shame we didn't catch them in time," Peter stated. "I'd have loved to get another piece of those assholes."

Bethany Anne's eyes narrowed. "And so you shall, my little Pricolici." Her eyes started to glow red. "So you shall."

The men turned to look at Peter. His eyes flashed yellow, and he had a predatory grin on his face.

"Send the first puck, ADAM," Bethany Anne instructed.

Inside the base, those on the first and second floors covered their ears when the first *BANG* resounded.

"Knock, knock," Baba Yaga whispered. "The Witch is here."

Several pucks and a significant amount of time later, the banging stopped, and those in the base wondered what the Etheric enemies were up to.

"You boys stay up here and pound away to make sure no one

leaves. Watch all the spy drones to the best of your ability." She looked at the map the spies had drawn, the infestation of the micro-sized drones having completed as much as the team needed to see. Baba Yaga turned to Peter. "Are you ready to finish this for your people?"

The seven-foot-tall Pricolici looked down at the woman with the white eyes who stared back at him and nodded. "Yessssss."

The guys watched as Bethany Anne and Peter disappeared into the Etheric.

"Well, shit." Stephen looked at the other guys. "There goes our fun. Anyone want to play poker?"

Darryl looked at Stephen with a smirk on his face. "Play poker with a mind-reading vampire?"

Stephen put a hand to his heart. "You wound me, sir."

"Not as much as you would wound my pocketbook," Darryl replied.

"I'm in." Scott stepped around the two arguing guys and walking over to where the cards were stashed.

"Hey!" Darryl called to Scott. "I didn't say I *wouldn't* play."

Behind Darryl, Stephen winked at Scott, who shook his head and smiled.

The Etheric Realm

Beside Bethany Anne, Peter was almost a statue as she sought the location of the main command center, chuckling evilly to herself the whole time.

Her method was to peek out of the Etheric, try to figure out where they were compared to the map in her head, and then pull Peter to another location and peek again.

It was their seventh time they had looked and Peter finally had to ask. "Whyyy arre youu laughinng?"

"Because," she answered in her gravelly voice, "I'm thinking what is going to happen when I find the command center."

"Whhat?"

Bethany Anne poked her head out one more time, but it stayed there a second longer than normal before she stood up, her eyes flaming red and her voice guttural. "You have ten seconds to get your pound of flesh before I arrive."

Peter looked down and smiled, his teeth showing, "Morre thann enouughh timme to explainnn myy annoyyyance."

Prime Quarter Leader Conclek watched the video take. They had tried fifteen different ways to shoot down the spaceship that was attacking them, but none of them had worked.

It was obviously a far more advanced ship than it seemed—which was not much more than a jumped-up merchant ship. Larger than normal, maybe, but its weapons were frustrating his defenses. He was pretty sure the Etherians were waiting until dark before they attacked. He had sent two detachments of troops to protect their energy generators and keep the lights on.

As well as making sure the appropriate teams had low-light gear.

They had set up locations to trap the enemy and blow the rooms on top of the attackers. They had pre-set multiple ways to block them in as well.

He and his people would take care of this Witch of the Empress, and he would *personally* piss on those bodies, and he would be damned if he wouldn't send *that* video to the news-groups as well. He wouldn't back down from a fight.

No way, no how.

The room, about thirty feet by twenty feet, was shared with his team's other eight commanders. Conclek had turned to look at a video feed when the roar shook them out of their inner thoughts.

Conclek was reaching for a pistol at his side, when a massive hand gripped his throat and lifted his massive armored body off the floor, shaking him. "YOUUU!" it screamed at him.

Conclek wasn't sure what the monster had said, but it knew who he was. His hand had just freed the pistol from its holster when the monster reached down, grabbed his pistol, and yanked it out of his hand. He was twisted in the air, and Conclek felt two slugs penetrate the back of his armor.

He tried to yell, but he was struggling with breathing just then. Next thing he knew, he had flown over a bank of video screens and crashed into someone behind him.

Bethany Anne *pushed* Peter into the command room and started counting to herself as she pulled in energy. "One Mississippi." She pushed a button on her holster and her Etheric Sword hilt popped up. "Two Mississippi." She grabbed the hilt and fed energy into the blade, causing it to light up. "Three Mississippi… WHOTHEFUCKAMIKIDDING? Ten Mississippi, *here Baba Yaga comes!*"

She stepped into the utter chaos of the command room.

"Wow!" She dodged the Leath Peter casually threw behind him. Bethany Anne slit the flying Leath open through his chest armor as he flew past. "Pay attention to your surroundings!" she called.

Peter picked up a heavy desk and slammed it into a Leath who was trying to get to the command center's exit.

Baba Yaga made a face. "I don't think he's going to make it."

"Nonne wiilll maakke itt!" Peter growled. He heard Bethany Anne's sword slashing in the background as he caught up with the commander. "Come back herrrre," he snarled, and slapped a weapon out of the commander's hand. Peter had no clue where he had gotten it from. "Iit's nottt niccce tooo shoottt meee," he told the commander conversationally as he grabbed his armored arm and raised it, then slammed it down on a desk. He did it once, twice, and on the third time it broke the desk.

"Dammmnn," he remarked. "Theey maakke goood arrrmor."

Three impacts caused rocks to shower the room, and Peter knew it was now just the two of them alive with this asshole.

Baba Yaga had finished those who had still been alive.

Peter picked up the commander by his armor's neck and the Leath smashed a fist into his ribs, cracking two. "Bassstard!" Peter threw him across the room to land on a desk, and the commander slid across it and slammed into the wall beyond.

Conclek knew for certain he was going to die, but at least he had hurt the monster. *That punch had to have done some damage*, he thought, as he heard the crunch on the alien's skeleton. He had rolled up and was steadying himself when a new face popped over the desk that had cushioned his fall somewhat.

It wasn't the monster, but rather it was a dark face. *An evil face*, he thought. He swallowed, transfixed, as it grinned; he could see the mouth full of pointed teeth. The thing casually swung a flaming red energy sword and sliced the desk in half, shoving the pieces aside.

She spoke a language he understood, at least well enough. "Let me introduce you to the Empress' Prime Guardian." The monster joined her in looking down at him. "You are responsible for failing to teach your people to properly respect their enemies, and therefore you have sentenced all on the planet to death."

Conclek glared at her, not willing to speak to the apparition.

"Keep him here." She turned her sword off and locked it back on her leg. She walked toward the computers and video monitors. "ADAM, what can we figure out about this technology?"

She flipped a couple of switches. "Nope." She flipped a couple more, noticing a second steel door starting to close. "Still not the right choice, ADAM." Her eyes turned to another console, and she walked over and punched a couple of buttons. "Good enough," she commented and then hit one more.

This time Conclek was surprised to hear her speak in his language. "This is Baba Yaga, the Etheric Empress' Witch. Pay attention as we kill your commander…" She walked away from the communications station.

ADAM, pass on to the guys that they are to move away since we are going to puck the fuck out of this location.

>>**No going from room to room for fun?"**

Hell, no. This is a death trap for both sides. I think we will have to be content with killing this asshole and making this a gravesite.

>>**They are informed, and are preparing for your return.**<<

Bethany Anne thought about that for a moment. *Preparing?*

>>**Cleaning up, is more like it.**<<

She shook her head and then nodded when she heard the sounds from outside. First came aggravated snarls, then banging as those outside worked to get inside the command center.

She walked back to Peter and the commander. "Peter?"

Peter looked down, "I'dd liikke himmm to suffferrr, buutt wee caann'tt leett himmm looosse."

"Oh, well. Then change," she told him. He looked at her for confirmation, and seconds later he was back in his human form. She pulled her sword's hilt back out, aiming it away from Peter and infusing the blade with energy. "I'd suggest," she handed it to him, "you don't let that touch you. Take off his hands and it will cauterize…"

Before she could finish the statement, Peter had taken off both hands and a leg at what would be his knee on a human. The commander's screams of pain reverberated through the room. "Okay, I guess that works, too."

Conclek couldn't believe how easily the energy blade had sliced through his armor, which was busy pumping him full of painkillers. He was just getting his focus back, even if it was a little fuzzy when he looked up at the two standing above him. Where the one called Baba Yaga had been, there was now a different woman. A beautiful woman.

One he recognized, his eyes opening wide. She had a blue ball of energy in her hand.

"*You!*" he spat.

"Know the truth," her voice was not as gravelly as before but close enough, "and take it to your grave." She hit him with the blue ball and his body spasmed. "That will keep you quiet."

Bethany Anne, Empress of the Etheric Empire, reached out and took the sword from Peter. Shutting it off, she slotted it back into its compartment, allowing it to disappear behind the protection of the armor that closed over it. She reached out and took Peter's hand. "**ADAM, send the pucks**," she commanded as the two of them disappeared. The banging on the door continued while the commander convulsed on the floor, unable to move as rock from the ceiling started to fall.

CHAPTER TWENTY-FOUR

QBBS _Meredith Reynolds,_ Open Court

Bethany Anne stood on the podium that had been built for her in the middle of the bottom floor of the open court, surrounded by her people—her Guardians and those who had passed the security checks. She looked out over those standing on this level, as well as turning her head to look up at the Etherians on the higher levels of the Court.

"Merrek is now free of Leath. The last thousand or two were entombed forever as a pointed reminder that you do not disrespect my warriors." Her eyes glimmered red, sparking from time to time. "We have personal confirmation of their deaths, and have provided video of what happened to all news agencies which adhere to the truth."

She turned to her left, then to her right.

"The Leath military treated our fallen in the most despicable way possible, and we have replied. We killed everyone responsible for committing the atrocities, and other Leath who had worked to subjugate Merrek to satisfy their own ambitions."

Bethany Anne's speech was being broadcast galaxy-wide as

fast as the news agencies could send it to their relay sites and through the gates to continue beyond the Yollin system.

"However," she continued, and then her visage changed, her eyes taking center stage as they glowed with power, "let me explain that my real fight is with the Kurtherians of the Phraim-'Eh clan, one of the Seven Kurtherian Clans. The Etheric Empire has declared war to the knife with *that* clan, not with the Leath who have been subjugated by these aliens, acting as their 'gods' for generations. To those Kurtherians, I say: know that I am committing our complete focus to your *eradication*, to uprooting you and killing you one by one, however long it takes. Should you seek safety, I will attack your location until I find you and kill you."

Her face crackled with energy, vehemence dripping from her words. "I have been granted a long life, and I will use that life to make sure you suffer for killing my people both on Earth and in space. Every member of your clan is now our enemy. You wanted to see if you were good enough to help a species? Well, you failed. Congratulations! You now have the attention of the Etheric Empire and the Queen Bitch."

Her hair floated in the calm air as the cameras focused on her face. "*Baba Yaga is coming,*" she assured the galactic audience.

She turned and walked off the stage, the roaring of her people signaling their willingness to continue the fight.

Whole space systems learned an important lesson that day: that their people should never, *never*, disrespect the Etheric Empire's warriors.

QBBS Asteroid *R2D2*, R&D

Bobcat looked down at his tablet, up at the images projected above it being discussed by Tina and Marcus, and back down at his tablet.

William was sitting on a stool, shaking his head. "Sonofabitch."

"It's fucking genius," Bobcat breathed. "Holy shit on a popsicle stick."

"Okay, that's just gross," Tina told him, making a face.

"Yeah, but it has a nice cadence," Bobcat pointed out. "Now focus. Why did you go this route?"

She pointed to the third set of figures. "This was where Marcus found my mistake, but it was also the area that just... just..." She stopped a moment.

"Felt right?" Bobcat asked. "Where your gut was saying you needed to look?"

She tilted her head and shoulders left and right just a little before shrugging, "Yes?"

"Good!" Bobcat smiled. "It's fucking beer-thirty somewhere, motherfuckers." He grinned and reached for the beer he hadn't yet opened. "R2, I need Bethany Anne."

"She asks if it is important. She is in the middle of something."

"Yes, it is. Tell her it has to do with portable Eat-Shit-and-Die weapons."

A microsecond later, the Empress' voice was heard in their meeting area. "Bobcat, you better not be fucking with me."

"No, my Empress," Bobcat told her. "We absolutely are not shitting you."

"Well done, then. Well done indeed!" she replied. "I'll be there to discuss it in six hours. Bethany Anne out."

There was silence in the team office as they each stood there thinking their own thoughts, just drinking up their success at cracking the impossible once again.

"What's wrong?" William asked Tina, who was wiping away a tear. Marcus stepped closer and put an arm around her, hugging her gently as she spoke. "I just realized I have now contributed in my own way to paying back those bastards on Merrek."

"Well," Bobcat spoke softly, "Baba Yaga did those jackasses

well enough, but with this breakthrough, we can create defense systems that will protect worlds for what are pennies on the dollar compared to what we have now." He used his beer bottle to scratch his cheek. "What are we naming it? If we don't do it ourselves, you know damned well Bethany Anne will call it something like Little ESD or Tiny ESD or something inane like that."

Tina smiled and wiped away another tear. "BYPS."

Marcus released his hug to look down at her and ask, "BIPS?

"No, BYPS." She chuckled. "Baba Yaga Protection System. The Witch of the Night, the Darkness of Space."

The men looked at each other, and William pointed to the screens they had been reviewing. "R2, print the records from Tina and Marcus. Print everything out so we can bind it. Put Project 'BYPS' on the cover sheet."

R2 replied, "Understood, William."

Bobcat held up his beer. "To BYPS!"

Tina, Marcus, and William grabbed their drinks and raised them in honor of Bobcat's toast.

"TO BYPS!" they agreed, Tina adding, "May she blow the shit out of unwanted Kurtherian assholes forevermore."

FINIS

AHEAD FULL

The Story Continues with book 19, *Ahead Full*.

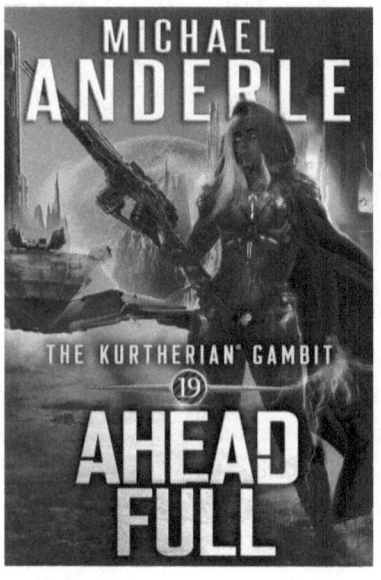

Available now at Amazon and on Kindle Unlimited

AUTHOR NOTES - MICHAEL ANDERLE

As always, I want to say THANK YOU for not only reading this book, but also reading through to these author notes, as well.

Today, I recorded the audio author notes for Release The Dogs of War, Book 10 in The Kurtherian Gambit series and I learned an important lesson.

I should be careful what I type in these author notes, for one day I will have to record them. Should I happen to put in really large multisyllabic words, I will have to *pronounce* them.

And there lies the sucky part. At least, it did today when my tongue tripped over speaking some of the words I typed nine months ago.

Perhaps I should gather a program that highlights any words with more than three syllables.

Oh well, I'm too lazy to deal with that, I'll just have to work on my reading abilities.

A *huge* "THANK YOU" to the Double-D's (Diane and Doreen - you might remember them from TS Paul's series The Etheric Academy) who helped me eons ago. Well, I suppose it was about five or six weeks ago, to express how to shape the emotion behind the Guardian Marines and their sacrifice. I hope I took the essence of our conversation, ladies, and did you proud with Brooklyn, Addison, Caden, Carter, and Chris.

Writing Might Makes Right

This book was both difficult, and enjoyable to write. The book was difficult to write because I had to start dealing with time lapses.

Easy because once I figured out Baba Yaga, it helped me nail down what was going to go on with Bethany Anne.

The challenge, like so many authors before me have encountered, is when your main character gets too high in rank, how do you allow them to go on these missions that could get them killed, when they SHOULD be working out how to be King, or Queen, Empress, General or Emperor?

It's hard.

However, I knew that I needed to explain how Bethany Anne, who was an unruly Empress in the last book, would come up with another way to get out and get to be herself, while still pretending she was being a good Empress, and staying back in the Meredith Reynolds.

Thus, we get her alter-ego, the Baba Yaga.

Now, the real Baba Yaga character is a bit enigmatic. She can be benevolent, evil or ambiguous. Rarely is she ever young or attractive. Pretty much the opposite of Bethany Anne.

I like the opportunity to keep her vague, in the shadows and out of the video if possible. Perhaps out of focus video like our versions of UFO video capture where (and why the hell is this always true?) the videos are out of focus, and always shaking.

I'm going to explore more of Baba Yaga, and I want to continue the line of questioning I asked back in book 01:

My thought behind Bethany Anne's character was 'what happens when you provide a person overly sensitive to injustice and give her the ability to kick ass and ignore the names? I'm sure she could effect change, but it doesn't automatically follow that it will be good change.

The fight she has might not be with a 'boss' at the end of each book, but rather with herself. Will she become that which she loathes? Will she be able to recognize humanity in enemies or will she become desensitized like Michael? How will her friends react if that occurs?

I think Bethany Anne is in a good place with her closest friends. However, the alien friends and enemies are starting to make up their own stories about the Etheric Empire. We start to understand where some of the other Species, and specifically those that wield their own power, are starting to band together against the two powers that are burning up space with their battles.

And their bloody peace agreements.

For those wondering, we have foretold how this ends, we are just playing it out.

For those pestering…ooops, sorry…. *Asking politely* WHERE IS MICHAEL'S NEXT BOOK? It is the next story I need to write: Darkest Before the Dawn - The Second Dark Ages Book 03 (Michael's next book). I will be working on that with collaborator Ell Leigh Clarke.

For those curious about the Kindles for the Military program – look in your email inbox for an update (for those on the email list.) The short message is I haven't stopped trying, but getting them over to the sandbox has been challenging. Right now, we have a fan who has contacts (I almost want to put air quotes around that, it sounds so cool) that might be able to move Kindles to a Red Cross location in Spain, and from there to locations that need it. I am still sending (as needed) Kindles to the Center for the Intrepid in San Antonio, Tx.

I have a Bethany Anne letter to write later for the next Ascension Myth book (Ell Leigh Clarke #6) which is due out Monday.

Further, on the family side, Joey Anderle (son and author himself) is safely setup at the University of Texas at Arlington and our last son at home, Jacob Anderle, will be heading to Texas A&M at Texarkana on Thursday.

Then, the mysterious beyond is waiting for me.

It has been almost twenty-five years since I didn't have one of the children at home and frankly…

I have no idea what is on the other side of that existence, anymore. *But I'm about to find out!*

Ad Aeternitatem,
Michael
August 22nd, 2017

BOOKS BY MICHAEL ANDERLE

Sign up for the LMBPN email list to be notified of new releases and special deals!

https://lmbpn.com/email/

For a complete list of books by Michael Anderle, please visit:

www.lmbpn.com/ma-books/

CONNECT WITH THE AUTHOR

Connect with Michael Anderle

Website: http://lmbpn.com

Email List: https://michael.beehiiv.com/

https://www.facebook.com/LMBPNPublishing

https://twitter.com/MichaelAnderle

https://www.instagram.com/lmbpn_publishing/

https://www.bookbub.com/authors/michael-anderle